DARK OMEN

A NORTHERN MICHIGAN ASYLUM NOVEL

J.R. ERICKSON

Visit
JREricksonauthor.com

AUTHOR'S NOTE

Thanks so much for picking up a Northern Michigan Asylum Novel. I want to offer a disclaimer before you dive into the story. This is an entirely fictional novel. Although there was once a real place known as The Northern Michigan Asylum - which inspired me to write these books - it is in no way depicted within them. Although my story takes place there, the characters in this story are not based on any real people who worked at this asylum or were patients; any resemblance to individuals, living or dead, is entirely coincidental. Likewise, the events which take place in the novel are not based on real events, and any resemblance to real events is also coincidental.

In truth, nearly every book I have read about the asylum, later known as the Traverse City State Hospital, was positive. This holds true for the stories of many of the staff who worked there as well. I live in the Traverse City area and regularly visit the grounds of the former asylum. It's now known as The Village at Grand Traverse Commons. It was purchased in 2000 by Ray Minervini and the Minervini Group who have been restoring it since that time. Today, it's a mixed-use space of boutiques, restaurants and condominiums. If you ever visit the area, I encourage you to visit The Village at Grand Traverse Commons. You can experience first-hand the asylums - both old and new - and walk the sprawling grounds.

DEDICATION

For my sister, Cherie.

PROLOGUE

The Northern Michigan Asylum
1966

Greta Claude

"I WON'T!"

Greta woke to the sound of Maribelle's shouts echoing up the stairs.

She blinked at the ceiling and sat up, pulling the blanket to her chin.

"You'll do as I say," their father, Joseph, bellowed.

Greta cringed at the sharp crack that followed and knew Maribelle's cheek was probably throbbing from the impact of Joseph's large hand.

Maribelle screamed and began to cry.

Greta jumped from the bed and raced down the stairs as the front door swung closed.

Through the window, Greta watched her twin sister, Maribelle, disappear into the grassy trail behind their house.

Joseph stood in the kitchen, his hands fisted at his sides. He turned and glared at Greta, and she shrank from his furious gaze.

"Go clean the basement," he snarled. "I'm going after your sister."

He stormed out the door, toward the wooded path that led from the caretaker's house, where they'd lived since birth, into the acres of forests surrounding the Northern Michigan Asylum.

"Don't hurt her," Greta cried out, but her voice was drowned by his heavy footfalls on the porch steps.

When she reached the concrete floor in the basement, the stench of blood and urine overpowered her. Other smells mingled with the odor; smells Greta had learned to associate with death.

Greta pulled her t-shirt over her nose, letting it hang there. She flailed her hand through the darkness, the drawn-out seconds in the black basement causing her heart to crash against her chest as if it too wanted to race back up the stairs and into the daylight.

She found the lightbulb string and yanked, illuminating the blood.

Dark and wet, it lay in a fresh puddle in the center of the floor. The body was gone, but drag marks left the pool and streaked toward the stairs.

Greta looked down and realized she was standing in one of the bloody drag marks. She peeled off her white socks, ruined, and stuffed them into the crumpled garbage bag her father had left.

She grabbed the bucket from the laundry basin and turned on the tap. Rust-colored water spewed into the bucket. She rinsed it and filled it again. The water had the sulfurous odor of rotten eggs, but was preferable to the fluids coating the basement floor.

As she wet a rag and returned to the blood, she hummed "Ring Around the Rosie," a song she and Maribelle liked to sing when they ran through the woods behind the asylum.

Greta sopped up the blood and dipped the rag into the bucket, wringing it and watching the red swirl into the brown water. When the brown water turned red, Greta emptied the bucket and refilled it.

She refilled the bucket five times before the pool of blood was washed away. She swept the bit of remaining water into the drain in the floor.

Greta stuffed the soiled rags into the black plastic bag, her eyes flitting over a single white tennis shoe, the laces stained pink. She tied the bag and then scrubbed her hands with lye soap until they were raw and tingling.

She turned off the light and hurried to her room, to put on a dress before Mrs. Martel, their home-school teacher, arrived.

Maribelle arrived only minutes before Mrs. Martel. She limped into the house with a tear-streaked face.

Greta could see a purple bruise spreading on Maribelle's knee.

"Come on," Greta insisted. "Let's clean you up, quick."

Maribelle cried quietly as Greta sponged off her face and quickly braided her unruly dark hair. She pulled Maribelle's nightgown over her head and cringed at hand-shaped welts on Maribelle's back.

"I hate him," Maribelle whispered. "I hate him so much."

1

Now

June 14th, 1991

BETTE DROVE THROUGH THE EIGHT-FOOT, wrought-iron gates marking the entrance to Eternal Rest, the cemetery where they'd buried her mother eleven years before.

Parking on the grassy shoulder, Bette popped the trunk and stepped from her car.

The cemetery was quiet at four-thirty in the afternoon. The trees watched, large and silent, as Bette pulled out the box that she and Crystal took to their mother's grave every year. It contained the Edgar Allen Poe poetry book they'd take turns reciting from, a handful of photographs, and Bette's letter to their mother. Crystal was bringing the flowers and she'd have her own letter.

Bette knelt in front of the marble headstone, heart shaped and engraved with her mother's name: Joanna Kay Meeks. December 15, 1947 – June 14, 1980. Their father's name, the death date not yet filled in, stood next to Jo's on the headstone, and Bette cringed whenever she saw it.

Bette and Crystal's father had offered to buy plots for his girls when their mother died, but they had both balked. At eleven and thirteen, they were hardly planning their future deaths.

As the minutes ticked by, Bette stood and paced away from the grave. She gazed at the winding road that led through the hilly cemetery, searching for Crystal's distinctive sky-blue Volkswagen Beetle.

Her sister didn't appear.

At five o'clock, irritated, Bette put the box in her trunk and drove to a payphone.

She dialed Crystal's number and left a message before calling her own number, on the chance that Crystal had gotten confused and gone to the house. Bette's machine picked up.

When an hour passed and still no Crystal, Bette drove home and called her sister again.

Crystal's machine picked up.

"Hi, you've missed me. Hopefully I'm on a daring adventure, but if all goes well, I'll eventually make it home to call you back."

"Crystal, it's Bette. Again." Her voice took on the high-pitched notes of early anxiety. "In case you forgot, we have dinner reservations, and we're planting flowers on Mom's grave tonight. You know, like we've done on June fourteenth for the last ten years."

Bette hung up and stared at her clock.

Their dinner reservations were in ten minutes and obviously they wouldn't be making it.

For another twenty minutes, Bette sat at the kitchen table, fuming, and silently willing the door to open and her free-spirited sister to come bouncing through with tales of rescuing a kitten in the road or driving a hitchhiker halfway across the county to make it on time for the birth of his child. Two stories which had actually happened, but never on the anniversary of their mother's death.

Crystal had never forgotten their mother's anniversary, and she'd never missed their yearly ritual.

As Bette tapped her foot and watched the clock, the sense of urgency in her stomach curdled into fear, and she realized that had been the root of her anxiety all along: not frustration that they'd be late to dinner, but fear. The fear crept up her legs and settled in the base of her spine. It clicked its fangs and tapped its sharpened claws. It would gnaw a hole right through her if she didn't do something.

The fear was unwarranted. Crystal was only an hour and a half late, but it had gripped Bette in its talons just the same.

A photo of Crystal and Bette, arm in arm, sat on the bureau next to the kitchen table. The bureau was filled with dishes, things their mother had loved and that Bette, still living in her childhood home, had never been able to part with.

She gazed at the silver-framed photograph. Crystal's red-gold hair hung long and wavy, flowing over each shoulder. Bette's own hair, also long, was stick straight and dark.

"Where are you?" she whispered to the picture.

Unable to sit still another moment, Bette stood and grabbed the phone, dialing her sister again and slamming the phone down when the machine picked up. Next, she called her father, gritting her teeth when his voicemail clicked on.

"Dad, it's Bette. Call me right away."

Bette walked stiffly to her car and climbed behind the wheel.

Though less than two years separated Bette and Crystal, Bette had often felt like a much older sister. She was the practical, sensible one. At twenty-four, she had a serious job as a research assistant for an anthropology professor, and she was well on her way to receiving her doctorate.

Crystal, on the other hand, had spent the first two years after high school traveling the world. She'd finally returned a year before and enrolled at Michigan State University. She worked a series of minimum-wage jobs and refused to do anything out of obligation. She loved to say, *"Should is not in my vocabulary."*

Bette let herself into Crystal's apartment with her spare key, sweeping through the space quickly. Crystal wasn't home, but Bette peeked into every room just the same.

In Crystal's bathroom, she spotted a damp towel and a long t-shirt, probably what Crystal had worn to bed the night before.

A hand-scrawled note was stuck to the vanity mirror.

"The day I met you, a part of me dissolved,

Slipped into the earth and rooted beneath you, grew up inside of you,

You are always with me now. I am always with you."

Bette read the words under her breath.

Weston Meeks hadn't signed his name, but he hadn't needed to.

Bette had heard how the man spoke to her sister.

The professor, who taught poetry at Michigan State University, had swept Crystal off her feet. Despite the age gap, ten years give or take, Crystal had fallen madly, stupidly in love with the man.

"Apparently, the feelings are mutual," Bette said dryly.

A calendar hung in Crystal's kitchen with a few notes scribbled in the small boxes. She didn't post her work schedule and probably didn't record half of her appointments. Crystal simply wasn't a planner.

She had however, noted the anniversary of their mother's death and written: "Evening with Bette."

Except she hadn't shown up, and her apartment was empty.

Bette walked across the hall to apartment four. It belonged to Crystal's friend, Garrett. Bette had only met him once. He was a beautiful gay man who dressed impeccably, and often sat with Crystal in their little apartment courtyard drinking wine and lamenting his latest break-up.

Bette knocked on the door.

She could hear music in the apartment. It sounded like Michael Jackson.

The door swung open and Garett grinned at her. He wore gym shorts and a tank top, wrist and ankle weights adorning his limbs.

"Bette!" he exclaimed. "How are you? I'm just getting my exercise in." He jogged in place, sweat glistening on his tanned face. "No Crystal?" he asked, making a sad face and peeking past her down the hall.

"No, she was supposed to meet me. Have you seen her?" Bette asked.

"Billie Jean!" he gushed. "This is my all-time favorite Michael Jackson song." He snapped his fingers. "I saw her this morning. I think she was going for coffee. We didn't chat long. I was itching to get a meatloaf in the crock-pot. My friend David's coming over tonight, and I'm hoping he'll see how domesticated I can be." He winked at her.

Bette shuffled her feet and glanced back towards Crystal's closed door. "Did she say she had somewhere else to go after getting coffee?"

He wrinkled his brow and shook his head.

"I'm afraid I barely let her get a word in edge-wise — hot date and all."

"All right. Thanks Garret. Tell her to call me if you see her."

"Sure thing, Betts." He grinned, giving her a salute and closing his door.

Bette left the apartment building and stood in the parking lot. Crystal's blue VW Beetle was nowhere in sight.

Bette climbed into her own car and drove to the coffee shop.

Crystal worked at Sacred Grounds part time, mostly on

weekends, but she was friends with the other employees and dropped by at least once a day for a cup of coffee or to chat with her friends.

Rick stood at the counter, wiping down the surface. Crystal had told Bette that Rick had an obsession with Nirvana and in particular Kurt Cobain. He'd even grown out and dyed his hair to match the singer's dishwater-blond, uncombed look.

"Hey Bette, how's it going?" he asked.

Bette glanced quickly around at the tables.

"Has Crystal been in?" Bette asked, moving closer to a booth in the corner where a redhead sat with her back to the coffee counter.

The woman laughed and turned sideways. Her laugh was deep and gravelly, not like Crystal's at all, and when she turned Bette realized the woman was well into her fifties.

Rick nodded.

"She came in this morning and had a coffee and one of Minerva's famous butterscotch scones. We've got two left if you're interested." He pointed at the display case showcasing the sugary treats.

Bette's stomach felt like a block of cement.

"No, thanks. About what time was that?"

Rick turned and looked at the Cheshire-cat clock that hung over the trays of variously colored coffee mugs.

"I'd say nine-ish."

"Okay, thanks." Bette started toward the door and then turned back. "Was she alone?"

Rick scratched his stubbly chin and nodded.

"Yeah. Her friend was in here. Um, her name starts with a G. Grace, maybe… But Crystal didn't stay for long."

"Okay, thanks."

Bette walked out to her car and slid behind the wheel.

Grace… Bette searched for the friend in her mind. Someone

that Crystal met at the bookstore, at college, maybe at Hospice House. Impossible to say. Crystal had a thousand friends, and she made them everywhere. Bette often joked that Crystal couldn't get a tank of gas without making a new friend.

Bette drove to The Reader's Retreat, a used bookstore on Pearl Street. She parked and pushed into the dimly lit space, which smelled of coffee, incense, and old books.

The shop's owner, Freddie, had fallen in love with Crystal the moment he'd seen her despite being thirty years her senior, married and with six kids. Theirs was a love affair that existed only in Freddie's mind, and he wasn't afraid to say so. Crystal worked the third weekend of every month at the store in exchange for free books.

Freddie sat in an overstuffed chair; a box of books balanced on the scarred coffee table before him.

"Bette," he said, smiling and blowing a layer of silt off the book in his hand. "If I wasn't just thinking of you not ten minutes ago. Lookie here." He stood and shuffled behind the heavy oak desk where an ancient typewriter sat next to an equally ancient cash register. Freddie's was the only business in Lansing that refused to accept credit cards.

He held up a copy of *On the Origin of Species* by Charles Darwin.

"It's a fourth edition. Impeccably cared for. Look at that binding. Not a single crack."

Bette nodded, barely looking at the book over which she normally would have salivated.

"It's beautiful, Freddie, but I'm looking for Crystal. She was supposed to meet me almost two hours ago and never showed. Has she been in today?"

Freddie stared at her, not believing her lack of reaction to the treasure in his hand. When she continued to wait silently, he set the book on his desk and returned to his chair.

"Not so much as a crimson hair has passed through that door in two weeks. She's been busy with that new flame, I'm sure. A sword to the heart, I might add," he said, clutching his chest as if mortally wounded.

2

Then

Crystal watched Professor Meeks stride into the auditorium, his smile easy, chatting with a student who followed him like a duckling after its mother.

"Welcome to Poetry 101," he announced, striding to the blackboard behind him. "I'm Professor Meeks, and I'll be the guy trying to look like a beatnik up here at the desk all semester, or so I've been told."

The class laughed.

"Truth be told, had I been born in the age of the beatniks, I would surely have joined them. Instead, I've been blessed with the lot of you."

He started to go through the syllabus outlining the poetry they'd focus on that semester.

Meeks seemed to be in his early thirties. His sandy brown hair brushed his shoulders, and a neatly trimmed beard covered the lower half of his face. He was handsome and looked the part of a shaggy poet. Crystal imagined him sitting at a scratched wooden desk drinking scotch and pouring his soul into a tattered notebook before collapsing into bed, exhausted.

He'd have only a shred of passion left for teaching, but he'd stretch and warp it until he could cast a luminous veil over every student in the room.

He wore dark jeans and a t-shirt covered with a wrinkled-looking blazer. As he spoke, his hands flew nearly as fast as his lips, and the students in the room watched him, rapt.

Crystal had read both of Professor Meeks' poetry chap-books, crying during each as she'd sat at her favorite coffee shop listening to Christmas music and missing her mother. Poetry and memories of her mother walked hand in hand in Crystal's life. The poetry could be unrelated, about seagulls or lemons, and still she'd find the words curving into the shape of her mother's smile or softening like her hands.

Meeks wrote about abandonment, fear, travel and love. It was the love poems that had struck her like a bell deep in her ribs. The reverberation continued for days after she'd read them. She'd been excited to meet the man who'd put the heart's longings, the sheer magnitude of them, onto a one-dimensional page.

When his eyes fell upon Crystal, he paused, his sentence cut in half, the silence stretching out long and empty.

He ducked his head, breaking the stare, and chuckled.

"Sorry folks, lost my train of thought there."

As the lecture continued, Professor Meeks kept his gaze averted. Whenever he drifted toward the right side of the stadium seats where Crystal sat, he'd pause as if realizing his mistake and shift his eyes left.

When class ended, Crystal made her way to the front of the room.

Up close, she saw thick dark lashes fringed the professor's blue eyes.

"Professor," she said.

He glanced away from the boy he'd been talking to, and his smile faltered as if he'd been struck silent for a second time as he stared at her.

The student glanced at Crystal as well and then back at the professor.

"I'm just nervous," the boy said, tugging on the collar of his gray polo shirt. "I've never read any of my poems out loud. My girlfriend says Open Mic Night is the perfect time to share, but... " He grimaced as if the mere suggestion brought him physical pain. "I'm sick at the thought of it."

The professor smiled and put a hand on the boy's arm.

"Forget the crowd, Ben," Meeks said. "Choose one person. Better yet, bring your best friend or your girlfriend. Bring the person you can read the poem to and mean every word. Read to them and only them."

Ben swallowed a big shaky breath and nodded.

"Okay," he said. "Bring one friend. Thanks, Professor."

He nodded and headed from the room, continuing to mumble the advice to himself.

"Hi," Meeks said, returning his gaze to Crystal. "And you are?"

"Crystal Childs."

She held out her hand, though it seemed an awkward thing to do suddenly.

He grinned and shook it.

"Lovely to meet you, Crystal Childs."

Their hands lingered together, warmth coursing from his hand into hers. She gazed at him, their eyes, like their hands, lingering overlong.

He forced his eyes away as if with great effort and stared down at the desk where he shuffled papers together. "Are you looking forward to Poetry 101?"

She heard him trying to sound casual, forcing an ease that

didn't flow into his limbs. He looked stiff, awkward, as if he suddenly wasn't sure what to do with his body.

"I've been excited to start this class for weeks," she confessed. "I read *Musings in the Morning Light* and *Long Drives*."

He studied her, as if surprised by the admission.

"I must admit, it's rare that a student reads my work before the semester starts. I try not to force my own poetry on my classes. My goal is to teach you the greats."

"It was..." she murmured, "great." And it had been. She thought of the poem titled *Her*, a long list of words that described a mother present in the flesh, but never in the heart.

He took a step back as if the space between them had grown too small, though it hadn't changed.

"Thank you. I've been writing poetry for twenty years, and I still stammer when someone comments on my work. That's the beauty of it, though. The vulnerability. Of course, your experience of my poetry has nothing to do with me at all."

Crystal smiled and nodded, studying the fine bones beneath his large, long-fingered hands.

"That's why I'm drawn to poetry. It evokes something different in us all," she murmured.

"Exactly," he agreed, reaching to grab a planner on his desk.

His hand brushed Crystal's, and she shivered. The contact moved between them like an electric current. Soft and enveloping, as if someone had thrown a sheet, warm from the dryer, over top of them. For an instant they were together beneath that shroud, tucked safely, solidly, and then the door banged open and a girl, probably a freshman judging from her frazzled expression and the campus map clutched in her hand, burst in.

"I'm sorry. Is this Poetry 101?" she squeaked.

Professor Meeks blinked, took another step away from Crystal, and nodded.

"Yes, you're in the right place. Grab a seat wherever," he told her.

He returned his gaze to Crystal and now he didn't break away from her eyes.

"I have to..." he gestured at his notes as if in explanation.

"Yeah, absolutely. I'm sorry to have kept you, Professor Meeks."

"Wes," he told her, reaching out as she turned and touching her wrist.

He looked surprised that he'd offered the word, his name, to a student he'd only just met.

"Thank you, Wes," she said and left.

She paused at the confused student who peered at the two hundred seats in the room as if her seat choice was the first question on the exam, and she was bound to fail.

Crystal pointed to the upper back section.

"They dim the lights for slides. You're practically invisible up there," Crystal told the girl, who gave her a timid smile.

"Thank you," she whispered, clutching her map and hurrying up the stairs.

As Crystal slipped into the hallway, she glanced back and saw Wes watching her.

3

Now

Bette drove to the Hospice House where Crystal worked several nights a week. They hadn't seen her.

She returned to Crystal's apartment, where she called every name and phone number listed in her address book. Crystal had owned the address book since high school, and it wasn't up to date. Several of the phone numbers were disconnected. A few of Crystal's old friends admitted they hadn't spoken to her in years.

Finding Weston Meeks' number nowhere in the book, Bette called Michigan State University and left a message on his office machine.

After exhausting every avenue, she pulled in to the East Lansing Police Department.

"I need to report my sister missing," Bette told the woman at the desk.

The woman studied her, and perhaps seeing the alarm Bette felt was written across her face, she stood.

"Just a moment, please," she said, disappearing behind a wall.

Bette heard voices beyond the wall and imagined a sleepy police station with men drinking cold coffee and telling stories of their latest traffic stops.

Several minutes passed, and the receptionist returned with a man in police uniform.

"Hi, ma'am. I'm Officer Hart. Come on back, and I'll help you out.

Bette followed him around the wall and was surprised to see an array of neat cubicles, many decorated with family photos or posters of superheroes and movie characters.

The deputy led her to his own cubicle, which contained a framed photo of a dog wearing a red bandanna next to another framed photo of an older man and woman smiling as they stood in front of a sloping vineyard.

"Your sister is missing?" the man asked.

Bette sat in the hardback chair next to his desk and nodded. She clasped her hands in her lap, weaving her fingers together to keep them from shaking or tugging and pulling at her long dark hair. She was a nervous fidgeter, prone to anxiety in normal circumstances and practically a bouncing ball during moments of crisis.

"Yes, her name is Crystal Childs. C-R-Y-S-T-A-L. She's twenty-two years old, long red hair, green eyes. She drives a 1979 Volkswagen Beetle. It's a light-blue convertible with a black top."

"Okay, hold on. You're talking faster than I can write." The man jotted the words down in a scrawl that Bette doubted he'd be able to read after he finished.

"When did she go missing?"

Bette looked at the clock. Three hours since their scheduled meeting time, but who knew how long her sister had actually been missing. Five hours, eight. The last person Bette had spoken to who confirmed seeing Crystal that day was Rick at the coffee shop. That had been at nine a.m. — nearly eleven hours before.

"I'm not sure. She was supposed to meet me at five. That was three hours ago."

The deputy paused and looked up at her.

"She's been missing for three hours?"

Bette watched him lay the pen down.

"Pick that back up," she snapped, grabbing the pen and holding it out to him. "Fine, never mind. The last time I saw her was Wednesday afternoon. That was three days ago. She's been missing for three days."

The deputy took the pen and sighed.

"Ma'am—"

"My name is Bette," she snarled.

"Okay, Bette. I understand it's frustrating when someone misses an appointment. I get it. I have a sister and she's notoriously late for everything. I kid you not, I'm still shocked she arrived on time for her own wedding. But I can't file a missing person's report on a twenty-two-year-old woman who hasn't been seen in three hours. The Chief of Police would not look kindly on that. You see, there's hours and resources that go into missing person's cases."

"Do you know how many people are" —he paused and made air quotes— "'missing' every single day? How many husbands come home late from work, or how many kids ride the bus home with their friend and forget to mention it to their parents? Do you know how many actual crimes wouldn't be solved if we had every deputy in our department tracking down sisters who missed dinner dates?"

Bette stood so abruptly her chair smacked into the cubicle and sent it wobbling. The officer also stood and grabbed the top, righting it before it could tip over.

She'd made it halfway to the front door when he called out.

"Wait. Ma'am, Bette, just hold on a sec, okay?" He hurried to catch up with her, his face flustered and embarrassed.

Bette glared at him.

"Let me take the information down. I can't put it into the system for twenty-four hours, but there's no reason for you to have to come back in. I can put a BOLA out to the guys on duty tonight. If anyone comes across her car, we'll call you."

Bette stood, arms rigid at her sides, her blood coursing in hot rapid gusts behind her eyes. She'd always had a short fuse, and instead of sadness tended towards anger when faced with a dilemma. Anger or panic.

She said nothing, but followed the officer back to his desk. She didn't sit but stood above him as he wrote.

"A blue Volkswagen Bug. Anything distinctive about the car?"

"A blue VW bug is pretty distinctive, don't you think?"

He smiled, but quickly wiped the look when he saw her expression.

"Sure, okay. Got it. Anything else suspicious? I only ask because you seem awfully upset about a woman who's only been missing for three hours."

Bette stuffed her hands in her pockets to stop their shaking.

She didn't have Crystal's insight, her ability to sense someone's favorite candy or if a person might get in a fender bender that afternoon, but her body perceived something. It always had, though she'd spent most of her life writing the feelings off as anxiety or neurosis. Crystal never tuned any of it out, but Bette found the feelings unmanageable, a nuisance, really.

But the fear that left her arms and legs quaking was not paranoia, and she'd had it twice before. Once on the day of her mother's death, and the second time when… no, she wouldn't go there. She shook her head.

"I just know my sister. Okay? She calls if she's going to be ten minutes late. She can be flakey about some things, but she's punctual. Today is the anniversary of our mother's death and we spend it together every year. It's a big deal. Get it? She wouldn't miss it; she wouldn't be late. Not unless something drastic had happened. There's something wrong, and you will be looking for her. This whole place will be looking for her."

Bette wished she hadn't said the words as she hurried into the warm summer evening.

The loud rattle-like call of katydids reverberated from the trees surrounding the parking lot.

Crystal loved katydids. She'd even named one of their cats after the loud insects, which at times had driven Bette to insomnia in the summer, when they were especially loud. She'd taken to wearing earmuffs to bed to drown out the sound.

She shivered and climbed into her car, heading for home.

4

Then

Crystal chose her usual table near the stone fireplace in Luna's Cafe. The embers crackled and popped, and she gazed at the orange flames leaping into the dark cavern of the chimney. As she pulled off her coat, the door to the coffee shop opened, and Weston Meeks stepped inside.

A light dusting of snow coated his hair and the shoulders of his dark coat.

It was most likely the final snow of the winter. One of those freak storms that arrived at the end of March to remind them that Mother Nature always got the last word.

Crystal had been attending Meeks' class since January, but she'd never run into him outside of class.

Weston leaned over and shook the snow from his hair. When he looked up, he saw her. She smiled and waved him over.

"Join me," she told him, as he walked to her little table.

"Are you sure? I don't want to interrupt your quiet evening."

"If I wanted a quiet evening, I would have gone home," she said, settling into her chair.

The waitress, a petite Goth girl with black lips and black hair, stopped at their table.

"Hi Polly," Crystal said. She frequented Luna's Cafe and was on a first name basis with all the staff.

"Hi Crystal, what can I get ya?"

Crystal smiled. "I'll have a cafe au lait, and he'd like espresso straight up with two sugars."

Weston gaped, glancing from her to the barista before nodding yes.

"How did you do that?" he asked.

"What?" She winked at him and picked up the menu, though she suddenly had no appetite.

"How did you know what I wanted? I mean, I'd say you guessed, but how could you have guessed that?"

"Maybe it was on your website at the college. Or I could have overheard you talking about it in class one day."

He frowned, and Crystal watched him consider both possibilities. He shook his head.

"No, no way."

Crystal leaned across the table and whispered. "I'm magic."

His eyes widened, and he glanced at her hands. She wondered if he expected to see a wand clutched in her fingers.

"Or I'm just very perceptive," she added.

"I don't think anyone is perceptive enough to be that accurate. Come on, tell me," he said, peeling off his black scarf and draping it over his chair.

"Maybe," she said. "Not tonight, though. Tonight, I want to hear about your poetry."

He studied her, and she could see he didn't want to let the subject go — but finally he leaned back, conceding defeat.

"I've been writing poetry since I was ten," he said. "The year my parents got divorced, followed by my mother moving to California. I needed an outlet. I lived in Detroit. Most angry kids got into fights, but the neighbors in the apartment above ours had immigrated from Chile. Their mother, Camila, had four children. She started to bring me empanadas and read me the poetry of Pablo Neruda. I got hooked on both. I've been writing poetry and music ever since."

"Neruda wrote beautiful poetry." Crystal smiled. "I spent a few months in New Orleans, and I saw an exhibition of Pablo Neruda while I was there."

Weston's eyes twinkled as if speaking of a poet he loved made him come even more alive.

"What's your favorite by him?" he asked.

Crystal drew a deep breath and closed her eyes, remembering the displays, the huge canvases covered in black calligraphy. She'd read the poems for hours returning to one in particular again and again.

"*Tonight I can write the saddest lines*," she recalled.

He quoted a line further into the poem, "*I loved her and sometimes she loved me too*." A flush rose to his face as he said the words.

His eyes found hers and all the sounds and movement in the cafe seemed to stop. Even her breath, the steady lilting sound, disappeared.

"Café au lait," Polly announced, sliding a purple mug, resting in a green saucer, onto the table.

Crystal blushed and smiled up at her.

Cafe Luna refused to serve customers on matching dishware, one of the many reasons Crystal loved the coffee shop.

"And espresso with two sugar cubes," Polly added, pushing Weston's drink in front of him.

He smiled and lifted the tiny black-and-white, spotted espresso cup off the dainty orange plate and laughed.

"I like your style in here," he told Polly.

She winked at him.

"We celebrate diversity at Cafe Luna." Polly ambled away, her big combat boots enormous on her tiny body.

Weston directed his attention back to Crystal. "I've never been in here before. I think I like it."

Crystal studied him. For an instant she'd felt… a secret tucked in his chest and throat. A shadow slipping back and deep, hiding from the part of her that sensed people's mysteries. The part of her that knew he drank espresso with two sugar cubes, that he loved dogs, but didn't own one, and that he ran from the past as if it wanted to devour him.

"Do you write poetry, Crystal?" he asked, lifting the little silver spoon and swirling the sugar in his cup.

She nodded. "I do. I believe poetry is in everything, music, conversations, the rustling of autumn leaves, making love."

He stared at her and then rubbed his hands together as if he'd gotten a sudden chill.

"I agree, completely," he said. "I tell my students poetry is swimming in the ocean, walking in the woods, hugging your child — all of it is writing a poem. We just don't always commit the experience to the page, but when we do, we have the chance to touch people in a way that rarely translates in conversation."

"I love that," she murmured. "I'll have to take your advanced poetry class next semester."

"Yes, you should," he said. "What are you going to school for, Crystal?"

She dipped her face forward, feeling the frothy cream stick to her nose.

When she lifted her head, Weston grinned.

"Professional circus clown," she confessed.

He laughed.

"I didn't know we offered that at Michigan State. I must look into expanding my portfolio. Really, though. Do you want to be a writer for a living? A poet?"

She stirred her drink. "I love how earnestly you ask that question. Most people are filled with such doubt when referring to writers and poets professionally. But you're completely sincere."

"My dad reacted that way. I guess that's why I'm a teacher. At the end of the day, I still had to pay the bills."

"I rarely do anything because I have to pay the bills. If I don't love it, I don't do it."

"Do you work now?" he asked.

She wiggled her fingers. "My sister says I hummingbird."

"I'm intrigued," he admitted.

"I work at a coffee shop, not this one, and I work occasionally at a used bookstore. I work two days a week at Hospice House in downtown Lansing. In the summer, I work on a lavender farm part time. Hence, I flit from place to place like a hummingbird."

He chuckled. "My head spins just hearing about all those jobs. How do you keep track?"

She paused and tilted her head, swaying slowly in her chair. "*The Man I Love*," she murmured.

His eyes widened.

"Billie Holiday." She gestured to the speaker behind them.

She watched him incline his head as if straining to hear the low, sweet melody, and then his face softened when he caught the tune.

"Yes, right there," she told him. She closed her eyes and listened, drifting for a time on Holiday's yearning.

When she opened her eyes, Wes watched her with unshielded desire.

Another long stare. She took in the heart-shaped curve of his upper lip, his slightly crooked front tooth and most dazzling, the flecks of firelight in his blue irises.

"That's how I keep track," she offered, feeling the same fire in his eyes leap high into her throat and crawl to her face. "I live in the moment. That's it. I don't organize my life; I don't create routines. Every day is new. I greet the morning unburdened by habitual ways of being. We never know how much time we have left in this life. I try to live every day like it's my last."

Wes leaned back in his chair, his coffee forgotten. "I want to do that. My alarm goes off every morning at six fifteen a.m., and I operate on auto-pilot until noon," he said. "I can't remember the last time I had an original thought while drinking my coffee or even tasted it!"

Crystal inhaled the scent of her café au lait, the slightly sweet froth and the deeper, darker coffee aroma at the center.

"Do it right now." She gestured at his cup. "Lean in and smell it."

"I already drank it," he laughed.

"But it lingers. Go on, inhale the memory of it."

Wes leaned over his cup.

"Close your eyes," she told him.

He did.

"Tell me about it."

His long lashes fluttered on his cheeks, and a small smile curved his parted lips. It was a playful smile, but Crystal had serious intentions. She'd known this man would come into her life for years. That he was *the one,* to use that naïve and often misunderstood label.

It wasn't girlish vanity that told her Weston Meeks was meant to be in her life. It was the same ability that told her he loved espresso with two sugars, that he had secrets he wanted to share but feared the repercussions if he did so.

"Rich," he said, breathing deeply. "Like dark chocolate melting on your tongue as you lean in close to a wood fire…" he trailed off and opened his eyes.

They sat that way, staring at each other, silent, until the waitress arrived to refill their waters.

Weston laughed and brushed a hand through his long hair.

"Thanks," he told Polly. He returned his gaze to Crystal's. "I don't think I've ever truly appreciated my espresso until this moment."

Crystal smiled. "It's amazing how vibrant the world is when we pay attention."

He nodded and gazed around the coffee shop. She watched his eyes linger on the brightly colored paintings on the wall before drifting to a clear display case filled with bowls of fresh fruit.

"It's also amazing what the fire does to your red hair. You look like Brigid, the Celtic goddess with flaming hair," he told her.

"The goddess of what?"

"Fertility," he admitted. "And interestingly enough, poetry."

"Then she must be a kindred spirit," Crystal agreed. "Do you love your job, Professor?" she asked.

He looked at her and nodded slowly, as if not entirely sure how to answer the question.

"Yes. I have days where I long for a more creative life, I guess. I miss playing music and staying up all night writing poetry by candlelight. Maybe I'm just guilty of painting the past in a golden light. *I am just the same as when our days were a joy, and our paths through flowers,*" he murmured.

"That's lovely. Did you write it?"

He smiled and shook his head. "Not at all. It's from the poem *After a Journey* by Thomas Hardy. Hardy wrote often of the past and his yearning for times gone by. You'll learn about him. I teach him every semester in my classes. Probably because his poetry resonates with me."

"You long for the past?" she asked.

"Not really. I have an ugly past. I long for my dream of the past. I'm a liar, you see. I remember it differently than it was."

"I'd call you a dreamer, not a liar," she disagreed. "Maybe

your subconscious is trying to help you change the present so you can have a golden past someday."

Again, their eyes met. Neither of them spoke, and Crystal's breath caught. She wanted to freeze the moment, the warm light from the faux Tiffany lamps, the smell of coffee, and the sense that something extraordinary was about to begin.

The bell on the door jingled and a man and woman, arm in arm, burst into the cafe bringing with them a flurry of snow.

Weston stared at the door and Crystal knew he was going to leave.

She smiled up at him as he stood.

"This has been really wonderful, Crystal. I have to go, though. I have class bright and early."

"Until next time," she told him, offering her hand.

He took it, but didn't shake it. He held it tightly and then released her, slipping into his coat as he hurried toward the door.

5

Now

WHEN BETTE REACHED HOME, she paused with her blinker on, staring at the empty driveway, the driveway of the home she and Crystal had grown up in.

Bette's shoulders sagged. She'd hoped to see Crystal's VW Beetle parked there, hoped to walk into the house to find her sister boiling water for tea and rattling off a thousand excuses for her tardiness. But the driveway stood empty.

In the entryway, the little red button glowed on her machine.

"Please be Crystal, please be Crystal," she repeated as she hit play.

"Hi, Bette, it's Dad. I just got home and listened to your message. I haven't seen Crystal. Is everything okay? Call me back ASAP."

Message two:

"I'm calling for Bette Childs. This is Gloria at the Lansing

Public Library. The books you put on hold have come in. You can pick them up anytime."

No more messages.

Bette slumped over the machine.

She picked up the receiver and dialed Crystal's number. It rang five times before her machine picked up.

She listened to Crystal's cheery message, imagining her sister recording it as she doodled flowers on the notepad next to her phone.

"Crystal, it's Bette. I'm starting to panic now, okay? I just reported you missing at the police station and I really need you to call me back. If you get this, when you get this, call me back. I'm serious. Don't even stop to pee. CALL ME BACK!"

Bette set down the receiver and walked into her living room where her two cats, Chai and Oolong, lay curled into a single ball of gray fur. Chai's head perked up when she entered, but when Bette didn't whip out a can opener or shake the bag of treats, she nestled her face into her sister's back and returned to her nap.

Without turning on the lights, Bette walked to the easy chair by the window and sat down. It had been their father's chair. It was old and ugly, with the seams frayed and one side bearing deep scratches from her cats' claws. She should have gotten rid of it, years earlier, when their dad left the house and abandoned the chair. But she couldn't let it go. She had memories of the chair. Memories of sitting on her mother's lap, fighting for space with Crystal as their father climbed a ladder to put the star on the Christmas tree.

Bette rocked back and forth in the chair, listening to the creaks and groans, unable to stop her legs from trembling. She braced her hands on the worn armrests, feeling the wood frame poking through.

Beyond the window, the street lay dark and quiet. Occasionally headlights passed. Sometimes two or three minutes elapsed between cars, and every set of headlights made her tense, her fingernails digging into the chair; but each car drove by, disappearing into the darkness.

Crystal had spoken of dying young for as long as Bette could remember. She'd been saying the words years before it was cool —*only the good die young*, and all the nonsense teens started to pick up as more and more rock stars perished before they reached twenty-five.

Bette remembered Crystal leaning close to their mother's casket at the funeral and whispering, "I'll see you soon, Mama."

It had upset Bette so much she'd run from the funeral home and taken shelter in the foyer, where her mother's best friend, Lilith, had stood talking to Bette's Uncle Jerry.

"But that's just Crystal," Bette insisted to the quiet room.

Chai looked up, eyes going hopefully to Bette's hands before again returning her face to Oolong's fur.

A car passed, break lights shining, and Bette jumped up, ready to run to the front door. The car pulled into Bette's driveway and her stomach leapt into her throat.

Mingled joy and anger erupted in her mind as she flung the front door open, but the car had already begun to reverse into the street. It was only a stranger turning around. She watched it drive several houses down before pulling into the Hammonds' residence. Their boys, who had gone to school with Bette and Crystal, were both grown and away at out-of-state universities.

Bette watched the doors of a car that was not Bette's swing open. An older woman climbed out, reaching back in for a paper bag before walking to the front door.

Bette stood on the doorstep, watching driveways illuminated by porch lights. A few people were out and about. Cecilia Gomez walked an envelope to her mailbox. When she spotted Bette, she lifted her hand and waved.

Bette waved and slid into the house, unable to close the door behind her. She left it open. The night breeze ruffled the papers on Bette's kitchen table and sent them in a whoosh to the floor.

The phone rang, and she jumped, running to the kitchen and startling both cats who stood, backs arched, as she snatched up the phone.

"Hello!" she half-yelled.

"Bette?" her father asked slowly. "Is everything okay, honey?"

Bette sighed.

"Dad, have you talked to Crystal?"

"No, not for a few days. She called me on..." He paused, and Bette assumed he was looking at the day planner next to his phone. He was a meticulous record keeper. He wrote down appointments, phone calls, even what he ate for breakfast most days. "Tuesday."

"Not since Tuesday?" Bette sagged against the wall.

"What is it, Bette? Is something wrong with Crystal?"

Bette imagined their father, the person she could thank for her neuroses, on the other end, tapping his fingernails on the side table next to his reclining chair. His dog Teddy would be snuggled in the chair beside him, head resting on her father's lap, ears perked when he sensed Homer's distress.

Bette wanted to lie and appease him. She'd done it a thousand times before. She'd learned to manage her father's emotions, in the years after their mother died, when a spat between her and Crystal might send him pacing up and down the driveway for more than an hour, hands jittery, anxious eyes watching the house for signs of the inevitable storm.

But that night she couldn't bring herself to tell the lie. She needed someone to commiserate with her, she needed someone who would understand.

"Dad," Bette paused and took a deep breath. "Crystal is missing."

She couldn't hear the tapping, but she imagined his fingers, drumming seconds before, suddenly pausing in mid-air.

"What do you mean, she's missing?"

"Well today is—"

"I know what today is," he said.

Homer never spent the anniversary of his wife's death with his daughters, not since they were girls, but he marked the date in his own way. The year before he'd been leaving the cemetery just as Crystal and Bette had arrived with flowers.

"She was supposed to meet me here at the house at five," Bette explained. "She never showed. I've been to her apartment, the Hospice House, the bookstore, the coffee shop. Nothing, not a trace."

On the other end, her father's chair creaked.

"Get down Teddy, there you go," her father told his dog. "Have you called her girlfriends? Or how about the boy across the hall? The one who came to Thanksgiving last year. What's his name again? Grady?"

"Garret. Yes, I've talked to everyone. The last person to see her was a guy from the coffee shop, Rick. She got a coffee at nine this morning. That's all I've got."

"How about the boyfriend? Western? She seemed quite taken with him."

Bette sighed and tugged on the phone cord. "Weston Meeks. I don't have his number."

"Don't have his number? Well, look him up in the phone book, Bette. He probably knows right where she's at."

"I tried to look him up in the phone book. His number wasn't listed. I called the university where he works and again, no number on record. I know he teaches Poetry 101 on Monday at nine a.m., but that's days away."

"Monday morning?" Her father thought out loud. "I'd best drive up. Right? I mean if she's been in an accident ... Yes, okay, I'm on my way."

Bette didn't bother arguing with her father. He'd made his mind up the moment she said Crystal was missing. His doggedness made him a good archeologist. He didn't let things go, and she needed a partner. She couldn't go it alone on this one.

"Dad, I already went to the police."

Silence on the line.

"Okay. That was the right thing to do. I'm leaving now."

6

Now

Bette walked down the driveway and looked in the mailbox, though she'd already retrieved the mail that day. It had been a stupid thought. Maybe Crystal had tucked a note in the mailbox, in such a hurry she hadn't even bothered to walk it up to the house, but no. It stood empty. A little black cavern of nothing.

She walked back to the house and then returned to the road. On her next lap, she slipped into the side yard where a shed, formerly the sisters' childhood playhouse, held the push lawn mower, rakes, a snow shovel and the necessities of a life. Bette had arranged the tools by the season. A section for winter items, including the bags of salt and the shovel, another section for the summer with pouches of flower seeds and her mother's big red watering can.

Their father had left it all when he moved out, opting for a condo near the Archeology Association he'd joined after his work as a professor ended. He left everything except a photo album, his clothes and a handful of knickknacks he'd purchased with his wife over the years.

He'd left many of his archeology books. He wanted Bette to have them. She'd followed him into the field, though her chosen focus was anthropology, the remnants of civilizations rather than their bones. He said they'd offer inspiration and reminders to keep going; you never knew what lay beneath another foot from the surface, *keep digging*.

It took her father an hour to make the drive to his former home. When he arrived, the hair on the left side of his head stuck out in tufts as if he'd been massaging and pulling at it on the drive, which he had, Bette knew. It was one of his nervous ticks, one she'd inherited.

"Hi Dad," Bette said, hugging him and walking back to the house with Homer practically stepping on her heels.

"Martin Henderson works at the university. I'll call him and see if I can't track down this Western person."

"Weston," Bette corrected.

"Sure, yes, Weston."

Her dad grabbed the phone in the kitchen and sat down at the table with a pen and a notepad.

Bette tried not to hover over him as he dialed the number, but she couldn't help it. Her lunch plates were still in the sink. She washed them, glancing back repeatedly and trying to make sense of the one-sided conversation as her father spoke into the phone.

Homer hung up. "He didn't have Weston's number, but he gave me the number for Jared Knudson. Apparently, they're chums." He dialed again. "Hi, may I speak to Jared Knudson please?"

His pen was poised and ready, but he looked momentarily crestfallen.

"Out of town for the entire week? Where? Mississippi.

Hmm... Could I get his number there? It is a matter of some importance. Yes, okay. I understand."

Homer hung up again and chewed the end of the pencil.

"He's visiting his ailing mother in Mississippi. His wife refused to give me his number, but said she'd ask him to call us back." He tapped the pencil against the wire binding on the notebook. "Someone has to know this guy."

He stared at the paper beneath him. He'd written almost nothing on it and then his eyes brightened and he slapped his forehead.

"Crystal!" he exclaimed. "Crystal knows him. His number is somewhere in her apartment. Come on." He stood and strode out the door.

Bette followed him. She'd looked for Weston's number earlier, but not thoroughly. At that point, she'd still assumed it was all a big mistake. Crystal had forgotten, or some unseeable thing had come up, preventing her from arriving.

It was still reasonable that she'd appear at any moment, filled with apologies. But that time had dwindled. They'd moved into dangerous territory — into that foreboding stretch that signaled something was wrong. If it had been anything within Crystal's control, Bette would have heard from her by now.

Bette's father drove, tapping on the steering wheel and pulling at his hair when they stopped at red lights.

"Have they added two minutes on to every red light in town? This is ridiculous." He thumped his hand on the wheel and the car shot forward the moment the light turned green.

Bette wound her fingers together and unwound them. She pulled at a string coming loose from her jeans. She looked out the windows, searching the people in restaurants, the faces of women walking to their cars, but none of them was Crystal.

When they opened the door to Crystal's apartment, her dad held out his arm.

"Disturb as little as possible," he told her, moving into the apartment light on his feet.

Bette surveyed the room.

The front door opened into a large combined kitchen and living room. Beyond that, a short hallway led to a single bedroom and a bathroom at the end. Colorful Indian tapestries hung from the yellow walls.

Crystal didn't have a kitchen table, but used a small island for eating. It was scattered with text books. Every chair had clothes slung over the back. Every surface contained books and journals.

Stained-glass hummingbirds, angels and flowers hung in her picture window. A pair of purple fuzzy slippers in the shape of Bigfoot's feet rested near her couch.

Homer walked to the hanging wicker chair near the picture window looking into the courtyard behind the apartments. A stack of magazines stood on a table, a book of poetry balanced on top. He picked up a pen and gently opened the cover of the book, allowing it to drop when he saw nothing of interest.

Bette headed straight to Crystal's room.

She eyed books and papers on the dresser. Clothes lay strewn across a chest and filled a hamper behind the door.

Beside Crystal's bed stood a nightstand holding a telephone, a notebook, and a paperback copy of *The Handmaid's Tale.*

Bette picked up the notebook and thumbed through the pages.

She read mostly scattered thoughts, things Crystal probably recorded when she woke in the night struck by inspiration for a poem. The series of numbers Crystal had been obsessed with most of her life was marked throughout the pages: *6251991.*

In the other room, she heard her father click play on the message machine.

"Crystal, it's Wes. I'm sorry, okay? Please just call me."

"Hi Crystal, it's Nina Henderson from Hospice House. I

wanted to let you know George Potter's son brought you a thank you gift. He might be sweet on you. No need to stop in and grab it. I'll put it in your cubby."

Two more messages from Wes, each sounding more urgent than the last.

"They had a fight," Homer said. "And she might have called you back if you'd left your unholy number!" He blurted, glaring at the machine.

Bette's father rarely swore, but when he did, his word of choice was *unholy*.

"I checked her address book. I don't think Weston's number is in this apartment," Bette sighed, tugging at her long hair.

"It's got to be. It's somewhere..." Homer's eyes scanned the room slowly, coming to rest on the corner drawer in Crystal's kitchen.

The infamous junk drawer, that dark burrow collecting the oddities people couldn't seem to throw away.

Homer went to the drawer and slid it open. It stuck. He tugged it and then carefully reached a hand inside, pushing the contents around until he managed to open it all the way. He laid a clean dishtowel on the countertop and started removing items, one by one.

Unable to stand and watch without helping, Bette joined him.

Her dad extracted six pens in various colors, and two pencils, one with the eraser broken off. He took out a necklace tangled into a pile of cheap silver with a small butterfly pendant. He removed three batteries in various sizes. The first bit of scrap paper contained a scrawled recipe for coconut lime banana bread.

He found a broken Christmas ornament of a puppy wearing a Santa hat; its foot was missing. Peppermint candies, loose change, a wadded-up dollar bill, three playing cards and a brochure for bungee jumping all came out of the drawer.

He pulled out a scrunched napkin from Luna's Cafe. When he gently unfolded the edges, Bette saw the phone number emerge beneath the name "Professor Meeks" and next to that, with a smiley face, "Wes."

"That's it," she shouted, ripping the napkin out of his hand and running to the phone.

Her father said nothing, but smiled grimly and began to put the items back in the drawer.

Bette snatched up the receiver and punched in the phone number.

After three rings, the answering machine picked up.

"Hi, you've reached the phone of Weston Meeks. I'm currently unavailable. Please leave your name and phone number and I'll call you at my earliest convenience."

"Weston, this is Bette Childs, Crystal's sister. Crystal is missing. I need you to call me as soon as possible at 517-676-4037."

She hung up.

"Let's go back to your house and send Mr. Meeks an email at the University," her dad said.

~

WESTON MEEKS DIDN'T CALL BACK until the following evening.

"Bette, this is Wes calling. I just got back into town and listened to your message. Have you found her?" he sounded agitated, scared even.

"She's not with you?" Bette demanded, planting a hand on the wall as a dizzying sense of falling coursed through her. "When's the last time you saw her?"

"On Wednesday," Weston admitted. "I haven't seen her since then. I had to go back to Traverse City to teach on Thursday and then I got sick."

Homer stopped next to Bette and held out his hand.

She gave him the phone.

"Weston Meeks?" Homer asked in his usual dry tone. "This is Crystal's father, Homer. Bette and I would like to speak to you in person. Can you meet us in one hour?"

No answer. Finally, the voice returned.

"Sure, yeah."

"We'll meet you at Captain Mike's in Old Town. In one hour, which is," Homer lifted his wrist and gazed at his watch, "six-seventeen."

He hung up the phone and looked at Bette, his forehead wrinkled with worry.

7

Then

CRYSTAL PARKED her VW bug and climbed out.

Thick gray clouds muted the light of the day. A thin drizzle fell, and she tilted her face up, allowing the rain to wet her cheeks. It had been an unseasonably warm few days in Michigan, and much of the snow, piling in drifts since January, had melted. As March came to a close, she imagined the spring. The return of green, of flowers and sunny skies.

The Crow Thieves were doing an unplugged show at a coffee-shop pub combined that served the best Aztec hot chocolate, something she had first discovered in California and been delighted to find in Michigan.

As she hurried down the alley and into the parking lot behind the pub, she spotted a familiar figure jogging from the other direction.

Weston Meeks.

He didn't notice her.

She slowed, watching him.

He wore ripped jeans and an itchy-looking wool sweater. He'd tied his shoulder-length hair back. His beard and mustache looked recently trimmed.

Weston stopped at the door and pulled the handle. It didn't open. He leaned in, reading a white sign plastered to the glass.

Crystal started walking again.

He looked up, surprised as she approached.

"Hi." He grinned.

"Hi," she laughed. "Small world."

"Are you here to see the Crow Thieves?"

She nodded.

"Well, I hate to be the bearer of bad news, but they canceled the show because of a power outage in the building." He tapped on the door where the taped sign hung.

"Bummer," she admitted as a crack of thunder split the sky and stole her comment.

As if summoned by the thunder, the drizzle turned into a downpour.

"Whoa," Weston yelled, but she barely heard him as rain pelted the street and buildings around them.

In seconds they were both soaked.

Crystal regretted the too-thin jacket she'd chosen based on the warmer temperatures as the cold rain saturated it and the shirt beneath.

Weston cupped a hand over his eyes.

"I walked from campus," he yelled.

"I'm parked over there," she shouted back. "I'll give you a ride."

They ran through the rain thundering onto the pavement. It hit the hard surface and splashed up, soaking their shoes and pant legs.

When they reached Crystal's car, she grabbed the door handle and yanked. The door didn't open.

"Oh shit," she whispered, leaning close and spotting her keys still dangling from the ignition.

Weston had wrenched up his sweater to create a small and ineffective cover for his head.

He recognized the look on her face and laughed.

"Locked out?" he yelled.

She nodded.

"My office is two blocks that way." He pointed towards the Michigan State University campus. "Let's make a run for it."

He offered his hand, and she grabbed it, not thinking about the stares if anyone spotted a professor and student running hand in hand through the wet grounds. Who would see them anyway? The street was empty; the campus deserted at five o'clock on a Sunday afternoon.

As they ran, Crystal's hands slid inside Weston's. It was a raw, exhilarating sensation. The wetness threatened to separate them, but she held on, refusing to let her fingers slip from his.

He ran up the cement steps to the huge brick building that served as the offices for most of the English staff at MSU.

They pushed through the door, and as it closed behind them, the roar of the storm died.

Inside, the long, high-ceilinged corridor was dim and quiet. Only a single lamp illuminated the hall.

"I'm on the second floor," Wes explained, heading toward a wide staircase with a bit of threadbare carpet running down the center.

They still held hands, and the electric buzzing between their palms seemed to intensify in the hushed space of the building's interior.

She swallowed the lump of nervous excitement lodged in her throat.

When they reached a door in the second-floor hallway, he pulled his hand from hers, reaching into his pocket for a keyring.

She held her hand in the air for a moment longer, the space where his had been empty and cold.

"Come on in," he told her, pushing into the office, and laughed. "Welcome to my cave."

The space was small, made smaller by the bookshelves on either wall crammed with books and binders. A desk sat in the back of the little office, a brown leather chair behind it. Much of the desk's surface was consumed by a large desktop computer. A leather couch faced the desk. Behind the chair, a window looked over the sodden campus.

"I've got a space heater," he told her, reaching behind his desk and pulling out a small black box.

He plugged it in and set it on top of his desk, directing the blasts of warm air towards Crystal.

"Mmm, that's perfect. Thank you," she said, shivering.

She hadn't noticed the cold until he took his hand from hers. Now her teeth chattered, and her wet clothes felt like ice blankets draped over her goose-pimpled flesh.

He wheeled his chair from behind his desk, placing it near the corner of the couch.

"I think I have..." he mumbled, digging around in a duffel bag in the room's corner, "...extra shirts!" He held up two MSU Spartans sweatshirts. "They give these to the staff as Christmas gifts every year. I don't even take them home anymore. I just drop them at the thrift store or give them to students."

"Thank you," she told him, pulling her coat away from her skin and fanning it in front of the heater.

"There's a bathroom down the hall," he told her, watching as she peeled off her soaked jacket. "Or I can just turn around."

She saw the blush rising up his neck. Her own blood coursed hot and close to the surface of her skin.

"I don't mind," she told him.

Before he could protest, she pulled her blouse over her head.

She wore her white satin bra. Not a pretty bra, but a well-worn and somewhat tattered undergarment with frayed elastic and a clasp broken on the back. She didn't care.

He blinked and looked away, shifting his eyes toward the floor.

Shivering, she stepped toward him. She took his prickly sweater in her hands and pulled it up.

As it rose toward his face, he looked at her, their eyes meeting before she drew the sweater over his head.

A swath of dark curls covered his chest.

His eyes found her again, and for several seconds they stood staring at each other, their desire expanding until it filled the room.

Weston broke the stillness. He put a hand on the small of her back and pulled her against him, crushing his mouth into hers.

They kissed until her mouth was raw and sore. His hands roamed over her face, her hair, and her back. His mouth moved from her lips to her nose and jaw, and finally to her neck.

They would have gone further. They nearly did.

A phone rang in the office next door. The shrill sound startled them both.

Weston paused, his mouth hot on her shoulder. He continued lower, kissing her chest, moving toward her breast.

But then it rang a second time and someone answered.

"Hello?" The wall between the offices muffled the woman's voice.

Weston stiffened and stood.

His hands slid away from Crystal's back.

She didn't reach for him, though she wanted to. His nervous, dazed expression told her the magic of the moment had slipped away.

He peered at the floor and rubbed his jaw before returning his eyes to hers. He looked ashamed.

"I—" he started.

She watched the apology forming on his lips and placed her hand over his mouth.

When she took it away, she put a finger to her lips.

She slipped the MSU sweatshirt over her head and stepped close to him, kissing him fiercely.

Without another word, she walked out the door and down the hall.

The rain had subsided, and Crystal ran across campus to the Union, where she ordered a coffee and sat in a little plastic booth watching the traffic crawl by on Grand River Avenue.

Her body seemed light and fluttery. If she stood naked before a mirror, she imagined she'd witness all the little atoms popping and whirring. She reached beneath her sweatshirt and touched the space on her shoulder where he'd last kissed her. She could still feel the impression of his mouth, not on her skin, but in her, as if for those drawn-out moments they'd melted together.

After an hour, when the buzz had worn off, she called Bette.

8

Now

Bette sat elbow to elbow with her dad in the little dive bar called Captain Mike's. Prior to that, it been named Captain Kurt's, and before that Captain Craig's.

Despite the change in ownership and a slightly modified name; the nautical decor, the dim lighting, and the rank smell of beer spilled onto old carpeting remained.

"Why'd you choose this place, Dad?" Bette asked, grimacing when her arm stuck to the grubby table.

He looked at her, surprised.

"Captain Craig's? This place is great. Your mom and I used to come here all the time. She went into labor with you at that table right over there." He pointed to a table in the corner, occupied by a group of middle-aged men drinking tall glasses of beer and arguing about the baseball game playing on the little TV above the bar.

"How charming," she grumbled.

"Plus, this place puts people at ease," Homer added. "Lots of cozy corners. It's loud enough. Setting is important when you interrogate someone."

"Interrogate?" Bette asked, surprised.

"I think it's an appropriate description," he replied.

The waiter, a middle-aged man with the weary gaze of a guy who'd spent too many years working in a bar, stopped at their table.

"What can I get ya?" he asked.

"A ginger-ale for me," Homer said.

"I'll have water, please. With lemon," she added.

Homer shook his head. "Make hers something dark, Coke or Pepsi."

"Eew, no," she argued.

Homer put a hand on his daughter's arm.

"They look like alcoholic drinks. We want to put him at ease, Bette. I want him to order a drink and he'll only do that if he thinks we've done the same."

"Fine, Cherry Coke, then," she told the waiter.

"And put them in short glasses, please," Homer added.

The waiter brought their drinks, sliding them onto the table as Weston walked in.

Bette did a double take when she saw him. His long hair had been sheared above his ears and his beard was gone.

"That's him," Bette mumbled under her breath. She saw her father train his eyes on the man who had entered.

He looked like a clean-cut college boy rather than the scruffy hippie-type Bette had met weeks before. He wore dark jeans and a green Michigan State University t-shirt. The removal of his facial hair made him look younger, more like a student than a professor.

He spotted Bette and smiled tensely, waving.

Sliding into the booth, he held out his hand.

"Hi, Mr. Childs. I'm Weston Meeks. It's a pleasure to meet you."

Homer extended his own hand, shook Weston's, and then signaled to the waiter.

"What will you have?" Homer asked as the waiter returned.

Wes glanced at Homer's and Bette's drinks.

"Ummm... I guess I'll have a scotch and soda. Thanks."

The waiter nodded and left.

"Let's get right down to it," Homer said. "Crystal was supposed to meet Bette yesterday at five for the anniversary of Joanna's death. This is a big deal. They do this every year. They go to dinner and then to the cemetery. Were you aware of that?"

Weston blinked at Homer.

"Umm... yeah. No. I didn't know they went to the cemetery every year. I knew the anniversary was coming up because Crystal told me last week."

"But she didn't show," Bette said. "And she'd never miss it." Her voice was rising, and Homer rested his hand over hers, a silent signal for her to stop talking.

"Crystal is spontaneous. That is true," Homer relented. "But more than that, she's considerate. Under no circumstances will Crystal hurt someone's feelings or stand them up. So, when she missed her scheduled date with her sister, Bette was immediately alarmed."

"Yeah, of course," Wes agreed.

Bette gazed at the glass but noticed Homer kept his focus on Wes.

Homer stared at the man intently. "Do you know where Crystal is, Weston?"

The waiter returned with Weston's drink and he took a sip before answering.

Wes shook his head. "No, not at all. Like I said, I haven't seen her since Wednesday."

"Have you spoken with her since then?" Homer continued.

Wes shook his head again, picked up his drink and finished it.

Homer signaled to the waiter.

"Oh, no, I'm fine," Wes argued, but Homer ignored him.

"A refill, please," Homer said, gesturing at Weston's glass.

"No, I haven't talked to her. I tried to call her a few times, but—"

"But she didn't answer and didn't return your calls?" Homer asked.

Wes nodded.

"Is that usual, Weston? To not speak with my daughter for three days?"

Wes opened his hands.

The waiter returned with his second drink, and he immediately clutched it.

"Not really. We talk most days, but... well, sometimes we don't. It just depends..."

"On what?" Homer inquired.

"I'm sorry?" Wes asked, and when he lifted his glass, Bette saw a slight shaking, though he tried to hold the glass steady.

"What does it depend on?" Homer asked.

"Oh, well. I mean if I'm busy or she's busy."

"So you're saying it has happened before since you started dating? You've gone three days without talking to Crystal?"

Weston's eyes shot towards the bar, scanned the other people, and returned to Homer before flicking down to his glass.

Bette realized Weston was struggling to look Homer in the eyes.

"No, not really. We talk almost every day."

"I see. And where do you think Crystal is right now, Weston?"

Wes's gaze jerked up and he glanced at Bette before taking another drink.

"I... we sort of had an argument. I thought she needed a couple of days to cool off. Maybe she took a drive somewhere. She has friends out west..."

Bette sputtered, planting both hands on the table. "Are you kidding me? Crystal would never hop in her car and drive out west without telling any of us. That's insane!"

Again, Homer's hand crept to hers. He gave her finger a little pinch.

She shot him a furious look.

Wes looked back and forth between father and daughter.

"I didn't know you hadn't heard from her," Wes explained. "I assumed she was only ignoring me."

"And what exactly did you fight about?" Homer asked.

Weston blushed and looked away. "Nothing really. Just... The usual couple stuff."

"No, I'm sorry, you must elaborate," Homer insisted. "Couples are very unique after all. I'd imagine the arguments myself and my wife had were very different than those between you and Crystal."

Weston shifted his hands into his lap.

"I had to go out of town next weekend, and that bothered Crystal. Her friend is in a play at the Wharton Center and she hoped we could go together. She got upset about it and left."

"That doesn't sound like Crystal," Bette interrupted.

"I have to agree with my daughter there, Weston. Crystal is not one to get upset about such things."

Weston sighed. "She did. I don't know why. Maybe there were other things she didn't say."

Officer Hart met Homer and Bette in the lobby.

"Come on back," he told them, leading them to his cubicle. He dragged an extra chair from a nearby desk. "I put Crystal's information in the system as a missing person's case yesterday and there's a Be On the Lookout for her car. No sightings have come in. Based on the information you've provided we're going to escalate to a potentially endangered missing person, but this can be deescalated any time if we receive information that implies Crystal left of her own free will."

"She didn't," Bette insisted, "and we just questioned her boyfriend. He cut his hair and shaved off his beard, and he was clearly lying."

Hart frowned. "You questioned him?"

"We simply had a drink with him to ask if he'd spoken with Crystal," Homer clarified.

"Okay. Well, that's our job from now on. Got it? I need a list of her co-workers, last people to see her, friends, everyone," Hart said.

He handed a sheet of paper and pen to Bette and she started writing.

9

Then

CRYSTAL DIDN'T SEE Professor Meeks until class that Wednesday.

He kept his gaze carefully averted from her own, but slipped once, and when their eyes met, he lost his train of thought as he'd done previously in his lecture. He apologized, returned to a stack of notes on his desk and veered into a topic about opening lines.

"Unlike books, poems do not have to make their intentions known in the first line," he told the class. "Though I challenge you to do so. Consider *Merciless Beauty* by Geoffrey Chaucer: *Your two great eyes will slay me suddenly. Their beauty shakes me who was once serene.* From those two lines, what do you think the poem is about?"

A girl in the front row raised her hand.

Weston nodded at her.

"I think it's about unrequited love," she said.

"Good. Why?" he asked.

"Well, he writes that her beauty shakes him when he was once serene. So, he's in love with her, but it's not reciprocated because he's using words like slay and shake."

"Very good." He pointed to another student with his hand raised. "Tell us your thoughts, Ronnie."

"I thought maybe he was facing down a dragon," the student said. "Or a Medusa. I mean, Medusa turned men to stone when they looked at her, right? Maybe he's talking about a literal she-monster."

The students laughed, Weston included.

"We know from history that Chaucer wasn't talking about a literal she-monster, whatever that is," Weston explained. "But I like where you're going, Ronnie. Poetry is meant to ignite something in each of us. We don't need the poet's reason for writing the poem. We need to discover what the poem reveals about ourselves."

Weston's eyes flicked up to Crystal as he spoke.

"The love might not be unrequited. Perhaps it's merely a love so passionate it threatens to burn the writer alive."

He glanced away from her, but Crystal felt the weight of his words.

When class ended, she packed her backpack slowly, slipping out the door as Weston quickly ended a conversation with a student, promising they'd talk more during his office hours the following day.

She left the building and walked across campus.

The cool April sun turned the puddles of melted snow into thousands of shimmering mirrors.

Crystal heard Weston's footsteps behind her.

She strode into the library, pausing to glance back at him. He still followed, his leather bag slung over one shoulder. He pretended not to see her, though a little smile played on his lips.

She took the staircase at the back of the building, going to the fourth floor. The rows were mostly empty. The only sounds came from the heat pushing through the metal vents overhead.

Crystal walked into an aisle and pretended to look at a book.

She didn't turn when he entered the row, stopping beside her and studying the shelves.

Crystal didn't move. Her shoulder pressed against his. She waited, the seconds stretching out until finally his hand slipped around her waist.

"My nights have been centuries since I last touched you," he whispered, leaning so close she felt his breath in her ear. "A jumble of endless hours with your face, your breath, your smile violating my every thought."

He stepped in front of her, sliding his other hand to her back.

"I missed you too," she murmured.

He kissed her, and some part of her collided with him in a space beyond their physical bodies, as if her soul had stepped out and embraced his.

They were in the annex, a rarely used section of the library that was filled with narrow aisles, between shelves and books that looked like they hadn't been checked out in decades. The annex had the musty, woody smell of ancient books.

As she tilted her head back and Weston pressed his mouth into the hollow beneath her throat, she saw an ocean of dust sparkling in the single beam of sunlight coming through the tall window at the end of the annex. The dust, more like a thousand sparkles, shifted as if all the tiny particles were on a journey out of the annex and into the daylight.

"My flame-haired goddess," Wes whispered, kissing her collarbone now, pulling her blouse open and moving lower. "You've put a spell on me."

An aisle over, someone pulled a book roughly from the shelves. A woman's high, annoyed cough followed.

Crystal clamped her mouth shut, straightening as Wes paused with his lips on her chest.

The moment was reminiscent of their last encounter in his office and, for a moment, Crystal feared Weston would get spooked a second time.

He looked up at her, biting his lip to keep from laughing.

Relieved, Crystal's own laughter gurgled and burst forth before she could rein it in.

The woman made an irritated sighing sound as if she'd just discovered two children drawing nude pictures in the books.

Crystal heard her move down the carpeted aisle.

Before the woman passed their row, Wes grabbed Crystal's hand and dragged her deeper into the annex.

"Come on," he whispered.

He tugged her down a narrow hallway.

"What's back here?" she whispered.

She'd only ventured into the annex a few times and had never noticed the dark hallway in the back of the section.

"Storage," he said trying doors, which proved mostly to be locked. The third one wasn't.

When he opened the door, they discovered a tiny room, not stuffed with books, but containing several worn armchairs.

"A daydreaming room," she whispered.

"A dream-making room," he corrected, his lips tickling the sensitive contours of her ear.

She shivered, and goosebumps rose along her arms.

He sat in a chair and pulled her onto his lap. As they kissed, he buried his hands in her hair, massaging her scalp, tilting her head back to run his fingers over her delicate throat.

They kissed for an eternity until the bright light of day softened and flowed in amber rivers across the shabby carpet.

"Come home with me," she whispered.

He pushed her long hair away from her face and studied her.

She saw something in his eyes, that murky secret crawling into the recesses, taking refuge from her gaze.

"Yes," he murmured.

10

Now

BETTE STOOD in the crowd of people. Police officers and volunteers swarmed the dirt parking lot that lined the wooded expanse behind Crystal's apartment building.

It was likely to be a futile search. If Crystal had wandered into the woods, her car would be sitting in the parking lot, but after four days and no leads, Bette managed to convince Hart to organize a search party.

Hart stood next to Bette, watching other officers dividing searchers into groups.

A bearded man, wearing a cowboy hat and a stained white t-shirt, broke from the throng of people and ambled over to Hart and Bette.

"Are you Officer Hart?" the man demanded.

"Yes. What do you need?" Hart asked, his eyes barely registering the man as he continued to scan the group of people.

"My name's Alvin," the man told him. "I found something."

He shifted his bloodshot brown eyes from the officer to Bette and then back to Hart.

"I'm sorry, just now?" Hart asked, paying closer to attention to the man before him.

"Last night," the man said. He spoke in a deep gravelly voice. "Real late. I called the police station, and they said the man working the missing girl's case would be here. So here I am."

Hart glanced at Bette and she thought he might ask her to leave.

She wouldn't go.

"I was parked up by Frasier Gorge last night around midnight. I sleep in my truck most nights and there's a gorge up there, a nice little spot to park and look out over the trees. I was sittin', havin' a smoke, when a little girl stepped out of the road and onto the dirt lot."

"Hold on," Hart said. "A little girl was out at Frasier Gorge at midnight?"

Alvin nodded and scratched his beard. "That look yer havin' right now about sums up how I was feeling. What in God's green earth is this child, no more than eight or nine, doing in these woods in the middle of the night? I had my windows rolled down, and she was singing that funny little song kids like, "Ring around the rosie, pockets full of posies-"

"I know the song," Hart interrupted before the man could sing the entire nursery rhyme.

"Anyhoo," Alvin went on, "I sort of craned around, looking for her parents or maybe an older brother. There're a few houses up that way. Not many, mind you, and most of 'em a good mile from that spot."

He stuffed his hands in the pockets of his worn blue jeans.

"That little girl walked right up to the lip of the gorge and stopped singing, and I thought she was gonna jump. I was about to hop out of my truck when she started throwing pebbles off the cliff into the canyon below. Ain't nothing down there but a bunch of woods, or so I thought. But as I'm sitting there, quiet as a cup of soup, I hear these little metal pings."

He paused as if to make sure they were still following the story. "Ping... ping... they went. Each time she threw a pebble, another little ping. Add I'm thinking, there's something metal down in that gorge. I'm a scrapping man. Something I do for a few bucks on the side, but I'm only half thinking that because I'm still wondering where this strange girl's parents are. Finally, I think I need to say something, so I gather myself and step out of my truck and... poof, she was just gone. Gone like a rabbit, I guess, into the forest."

"She ran away?" Hart asked.

Bette stood beside him, trying to puzzle the story together, her hands growing sweaty in the pockets of her shorts.

"I didn't see her run away, but she must have, because by the time I closed the door of my pickup, she was long gone. I listened real good, thinking I'd hear her in the woods, ya know? Twigs snappin', leaves crunchin'. But nothing, not a peep. I did a little walk around. Walked out to the road, walked into the brush a bit and finally decided she'd run off real quiet like, probably noticed me in the truck and got spooked."

He tugged on his beard. "The kiddies don't like this beard, or so my brother says; his young-uns run like wild pigs when I show up. I waited a few more minutes and then thought what the hay, might as well climb down that gorge and see what the girl had been hittin' with her rocks. I went back to my truck and grabbed my flashlight and walked down."

Alvin paused as a few other searchers moved closer. They too were listening to his story.

"About halfway down, I shined my light and spotted something blue. A light blue, but it was kinda covered over with leaves. I got all the way down and saw it was a car, a Beetle Bug or whatever they call those with the round top. This one had a black soft top, the kind that folds down. Anyway, there's a light blue Beetle sitting at the bottom of Frasier Gorge like somebody drove it right off that cliff."

Bette's knees buckled, and she hit the grass with a thud, sinking her butt onto her heels.

She shook her head from side to side.

"Homer," Hart called out, waving.

Bette's dad looked up from where he'd been cross-sectioning a map with another searcher. When he noticed Bette, he ran towards them.

"Gosh, I'm sorry, Miss. I didn't mean to—" the bearded man said, removing his Stetson hat and holding it over his chest.

Homer knelt and took Bette's hand.

"Are you having a panic attack, Bette?" he asked.

She shook her head and pointed a shaky finger at Alvin

Hart signaled to another officer.

"Radio the station. We've got a witness who found a blue Volkswagen Beetle at the bottom of Frasier Gorge. We need confirmation."

Homer looked up sharply at Hart's comment. He stood, Bette forgotten on the grass.

"Someone found my daughter's car? Who? You?" He turned to face the bearded man whose eyes darted between the police officers.

"Yes, sir. I found a little blue Beetle Bug at the bottom of Frasier Gorge."

Homer sprang forward and grabbed his shirt.

"Was she in it? Was Crystal in the car?" he demanded.

Alvin stepped back, blinking at Homer's hand as if a tarantula had leapt onto his chest.

"Homer," Hart said, touching him. "Please release this man's shirt."

Homer's shocked eyes turned to Hart and then back to his hand. He let the fabric go, his arm dropping heavily to his side.

"I didn't see anyone in the car," Alvin told them. "I read the paper. I saw the cops was lookin' for a little blue Bug so I didn't touch nothin'. I climbed out of the canyon and called the station first thing this morning. They told me to come here, so that's what I did."

~

More than an hour passed before Officer Hart returned.

Bette didn't have to ask if it was Crystal's car.

Homer stood, clutching his Styrofoam cup of coffee.

"The license plate is a match," Hart told him.

Homer crumpled the cup, cold coffee spilling over his hand. Bette watched his profile as everything contracted, his mouth and eyes screwing tight against the news.

Bette had known it was Crystal's car the moment she heard Alvin's story. Blue VW Bugs weren't common. Weston Meeks had taken Crystal to Frasier Gorge. There were too many coincidences for it to be a coincidence.

"Was Crystal...?" Homer asked, his voice almost too low to hear. He didn't finish the question.

Hart shook his head. "She wasn't in the car. We've done a preliminary search of the surrounding area, but a larger search is in the works. Right now, we've got to get the car out. In the meantime, the chief is organizing the search. There are already officers out there cordoning off the woods. Are you familiar with Frasier Gorge?"

Homer shook his head.

Hart looked at Bette.

"I've never been there, but Crystal told me about it," she said.

Hart's expression perked. "She liked to go there?"

Bette shook her head. "Weston Meeks took her there once for a date."

Hart frowned, but didn't ask more.

"We've canceled the search here. Frasier Gorge is a better use of our resources right now. If that's a dead end, we'll reconsider searching here, but..." He offered his empty hands. "In the meantime, you both might as well head home, eat some breakfast. I'll call if we find anything."

Homer's shoulders slumped, and he sat on the park bench next to Bette. He still clutched his crumpled cup in his hand.

11

Then

WESTON STOPPED MID-POUR, a glob of pancake batter splattering his bare foot.

He'd followed Crystal to her apartment the night before and neither of them had said a word as they walked up the carpeted stairs to the second floor. She'd unlocked the door and stepped inside. Before she'd even turned on a light, his hands hand found her. He'd stripped her slowly, whispering poetry as he kissed every inch of her skin.

They'd made love on her living room floor, and again in her bedroom. And one last time that morning before he jumped out of bed and announced he was making Crystal breakfast.

His hair, more golden than brown in the morning sun, rested on the smooth slope of his shoulders. The muscles in his back shifted as he lowered a ladle into the batter and poured it into the pan. It sizzled and popped.

He turned and caught her watching him.

"I ache for you, Crystal," he said as if in wonderment at his own emotions. "You're right there and still…" He put a hand to his chest. "It's as if you've awakened me."

Crystal sat naked except for Weston's "Get Lit" t-shirt, which he'd left discarded on her bedroom floor the night before. The chair pressed cold against her legs and bottom, but her body prickled at his words. She too felt the ache, the deep calling from within her. A foreign sensation, so alien she wondered if Wes had ignited an internal flame that had been dark her entire life.

How many men had she dated? A few she'd even thought she loved, but now… now she understood she'd been terribly wrong.

She stood and walked to him, softening against his hard chest, nuzzling her face into the crook of his neck. He held her, and his breath whooshed soft in her ear. The pancake in the skillet released a slightly noxious odor as it burned.

She didn't care. Neither of them cared. She'd never eat again if it meant they could stand there, suspended in time and space, holding one another.

The phone rang and she jumped, bumping his chin with the top of her head.

"No," he murmured, though she hadn't pulled away to answer it and she didn't intend to.

A charred odor drifted up from the pancake on the stove.

Weston slipped a hand away and deftly flipped it with the spatula revealing a blackened pancake.

Crystal giggled into his chest.

The phone rang until her message machine picked up.

They both listened to her voice on the machine followed by Bette's.

"Hey, call me. A girl I work with is having a birthday, and she loves pigs. I was thinking of giving her one of Mom's. The one with the top hat. Just a thought. If you don't want me to, I won't. Love ya, bye."

"Who was that?" Weston asked, still keeping one arm around Crystal as he attempted a second, less scorched pancake.

"My sister, Bette."

"And your mom has pet pigs? One that wears a top hat, no less?"

Crystal sighed against him. "Our mom died. Cancer took her when I was eleven. Her mother collected pigs, figurines, not the live ones, and my mom kept a lot of them after my grandmother died. Bette is now the keeper of the pigs."

"I'm sorry you lost your mom," he murmured, kissing the top of her head.

Crystal pulled away and looked into his eyes.

"Thank you," she said. "Do you still have your parents, Wes?"

He'd mentioned his parents' divorce, but she knew little else about the life of Weston Meeks.

He furrowed his brow as he flipped a pancake. This one formed a perfectly round golden disc.

"My mom left when I was ten. I have no idea if she's still alive. My dad died when I was seventeen."

"I'm so sorry," she said, squeezing him harder.

He stroked her back.

"It's been a long time. It hurt when I was young but getting older helped me see her side. Now that I'm a man, I've forgiven both of them. My mother for leaving. Life with my father was hard, and she never wanted to be a mother. My dad was a workaholic and a very distant person emotionally. He paid the bills, and that's about it. My mom..." he trailed off. "I think she just woke up one morning and decided she wanted a different life."

He pulled Crystal away and guided her back to her chair.

"I want to keep holding you," he assured her, "but if I do, we're eating blackened pancakes.

She laughed.

"Anyway," he continued returning to the stove. "She sent cards for the first few years and then…" He shrugged. "Nothing."

"Did you ever try to find her?" Crystal asked.

Wes nodded, turning the pan over and dropping the first edible pancake onto a plate before pouring another scoop of batter in the skillet.

"After my dad died, I hooked up with a band and we started touring," he grinned and looked embarrassed. "And by touring, I mean we drove around in a rusted van and begged dive bars to let us play for their drunken patrons. They paid us in booze." He shook his head. "The dark ages. During my infrequent days of sobriety, I made a few calls. I never found her."

Crystal tried to imagine letting her mother go. Had the woman tried to leave, Crystal would have chased her to the ends of the earth. But then, Crystal's mother would never have left, not of her own free will.

"I tried again a couple years ago," Wes said. "I was getting ready to turn thirty and… I wanted to know she was okay. I didn't care if we had a relationship. I just wanted to put the questions to rest."

Crystal waited, noticing the crease between his eyebrows, the stiffness that settled in his shoulders.

"Nothing. Not a thread of her anywhere. I searched through my dad's stuff. I still have a few boxes. I found some of the old postcards she'd sent and I tried to track her through those, but her address changed frequently. She just disappeared.

Crystal started to ask more, but he cut her off.

"Enough about me. Did you grow up here in East Lansing?" he asked.

"No, but nearby. Dimondale. It's west of town," she said.

"Sure, yeah. I've been to the village bar once or twice. A pretty happening town," he joked.

Crystal laughed. "Yeah, if you're ninety. I wanted to travel after high school. Once I saw more of the world, I realized how tiny Dimondale truly is. My sister still lives in our childhood home. She sort of followed in my dad's footsteps. He's an archeologist. She's an anthropologist. They're two peas in a pod."

"That's great. It fascinates me when people pursue the same careers as their parents. Does your dad dig up dinosaur bones? That kind of thing?"

Crystal laughed. It was the most common question asked when she told someone her father was an archeologist.

"He'd absolutely love that," she said, "but no. He used to do digs out of the country. He excavated skeletal remains in Australia and England with groups he was part of, but after my mom got sick, he shifted to a full-time teaching position and then a few years ago he retired. He's part of the Michigan Archeological Society now. Most of his work these days involves directing young archeologists as they dig up old civilizations here in Michigan. They find pottery and tools."

"Intriguing," he admitted, holding up a plate stacked with pancakes.

"Voilà," he announced. "I hope my goddess is hungry."

Crystal grinned and stood to grab syrup and butter.

"For you," she told him, "but I can make room for pancakes too."

THEY ATE at Crystal's little kitchen table.

Weston flipped the cover on one of her journals.

"What's this?" he asked, tapping the page where she'd written the series of seven numbers that had been plaguing her since childhood.

"I'm not sure," she admitted. "It's a number I've always had in my mind."

"But you don't know what it means?" he asked.

Crystal looked at the sequence, tilted her head sideways. Seven digits, seemingly random, and yet they'd been floating through her head for ages.

When had she first thought of the number? When she was seven or eight. She remembered carving the digits into an oak tree, something she felt guilty about later but at the time seemed okay. All the kids were doing it. Bette had carved, "Bette and Crystal 4 Ever" into the same tree and then added a crude heart around the words.

"Six, two, five, one, nine, nine, one," he read out loud. "It almost looks like nine-one-one in that part. A cry for help?"

He smiled at her in a mischievous way, a tell-me-more way, but a tremor crept down her spine at the suggestion. The numbers had been on repeat in her brain for years and yet, whenever she truly gave it her attention, a sense of foreboding surrounded the numbers.

"I do think they mean something," she murmured.

"Like what?" he asked.

He squinted at the numbers and then picked up a pencil. He wrote an F beneath the number six.

"What are you doing?" she asked.

"Lining them up with the alphabet." He finished and read the letters. "F - B - E - A - I - I - A. Fbeaiia? That mean anything to you?" he wondered.

She didn't immediately answer. As she'd watched him transcribe the letters, her hands had begun to shake. Now, as she stared at the incomprehensible message, the fear slid away.

He looked at her and she shook her head, standing and grabbing his plate.

"Nope. Doesn't mean a thing." And it didn't. But still, as she carried their plates to the sink, she found she didn't want to turn around and look Weston in the eyes.

12

Now

BETTE SAT near Officer Hart's desk.

She'd planted herself there nearly an hour before, refusing to leave until he told her what they'd found.

When he walked over, his eyes looked troubled.

"What?" she said, shooting to her feet. "Did you find her?"

Hart shook his head and set a folder of papers on the desk.

"No. There's no sign of her in the woods. We have a search group still out there and two dogs. They couldn't pick up a scent," he explained.

"But something happened?" Bette insisted, searching his face.

"We interviewed Weston Meeks. Bette, are you aware that Mr. Meeks is married?"

"Wait," Bette held up a hand, which trembled so badly she pressed it against her chest. "Did you just say he's married? As in he has a wife?"

Officer Hart nodded.

"Yes, he's married to—" He paused and looked at a sheet of paper before him, "Hillary Meeks. They have a house in Traverse City where she works as an ICU nurse at Munson Hospital."

Bette's heart raced beneath her hand.

"But they're separated, right? Or getting divorced?"

Hart shook his head, lips set in a small thin line. "No, they're not. We haven't interviewed the wife, but we will. Wes came clean. He admitted he's been having an affair, and that his wife knows nothing about Crystal."

Bette squinted at the table that seemed to blur and shift.

"Was he with her when Crystal went missing?" Bette stammered.

"He claimed he was in Traverse City all day Friday. He saw Crystal Wednesday, returned to Traverse City that evening. The following day, he developed some kind of stomach bug and spent the rest of Thursday and all day Friday in bed. He returned to Lansing on Saturday."

"Crystal said he teaches part time in Traverse City," Bette mumbled. "Just a few classes on the side. Turns out he's actually going home to his wife."

Hart nodded. "He divides his time. He was teaching at Northwest Michigan College and got the offer from MSU two years ago. It was a position too good to pass up, but his wife loves Traverse City and wasn't interested in moving. He spends three days a week in East Lansing teaching and the other four days at home. He's been doing that for two years."

Bette shook her head. "But he doesn't spend four days at a home," she said. "He spent almost all of his time with Crystal. Every time I called her, they were together. He wasn't in Traverse City."

"His wife has been traveling a bit over the last couple of months. That, combined with lies, made it work. He told her he was slammed with grading and exams, that he'd volunteered to work with a writers' group. He lied, Bette."

Bette sagged back into her chair, feeling suddenly sick.

She thought of Crystal's adoring eyes as she spoke of the man she'd claimed was her soul mate after they'd only shared a coffee together.

It had all been a lie, a total fabrication.

"It gets worse, I think..." Hart continued. "And this is between us, got it?"

Bette put her hands to her face, unable to look at him, unsure if she wanted to know how it could possibly get worse.

"A young woman disappeared from Traverse City two years ago," Hart confided. "She was Weston Meeks' assistant at the college. I have a friend in the force up there and I called him to see if Meeks had ever been in any trouble. No record, but my friend questioned Mr. Meeks extensively two years ago about his missing assistant. She disappeared without a trace. They've never found her."

Bette pulled down her hands and hunched over in her chair.

She struggled to breathe, to think, to piece together what he was trying to say.

Why would that be connected? Why would it matter? But she knew why. The fairytale man had lied to her sister; he had a wife, and now Crystal was missing—and she wasn't the first young woman to go missing in Weston Meeks' life.

"Was he seeing her? Were they having an affair too?"

Hart shook his head.

"They never found evidence of that, but she was very pretty, and apparently she worshipped the ground Weston Meeks walked on. It's not a huge leap to assume that something was going on."

Bette sat up and tried to channel her breath. It rushed in and got stuck in her throat as if her constricted diaphragm refused its passage. The room before her narrowed to a pinhole. Dark blotches shuffled at the edges of her vision.

"Bette?" Hart asked.

He stood and walked around the desk. He touched her arm and she blinked at him, but he was fading. She couldn't catch her breath. She hadn't had a panic attack in years and yet one was upon her, its concrete arms wrapped tight around her body hugging, squeezing until she'd suffocate and die.

Hart reached for his desk, grabbed something and shoved it into her face. He gently pressed the back of her head toward her thighs.

"Breathe into the bag, Bette, breathe," and as her breath whooshed into the paper bag, releasing a wave of crinkling, she remembered Crystal doing the exact same thing after their mother died.

"Breathe, Bette. It's okay, come on, just breathe," she'd whispered into Bette's ear. The sack had ballooned out, collapsed, ballooned again.

Hart's fingers brushed Bette's long dark hair from her face as if she were a co-ed who'd had too many plastic cups of cheap beer. His fingers felt cold and clammy against her neck, not unlike her own hands, tightly woven together in her lap. The sensation, the coolness of his touch, drew her back from the tunnel of dark she'd been slipping down.

As she blinked toward the paper bag, it slid into focus. The hysteria ebbed away and the overbright fluorescent lights filtered back in.

"I'm okay," she murmured, sitting up. "Thank you. I'm okay now."

Hart let go of her hair and removed the bag. He walked back to his chair and sat down.

"I'm sorry. That was too much, too quickly. I've been guilty of that before. Tactless, my ex-girlfriend called me."

Bette would have smiled but the muscles in her face felt

weak as if she were a mannequin in a wax museum. She managed a nod of her head.

"What now?" she asked, suddenly exhausted beyond measure. So tired and so afraid that she couldn't imagine walking into the dark evening, climbing into her car and driving home.

Hart glanced at the sheaf of papers on his desk.

"More interviews. I'm heading to Traverse City tomorrow with my partner. We're going to talk to Hillary Meeks and look into the case of the missing assistant. It's never good when we find another missing person's case related to a suspect, but it does strength the theory that Weston Meeks was involved."

"Suspect. He's a suspect?" Bette asked.

Hart nodded.

"He is now."

13

Then

"This love is better than books and movies. It's better than any fictional romance I've ever heard of," Crystal said, sitting on the floor in the living room and drawing invisible circles in the cream carpet.

That morning she'd arrived at Bette's house, formerly their childhood home, and Bette had been grilling her for details on Weston Meeks.

"Better than Ralph and Meggie in *Thornbirds*? No way!" Bette said, finishing her cup of coffee.

"Way better than that," Crystal insisted. "It's not forbidden." Though something tugged at her spine when she said the word "forbidden," that creeping sense of knowing. She pushed it down.

"Except it is forbidden, right?" Bette countered. "He's a professor. You're a student."

Crystal shrugged. "We're careful."

"Refill?" Bette asked, standing and holding out a hand for Crystal's mug.

Crystal handed it to her. It was pink with white polka dots and said "World's Best Mom." They'd given it to their mother for Mother's Day the year before she died. Crystal loved the mug and chose it whenever she had coffee in her childhood home.

"He sounds too good to be true. When will I meet the fairy-tale professor?" Bette asked.

Crystal watched her refill the coffees, adding milk and sugar to Crystal's cup. The sugar caught the sunlight filtering through the window. It fell like fairy dust, glittering and unreal.

"Too good to be true," Crystal murmured, returning to her carpet designs.

"Is he?" Bette asked, overhearing her.

She handed Crystal the mug.

Crystal took a drink. The coffee still tasted bitter. The fairy dust hadn't done the trick.

"No, he's perfect."

Bette rolled her eyes.

"Come on," Bette took a big swallow of her black coffee and set it on a coaster on the coffee table. "Tell me what's wrong with him. Not for my sake, but for yours. You need to ground this thing back in reality before the rose-colored bubble you've stuck your head into explodes."

Crystal laughed. "He loves fish, like loves it, loves it. We're going on a date tomorrow night to some place called Frasier Gorge, and he's bringing his specialty. Fish tacos!" Crystal moaned.

Bette made a gagging face. "You'll have to throw yourself into the gorge to escape them. Ugh! What kind of person chooses fish tacos as their specialty?"

Again, Crystal laughed. She and Bette both had a lifelong

aversion to fish, a repugnance born from all the fish sticks their father fed them in the years after their mother's death.

"Tilapia tacos," she added. "I've heard tilapia's not that bad, sort of tasteless." She wrinkled her nose and Bette nodded.

"Sounds delicious. This guy's clearly got issues."

Crystal stuck out her tongue and reclined on the floor, propping her knees up.

Chai jumped down from the couch and padded over, nuzzling her face into Crystal's hair.

"Hi, Chai baby. How's the best kitty in the whole wide world?"

"Don't let Oolong hear you," Bette told her. "She's already licking her tail bald. If she thinks you prefer Chai, she might start on her hind legs."

Crystal stroked Chai's back and then twittered her fingers at Oolong, who still lay stretched out on the couch.

"Come here Oolong, come get the petties."

Oolong ignored her.

"It's too late," Bette said. "She's a grudge-holder, that one. You'll be lucky to get a sniff on your deathbed."

"I guess I'll have to ask Wes to bribe her with some fish tacos."

Bette scowled and mimed sticking a finger down her throat.

"In all seriousness, Crystal. This guy sounds a little over the top. The poetry, the longing for you over centuries. I mean, who talks like that?"

Crystal turned on her side, propping her head in her hand.

"I love it. I do. I love him, Bette. I'm completely in love with him."

Bette raised her eyebrows but said nothing.

"Okay, well, how about his family? Or friends? Have you met anyone in his life?"

Crystal shook her head.

"His mom left when he was young. His dad was more of a

part-time dad who worked all the time. He died when Wes was seventeen and Wes started moving around the country, sleeping on people's floors, playing music and writing poetry."

"Which all sounds very romantic, but also means Wes has some problems. I mean you know that, right? Crystal, you have a better read on people than anyone I've ever met. He has to be affected by those things. A mother who abandoned him and a negligent father."

Crystal sighed, wishing for once that Bette could just accept someone at face value.

"He's good, Bette. His heart is good. He should be scarred by what happened to him. We're scarred by what happened to us. No one makes it to adulthood without being shaped by everything that came before. Should I judge him for that? Run away because he had a hard childhood?" Crystal demanded.

Bette sighed and held up her hands.

"Okay, I'm sorry. I don't believe in fairytales, Crystal. You know that. But maybe he's the real thing. I want to meet him, though. When are you bringing him over for dinner?"

Crystal grinned.

"Maybe this week. Let me talk to him."

"So, this is Frasier Gorge," Crystal said, marveling out the window as Wes maneuvered his Jeep Wagoneer up the winding forest road. "How have I never heard of this place?"

"Top secret," Wes told her. "The closest we get to the top of the world in the flat plains of central Michigan. I've heard it called a lover's lane. Maybe the universe didn't want you to discover it until you found your great lover."

"Mmm." She snuggled against him. "I can't imagine anyone I'd rather experience it with than you. Did you have a lover's lane in high school, Wes?"

He turned onto a grassy trail, his headlights illuminating a path barely carved from the dense forest.

"Sundrops Park," he said. "On most Friday nights, there'd be a dozen cars parked there, windows so steamed up, you'd think there were locomotives inside."

Crystal laughed and reached into Wes's lap, rubbing his thigh. "I've never seen the inside of a car when it's all steamed up. Maybe we could make that happen tonight?"

"Yes, please," he murmured, and kissed the top of her head. "Your wish is my command."

He parked the car, and Crystal climbed out. The forest bustled behind them, but in front of them, a grassy space, trampled by cars, sat overlooking the forest and sky. Frasier Gorge plummeted a hundred or more feet into more dense woods, green-black beneath the purpling sky.

A flood of exhilaration poured through her as she surveyed the miles of wilderness stretched before her and further, the distant lights of the city. It was a secret paradise, a cliff tucked amid long flat farmlands and concrete cities.

Crystal tilted her head to look at the sky. Wes walked behind her and pressed his chest into her back, wrapping his arms around her and tracing his fingertips over her jaw and down her neck.

He kissed her ear.

"Tell me what you feel," he whispered.

She craned her head back further, traced the curve of the sky with her eyes.

"Like a single fleck of dust floating down from the stars. Held, immersed, free."

14

Now

BETTE OPENED her door to find Officer Hart standing on the porch.

"I wanted to drop off this box of stuff from your sister's car. The Volkswagen won't be released for another week, but we've gone through this already. There's a journal, which we photocopied, and a few other personal items."

Bette took the box with trembling hands.

"Come in," she told him.

Hart followed her into the house.

Bette set the box on the table and peeled back the flaps. The first thing she saw was the faded photograph Crystal kept tucked behind her steering wheel, blocking the speedometer. It was an image of her and Bette, hand in hand, on a Lake Michigan Beach. Their mother had taken the photo. Their dad had been scouring the shoreline for Petoskey stones, wading knee deep into the water to pluck them from the sandy depths.

Gritting her teeth, she took the picture out. A faint residue of light powder smudged the edges where the police had dusted for fingerprints.

"I can't lose my sister," Bette gasped, clutching the picture. "I can't be without a mom and a sister. I can't, I can't, I can't..." Bette cried as she spoke, unable to keep it together, unable to plaster on her strong face.

Chai, distinguishable only by her single black ear, plodded from the living room and gazed mistrustfully at Officer Hart.

Everything within Bette twisted. She wanted to rip things from the walls. She wanted to pull out the pain, somehow make it stop, but she couldn't. There was no way to make it stop and proof, evidence, the truth, that might be worse yet. Right now, she held a shred of something, not hope, no, nothing close to hope existed in her tense, desperate body, but something... something other than complete despair.

Hart didn't touch her. He watched, tensed, his eyes filled with the unfathomable truth that Bette didn't want to see.

He regularly told people their loved ones were dead. She could see it on his face. He wasn't a stranger to her desperate grief.

"Can I call your dad, Bette? Or someone else? A friend?" he asked.

"My sister," she screamed, dropping the picture and pulling at her long dark hair. "Call my sister." The shriek turned into a wail and she crumpled to the floor, tucked her legs into her body and buried her face in her knees.

"Call my sister," she mumbled again because that was the only person who could make it right.

~

"BETTE, I'd like you go see Dr. Bliss," Homer said.

He'd walked in with paper bags of Chinese food as Bette was having a meltdown and had proceeded to brew a pot of coffee and see Officer Hart out.

Bette narrowed her eyes at him, her hands wrapped around her mug like it contained the last shreds of her sanity. She'd opted for the World's-Best-Mother mug that Crystal always chose when she visited.

"Are you serious?" she asked, barking a derisive laugh.

She and Crystal had joked many times about Dr. Bliss. His name alone ignited peals of hysterical laughter in the sisters. He was a dry, monotone man with painted pictures of elk hanging from his beige office walls.

Their father had chosen him as their child psychiatrist after their mother's death because he knew Dr. Bliss from the university. The doctor couldn't have been a more inappropriate child psychiatrist. He used words like bereavement and functional impairment. There hadn't been a single colorful item in his office.

"Dad, Dr. Bliss didn't help when I was eleven years old, and he sure as hell won't help me now," Bette snapped.

"Well, he could prescribe something for the anxiety. You don't look good, Bette. You've nearly finished the pot of coffee, and I haven't seen you eat all day."

Bette blinked at him.

"Who cares about eating? Do you?" She narrowed her eyes at the plate of Chinese food he'd barely touched.

"You can't help Crystal if you have a nervous breakdown," he said quietly.

Bette blinked at him, shocked and hurt by his words.

He wasn't entirely off base. Bette had suffered breakdowns before. The first occurred during her senior in high school when she was passed over for Valedictorian. The second when her first serious boyfriend, Elijah, died in a car accident.

Both instances landed Bette in the emergency room after hours of hysterical crying. The doctors sedated her, and when she woke, the terror no longer consumed her. She'd tried to explain the terror to Crystal later, the sheer horror that seemed to bypass her mental faculties and lodge in her body, trapping her in a stream of fight or flight. Except she couldn't fight or flee her failure, nor could she fight or flee from Elijah's death.

She'd come to understand the physiological responses to fear during her graduate work in anthropology. Humans and chimpanzees were the only species that regularly engaged in war. Thousands of years spent in an environment of battle and death had primed her to be ever vigilant and given her body's sympathetic nervous system full control when a threat arose.

Most people realized a threat was not imminent, and their nervous system acted accordingly, but Bette's body had malfunctioned somewhere down the line. She'd been part of the gene pool whose nervous system couldn't handle the constant release of adrenaline and noradrenaline.

Eventually Bette found coping mechanisms. Diaphragmatic breathing, walks in nature, and meditation, but Bette didn't do them regularly enough to ensure another attack wouldn't come.

Bette swallowed the last of her coffee and stood.

"I'm going to lie down," she told Homer.

She walked upstairs and collapsed onto her bed, head aching and eyes grainy.

She fell into a troubled sleep.

Hours later, Bette woke to voices and leapt out of bed before she'd fully opened her eyes. The door to her bedroom was cracked open, light spilling in from the hallway.

She ran from the room and pounded down the stairs, the light in the kitchen momentarily blinding her. For half a second she saw two figures, one a woman, and thought: *Yes, please,*

Crystal is home. But as her eyes adjusted, she saw it was not Crystal at all.

A tall woman with dark curly hair streaked with silver looked at Bette and then stepped into the hall, gathering her in an embrace.

Bette hugged Lilith, their mother's best friend, whom she hadn't seen in nearly two years.

Lilith had moved to Portland, Oregon five years after their mother had died where she opened a used bookstore. Crystal had cried like a child the day Lilith had departed. They'd always been closer, Crystal and Lilith, though Bette never doubted Lilith's love for both of Joanna Child's daughters.

"Lil," Bette cried, hugging Lilith fiercely. It wasn't Crystal, but it the closest thing to a mother she'd known in a long time.

"Shhh… Oh, Bette. How I've missed you girls. Oh, honey…" she murmured and smoothed Bette's hair, tangled from sleep.

~

"How did you find out?" Bette asked Lilith after Homer retired to bed.

Lilith sat on the living room floor, her legs crossed, a scattering of oracle cards spread on the cream carpet. Chai plopped on the floor and rolled across the cards, stretching her claws toward Lilith's leg. Lilith scratched the fur of her neck before scooting her aside.

"Your dad called me yesterday morning. I booked the first flight out. He'd waited to call. He said he kept hoping she would show up."

"Me too," Bette admitted. She'd also thought of calling Lilith but hadn't been able to make the dreaded call informing her of Crystal's disappearance.

"Can you talk about it?" Lilith asked.

Bette gazed at the cards.

They depicted colorful images of fairies and woodland creatures above words like *Surrender, Regenerate,* and *Higher Power.*

"It's so much worse than I ever thought it could be," Bette admitted. "Crystal fell in love with one of her professors. I met him. He seemed too good to be true."

"And he was?"

"He's married. He's been married for years. Crystal didn't have a clue. He has a whole other life in Traverse City."

Lilith frowned and shuffled the cards before setting them aside. She leaned her back against the couch.

"Crystal's always been such a good judge of character. She didn't have any sense that he was hiding something from her?" Lilith asked.

Bette shook her head.

"I don't think so. She was just… over the moon for this guy, Lil. I've never seen her like it. She couldn't see a flaw in him."

"Which is a sure sign of a fake," Lilith said. "No one is flawless. We're all human."

"Exactly."

"You think he hurt her?" Lilith asked.

Bette scowled. "Yes. I mean, it makes sense, right? He's married; he doesn't want the wife to find out. Plus, Officer Hart said the wife has money. If Meeks lost his wife, he'd lose the money too."

"Money," Lilith grumbled. "It's a sick fantasy."

Lilith stood and grabbed her suitcase, pulling out a dark-purple gift bag. "My partner is rather witchy. She's an herbalist. I brought you a few things."

Lilith handed Bette the bag.

"Your partner?" Bette asked. "Did you and Heather break up?"

Heather had been a chiropractor Lilith met soon after moving to Portland.

Lilith waved her hand.

"Ages ago. She didn't like dogs. Hagar growled every time she came over," Lilith told Bette. Her Dalmatian was named after the comic strip Hagar the Horrible.

Bette smiled. "How is Hagar?"

"Old." Lilith sighed. "He's gone blind in one eye. Irina, my new gal, has been treating him with turmeric and boswellia and other herbs. They seem to help with his arthritis but not much she can do at this point. Age gets us all if we make it that long."

Bette pulled two blue glass bottles out of the gift bag. Little red labels were attached to each bottle.

"Peaceful Tranquility and Sound Sleep," Lilith said, sitting beside Bette. "That Sound Sleep one saved my life after the store got broken into."

"Oh, wow, I forgot about that. Did they ever catch the guy?"

Lilith's store had been burglarized six months earlier, an especially scary event since she lived in an apartment above her shop.

"No. And he didn't get away with much. A few antique books and a hundred bucks, but I woke up to something rattling my doorknob. Somehow, I convinced myself it was the furnace kicking on. Turns out it was a guy trying to get in. I met Irina that week when I went into an herbal apothecary in town. It's a New-Age store that sells all kinds of stuff, but she produces all their natural supplements and was dropping off stock. We got to chatting and..." Lilith held up her hands. "The rest is history."

Bette smiled and leaned her head on Lilith's shoulder.

"I'm happy for you, Lil."

"Thanks, honey. I brought a bag for Crystal too. I really hope..." She didn't finish her statement.

Bette's eyelids grew heavy, and she allowed them to close. Nights of sleeplessness had begun to catch up with her.

"Here, open your mouth," Lilith said.

Lilith unscrewed the cap on the Sound Sleep bottle. "Two drops, and you'll be out like a light. Valerian root."

Bette opened her mouth, cringing as the cool liquid hit her tongue. It wasn't unpleasant. The woody taste lingered in her mouth after she swallowed.

"I'll see you in the morning, honey," Lilith told her, kissing her cheek as Bette stood on tired legs and walked upstairs to bed.

~

THE FOLLOWING MORNING, Bette found Lilith in the kitchen, brewing tea and baking banana-nut muffins.

Lilith had always been a baker. When their mother was dying, Lil set up shop in their kitchen and baked for days. The girls lived on oatmeal cookies and zucchini bread.

Their mother, who struggled to eat as the cancer stole the last of her appetite, still managed a few bites each day of Lilith's carrot-cake muffins.

The memories had forever ruined carrot cake for Bette, but Crystal still loved it and bought a carrot cake on their mother's birthday every year.

Homer sat at the counter, drinking coffee and sifting through the previous day's notes.

"Smells good," Bette said, yawning and stretching her arms overhead.

"You slept in," Homer said happily.

Bette looked at the clock over the stovetop and squinted at the little black numbers.

It was after nine o'clock.

"Valerian root," Lilith said, grinning. "Sit, have a muffin. They're coming out hot right now."

Bette sat at the counter, feeling energized for the first time in days.

Lilith pulled a pan from the oven and lifted a hot muffin

onto a plate. She dropped a tablespoon of butter on top and slid it over to Bette, doing the same for Homer.

"I brewed coffee too. Coffee or green tea?" Lilith asked.

"Coffee all the way, Lil. Green tea tastes like seaweed," Bette said.

Lilith grinned and shook her head.

"Seaweed that's chock-full of antioxidants, young lady. I'll make a convert of you one of these days."

Bette drank her coffee and leaned close to her dad.

"Yesterday was a blur. What have you got?"

He showed her his latest list, organized in neat bullet points.

"I've sorted the most important points from the day. In particular, I think we need to focus on canvassing Weston's neighborhood with fliers. We know she visited him two days before she disappeared, but who's to say she didn't go back the day of? Our best chance is to get eyes on this flier. I'm also curious about their trip to the UP. I'd like to know what the tour guide thought of them. If he saw any arguments."

Lilith looked at the page. "How about his wife? Has anyone talked to her?"

"Officer Hart said they were going to, but I don't have any news on that," Bette said. "I'd like to talk to her myself. I want to talk to everyone who knows Wes - his parents, his ex-girlfriends, his buddies. Anyone that might know what he did with Crystal—"

"Start with the tour guide at Michigan Mayhem," Homer said. "I'm heading to Kinko's in twenty minutes to print more fliers."

Bette remembered how Crystal had glowed when she returned from her weekend in the UP with Wes.

"I am so fucking in love," Crystal had shouted, telling Bette about the trip as they walked through an open-air farmer's market. Several of the vendors had laughed, and one older man had shouted, "With me, I hope."

Bette had cautioned her against falling too fast, but they both knew she'd surpassed that months earlier.

"Did something happen on their trip?" Lilith asked.

Bette shook her head.

"Not that she told me, but I think you're right, Dad. I'm going to go talk to the guide, but first I want to talk to Weston Fucking Meeks."

15

Then

"Wes, I'd like you to meet my sister Bette." Crystal wrapped an arm around Bette's waist and kissed her cheek through the sheet of dark hair that fell over her shoulder.

Bette held out her hand.

"So, you're the poet?" Bette shook Wes's hand.

He smiled. "I teach poetry, yes."

"He lives poetry," Crystal corrected, leaving Bette to wrap both arms around Wes's neck and kiss him.

The kiss was long and deep. The kind of passion that seeped from Crystal's pores, and that Bette had always found alien and uncomfortable.

"Don't forget to give his tonsils a wash while you're in there," Bette told her.

Crystal laughed and pulled away.

"They're squeaky clean," she promised.

Wes chuckled.

"Well come on, let's get out of this rain," Bette urged, throwing the door wide and spilling light from the hallway onto the porch.

She led them into the kitchen.

After Bette had taken over the house, she'd painted the walls in every room white. She liked color, a splash here and there in the form of paintings, but preferred blank walls. Anything more seemed to overwhelm her.

"I don't cook," Bette said over her shoulder. "But I picked up enchiladas from Vinnie's."

"Vinnie's? Sounds Italian," Wes said, shrugging off his coat and hanging it on the rack.

"He's a rebel like you," Crystal laughed. "His parents own a chain of Italian restaurants, so naturally he opened a Mexican restaurant down the street."

Bette eyed Wes. "You're the rebel in your family? You and Crystal make a fine pair, then. Though my father favored her despite her wayward choices. Her rebellion backfired."

"Mine was not rebellion. I just like what I like," Crystal insisted, slipping off her shoes and leaving them on the rubber shoe mat.

"I'm not sure rebellion is what I did," Wes offered. "Rebellion implies someone cared either way. I never had a mother prodding me to become a doctor, so the thought never even crossed my mind. But Crystal tells me you're an anthropologist? That sounds interesting."

Bette smirked. "It's not. To most people anyway. I can happily disappear into the black hole of studying genealogical records for days, but that would put Crystal to sleep in ten minutes."

Crystal yawned. "I'm like Pavlov's dog," she said. "As soon as Bette says 'genealogical records,' I doze off."

Bette grabbed a strand of Crystal's long red hair and pulled.

"It's that humming bird brain," Bette teased. "She can't

concentrate on anything for over five minutes, Wes. You've been warned."

Wes didn't respond but took Crystal's hand and turned it over, lifting it to his mouth and kissing her palm.

Bette felt a tug in her own heart, an unspoken wish for that same kind of intimacy, but she stuffed it down, heading for the stove.

WHILE BETTE FINISHED WARMING the food, Crystal tugged Weston upstairs.

"Welcome to the shrine," Crystal said, pushing open a door.

Wes stepped into the room.

"The shrine?" he asked, looking around.

"It all belonged to our mother. Over the years, we gradually moved it in here, Bette and I mostly, but sometimes my dad too. I'd come in here and sit in her chair, smell her clothes, touch the things she loved."

Wes walked to a high bookshelf cluttered with books, figurines and pictures.

He picked up a glass pig wearing sunglasses.

"I told you," Crystal laughed. "Her mother collected pigs."

Wes smiled and put the pig back down.

"She liked Poe?" he asked, trailing his fingers across several leather spines filled with the works of Edgar Allan Poe.

"Loved him. She used to recite *Dream within a Dream* to us before we went to bed at night."

"I stand upon the shore..." Wes murmured the first line, continuing around the room.

He picked up a silver photo of their mother laughing as she kissed Crystal's cheek. Crystal was three and her mother held her balanced on a hip. A wooden spoon, covered in chocolate frosting, poked from her free hand. Bette was standing on tiptoe, trying to lick the frosting as their mother's attention was on Crystal. They'd been baking a birthday cake for their father and all three girls had flour on their faces and in their hair.

"You look like her," Wes said.

Crystal gazed at the picture. She had her mother's coppery red hair. But Bette had her brown eyes.

Nearly eleven years had passed since their mother's death, and Crystal still felt a spasm of grief clutch her heart as she looked at the photograph.

"I like this room," Wes told her. "All I have left of my dad is an old pipe and a few pictures."

"What happened to all his stuff after he died?" she asked.

Wes shrugged.

"I don't really know."

"Dinner," Bette called from downstairs.

"That's our cue," Weston told Crystal, taking her hand.

~

"You took him in mom's room" Bette asked, when Wes disappeared into the bathroom.

Crystal looked up to find her sister grumpily opening a packet of sour cream.

"Sure, why not?" Crystal asked.

"Because you barely know him."

Crystal shook her head. "Just the opposite, actually. I feel like I've known him my whole life. I feel like I've known him in lifetimes before."

"But you haven't, Crystal. You've known him for two months," Bette snapped.

Crystal sighed, and moved closer to Bette, taking the sour cream packet from her hands and tearing along the perforated line. Their shoulders touched and Crystal pressed into her sister, leaning her head on Bette's shoulder.

"Thank you for always protecting me, Bette, for always protecting all of us. But you can trust him. I feel his goodness, just like I feel yours."

Crystal kissed her cheek and grabbed their plates, carrying them to the dining room table that Bette had cleared of books and paperwork for the first time in weeks.

"Time to switch the month," Crystal announced, pausing at Bette's calendar and pulling it from the nail it hung on.

She flipped it to June and returned it to the wall. It was a quirky cat calendar. June's cat was a fluffy Himalayan lazing on a white stucco porch. A glittering Mediterranean city sloped toward the sea behind him.

As she shifted her eyes to the grid of days, the black numbers began to ooze down the page. Crystal gasped and stepped back. The dark tendrils pooled on the floor and then snaked across the tile towards her bare feet.

"Crystal?" Weston asked.

She jumped and her hands shot out, pushing him roughly away.

His eyes widened and he stumbled, bumping into the kitchen island.

Crystal spun back to the calendar, but the days of the month had returned to normal. Nothing seeped down the page. The cat continued napping in the image above, oblivious to the woman in another world watching him on trembling legs.

"Are you okay?" Weston asked, not touching her but clearly wanting to.

Bette watched them both from the doorway of the living room.

"What happened?" she asked, eyes shifting from Crystal to Weston.

Crystal shook her head.

"Nothing, I-" she gestured vaguely at the calendar. "I thought I saw a spider."

Bette looked unconvinced. "Since when are you afraid of spiders?"

Crystal shook her head. "I'm not, it just startled me."

Weston smiled and pulled her against him.

"My spider-fearing fire goddess." He kissed the side of her head.

Bette looked like she might roll her eyes, but contained herself.

"Let's eat," Crystal announced. "I'm starving."

~

"So, what did you think?" Crystal asked.

She hadn't seen Bette for several nights — not since she'd introduced her to Weston.

Bette sat at her kitchen table, a flurry of notes spread out in front of her.

Crystal had stopped by after working at the coffee shop, bringing pastries and coffee to sweeten up her sister.

Bette stood and walked to the counter where Crystal had set the white paper bag. She extracted an almond scone and took a bite.

"He's okay, a little gooey for my tastes, but..." Bette shrugged. "He's better than the tuba player."

Crystal laughed and threw a dried cranberry from her own scone at her sister.

"Hey!" Bette said, scrambling to grab the cranberry. "I just swept."

"Better than the tuba player is hardly a compliment, considering the last time I saw him he was unconscious in my parking lot."

Bette laughed.

"You've always attracted the crazy ones," Bette said. "And you're the one who didn't call the cops when he started drinking from a bottle of tequila and playing his tuba beneath your window."

Crystal hung her head and laughed. "Oh God, he was crazy, wasn't he? But he'd been so nice to his grandmother at Hospice House. He had a good heart. I still believe that."

Bette rolled her eyes. "That's why you don't date people you meet at work. Obviously, you haven't learned your lesson since you're now sleeping with one of your professors."

Crystal grinned and hopped up on the counter, legs dangling over the side. "We're doing a lot more than that."

Bette wrinkled her nose.

"Eew," she said, shaking her head and returning to her chair at the table.

"Not like that," Crystal protested. "Oh, never mind."

Bette set her scone on a napkin. "Oh yeah, the love thing. You realize he's got a decade on you?"

"Nine years," Crystal corrected. "He's nine years older than me."

"Which puts him at nineteen when you were ten, which definitely classifies him as a pedophile."

"Stop," Crystal moaned, flicking another cranberry at her sister.

It bounced off her forehead and landed somewhere in her long dark braid.

Bette grimaced and picked at her hair until she found it.

Crystal looked at her watch.

"I've got to go. I told Linda I'd pick up a shift at Hospice House tonight. The new girl called in sick."

"Again?"

Crystal nodded. "She turns green every time someone throws up. I don't think she's cut out for hospice."

"Apparently not," Bette agreed.

"Hug me," Crystal said, stopping next to Bette and offering to help her up from her chair.

Bette took her hand.

"Are we hugging now when we say goodbye?" Bette asked, wrapping her arms around her younger sister.

"Yes."

They hugged for a long time.

Crystal pulled away, but paused at the doorway.

"I love you, Bette," she said.

"I love you too, sis. I hope nobody dies on you tonight."

Crystal blew her sister a kiss and walked out the door.

16

Now

Bette called the office of the professor she worked for and left him a message. She wouldn't be in for the rest of the week, maybe not the week after. Her sister was her only priority.

She drove to the gas station and filled her tank before walking inside to buy a bottle of iced tea.

As she stood at the glass doors, surveying the drink options, a reflection appeared in the glass beside her.

She considered apologizing, promising them she'd only be a minute, but Bette wasn't feeling friendly. They could wait.

As her eyes scanned the labels, her gaze drifted to the figure, expecting an adult man or woman. Instead, a child stared back at her through the glass. Not only a child, but a child dressed inappropriately in a pale nightgown, her hair in tangles.

Bette blinked at the girl and quickly opened the door, grabbing a sweetened black tea.

She turned, expecting the girl to be standing behind her, but the aisle was empty.

Standing on tiptoe, she searched for the girl but didn't see her. Rather than heading for the counter, she walked along the backs of the aisles and glanced down each one. Who took their young daughter out in a nightgown in the middle of the day?

Every aisle stood empty. She'd either gone to the bathroom or walked out the door.

At the cash register, Bette peered into the parking lot, but hers was the only car at the pumps.

"Where did that little girl go?" she asked the man who scanned her drink.

He was tall and slim with a dark goatee and wore mirrored glasses pushed up on his head.

"Huh?" he asked, glancing past her. "Dollar even."

She handed him a dollar.

"The girl in the nightgown. I just saw her back there." Bette pointed toward the cooler of drinks.

He lifted an eyebrow and smirked. "You might be imagining things, Miss. I see every person who walks through that door and not one of them today, yesterday, or even this month was a little girl in a nightgown."

Bette frowned, tempted to argue with him. The girl must have slipped in unnoticed. And back out again too.

She reached into her purse and pulled out a flier.

"Have you seen her?" She held up an image of Crystal, long red hair flowing over her bare shoulders.

He nodded. "On the news a couple nights ago, but she's been in here a few times. She came in around Christmas time. I remember because she was wearing a sweater with a big snowman on it."

Bette smiled. She knew the sweater well.

"You're welcome to post that on the bulletin board," the man told her, pointing at a large corkboard near the restrooms.

"Sure, thanks."

Bette hung the flier and left.

~

Bette found Wes eating eggs at a sunny little table by the front window in Luna's Cafe, the place where Crystal had insisted they shared a fated coffee only months before.

She wanted to flip his table over.

Bette stopped and gazed down at him.

He glanced up and his face paled.

"You're married?" she hissed.

He blinked at her, setting his fork down slowly as if sudden movements might cause the whole place to blow up.

"Bette," he said. "I... I was going to tell you. I was going to tell her. I just—"

"You just what?" she demanded, and her voice boomed across the small, quiet cafe.

"Please, sit down," he said. "Please, let me try to explain."

As she sat, he stood. She reached out and grabbed the hem of his button-down shirt.

He looked at her hand, surprised.

"I'm refilling my coffee," he assured her, nodding his head toward the coffee station. "Can I get you a coffee or a tea?"

"No," she snarled, releasing his shirt and not letting him out of her sight as he walked to the counter and filled his cup.

When he returned, some color had come back to his face.

"I was lost for a long time, Bette," he told her sitting down. "The black hole, I call those years now. I mean it, blackouts. It started when I was young, the drugs. I don't know how much Crystal told you about my past, but I was a wreck for a long time. I was a musician, a poet. I started drinking a lot, smoking reefer, nothing major. And then I met a guy in California and..."

He stopped, picked at his eggs, and not looking her in the

eyes, released the next words in a rush. "I got hooked on heroin. I got high during the day, played music at night, got high some more. By the time I left California, I needed a fix every day. I was convinced I'd be a terrible musician without it, a terrible writer. I'd lose my vision, my edge. I chased the dragon and lost myself."

Bette's mouth had fallen open at his words. Crystal had told her things about Weston, but heroin sure as hell hadn't been one of them.

"Are you trying to say my sister is aware that you used to be a junkie?" she demanded.

Weston looked like he might cry, and Bette was tempted to push further, to say the cruelest, most hateful things she could imagine until Weston Meeks was sitting across from her blubbering like a child.

He looked down, gazing at his half-eaten eggs. "Hillary, my wife, found me in Detroit. I had passed out on a mattress in an abandoned building, been robbed of everything except my book of poetry. I had track marks up and down my arms. I was twenty-one and looked forty. She was in nursing school down there. She shoved me into a cab and took me back to her place, detoxed me for two weeks. Hillary fought for me. A perfect stranger who saw something in me my own parents hadn't seen, that I hadn't seen. I think that's what I fell in love with most of all. And I did love her." He paused and looked Bette in the eye.

She glared at him, not moved by his story. It sounded like an excuse. As if he genuinely believed any explanation could justify his lies.

"And yet you cheated on her," Bette sneered.

Weston put his face in his hands and nodded.

"We've been together for ten years. The first few were good, great even. But then…" He looked into Bette's eyes. "We drifted. I started spending more time in East Lansing. She traveled more for work. She'd started taking on private nursing jobs. When I met Crystal…" He stopped, closing his eyes. "It was like being on the shore as a powerful hurricane gathers in the ocean. The hurricane is so strong it sucks the water from the shoreline. That's how I felt, this inescapable pull. I couldn't turn away."

Bette bit her lip and said nothing. She knew Crystal's magnetism. She'd felt it herself her entire life, the force that surrounded her sister, that had drawn more than a few obsessive admirers during Crystal's twenty-two years on earth.

"So it's Crystal's fault. Is that it? My twenty-two-year-old sister was so powerful that you — a grown man — couldn't keep it in your pants?" Bette gripped the edge of the table so hard her fingers ached.

"I didn't hurt her, Bette. I swear to you, I didn't."

"How can I possibly believe a word you say, Weston? You came to my house and had dinner. You lied point blank to my face and not only to mine, but to Crystal's, the supposed love of your life." She shook her head in disgust.

"I'm a coward. I… I knew when I told her the truth, I'd lose her. I never intended for it to go so far."

"The man with a thousand excuses," Bette taunted.

Wes sighed and pushed a hand through his hair. He paused and touched the short strands.

"Let's hear your excuse for that," Bette demanded.

He blinked and frowned.

"I… Hillary got gum in it," he confessed.

Bette laughed. "Are you fucking kidding me? Your explanation is that your wife got gum in it? Are you a ten-year-old girl?"

Weston's face turned red. "I know, it sounds ridiculous, but—"

"How about the beard, Wes? Why did you shave your beard?"

Wes scratched at his bare face. "My wife—"

Bette didn't let him finish. Furious, she stood and turned to leave, but Weston grabbed her arm.

"Didn't you know her at all, Bette? Your sister. Would she

have fallen in love with me if I were the man you're claiming? Would she have fallen in love with me if I were a killer?"

Bette jerked her arm from his grasp. "You won't get away with this, Weston. You think your pretty-boy bullshit makes you invisible, but I see you. I fucking see you."

She stormed from the table, breaking into a run as she fled the cafe.

By the time she reached her car, tears flowed in rivers down her cheeks. She struggled to breathe, to contain the sobs, the cries that would contort her face and wither her body. She needed to be alone for those tears, in the car, or better yet in her bed.

She drove fast through town, running a red light and narrowly missing a pickup truck. The driver laid on his horn and flipped her the finger.

Bette barely registered him. When she reached her house, she ran inside, pounded up the stairs and collapsed on her bed. The sobs came then. Loud, furious, sobs that could break a person in two.

She stood and wrung her hands, pacing away from the bed.

Her eyes fell on a picture of Crystal on her bedside table. The girls sat in a field of flowers back to back. Long black hair and long red hair pressed into one mane of dark crimson.

"Damn it. God damn it," she heaved, wanting to reach into the picture and pull her sister out.

"Crystal," she whispered. "Please…"

But the phone didn't ring as it had so many times in the past when Bette called out for her sister. Crystal knew when you needed her or if you'd run out of coffee creamer or if the dog in the shelter had parvo and you could adopt him, though he'd be dead within a year.

Bette remembered that sweet pup with the golden fur and the sad brown eyes, and she'd opted instead for the beagle dog, six months old, strong as an ox, as a gift for their father.

But they hadn't left the golden puppy. Crystal had rescued him. He'd slept in her bed for four months and then, one morning, he didn't wake up.

Bette slid to the floor. The pain clenching and unclenching, a constant desperate desire to know, to find her sister, to hold her. But no reprieve came. She could only sit on her floor, stare at her picture, and wish and wonder and cry.

"I could never do what you could," Bette murmured, the picture clutched so tightly she loosened her grip for fear of shattering the frame.

If Bette had gone missing, Crystal would know where to find her. She'd have driven to Bette without pause, but she wasn't Crystal, never had been and never would be.

17

The Northern Michigan Asylum
1966

Greta Claude

"SOMEDAY A WHITE HORSE is going to come out of those woods and rescue us," Maribelle said, lying long on a tree branch, stomach down, with arms dangling over the sides.

Greta sat on the ground pinching ants when they scurried up her tennis shoe. She crushed them and dropped their tiny bodies back into the grass.

"Rescue us from what?" Greta asked. "Daddy?"

"Daddy and this whole place. This whole evil place. Daddy's a liar," Maribelle whispered.

She sat up and climbed down from the tree, looking towards the path in the woods as if that white horse might just appear today.

They were twins; not identical, not in appearance nor personality. Greta's hair was silver white and Maribelle's was black as coal. Where Greta was subservient, Maribelle was defiant. Maribelle laughed loudly, twirled in the yard, snuck dolls out of the children's ward in the asylum so she and Greta had toys to play with. Toys they kept hidden in a hollowed log in the woods because their father forbid toys, especially dolls.

"We wouldn't have anywhere to go," Greta complained.

"We'd go to a castle. A beautiful castle perched on a cloud. You'd only be able to see it on clear, sunny days. The castle would be made from pink crystal, and the beds would be filled with fluffy feathers, and for breakfast every day we'd get bowls of melon and strawberry milkshakes. Only special people could see it. Daddy's eyes are black. When he looks at our castle, he'll see nothing but clouds." Maribelle tilted her face toward the sky and her long dark hair hung down her back.

"But how can you say that? This is our home. Daddy said a Claude must always stay here at the asylum, always pay homage to the land."

Maribelle scowled and kicked the base of the tree. She bent over and grabbed a handful of pigweed. She threw the leafy stalks to the side and crunched them under her flat black shoes.

When she stopped, sweat glistened on her face.

"Did you see the lady in the black dress?" she asked.

Greta nodded and flicked an ant off her wrist.

"She was pretty," Maribelle said, and her words sounded pinched, like she was trying not to cry.

Greta shrugged.

"Daddy has to feed the land, Maribelle," she said, avoiding her sister's tear-filled gaze.

"I found something in the basement." Maribelle sat down next to Greta and fished in the pocket of her dress. She pulled out a small gold ring containing a red stone and a white stone.

Greta glanced at it, and her eyes widened.

"You should have put it in the black bag," she whispered. "If anyone ever found it—"

"They'd know what Daddy did," Maribelle finished.

18

Then

"TELL me more about this sixth sense you have," Weston said. "How did you know that lady was sick today?"

Crystal and Wes had been grabbing salad fixings and wine from a little market near campus when a woman had paused in an aisle.

Moments before she collapsed, Crystal had walked close to the woman and snaked an arm around her waist. Weston had been startled, but almost immediately the woman's eyes rolled back in her head and she lost consciousness.

Crystal gazed at Weston's curious face and wondered how much she wanted to reveal.

"It's something I've always been able to do," she admitted. "I sense things. Today with the woman in the store..." She bit her lip, warmth creeping into her face. "I saw a shadow around her, a darkness. She's going to die."

"She's going to die?" he asked. "How can you know that?"

"I've seen the shadow before. I understand what it means." She said the words, but didn't look at him, feared he would sense all that she held back.

"You've seen the shadow and then those people have died?" he asked.

Crystal nodded. "Bette has likened the gift to being really good at trivia When does that ever come in handy unless you're on Jeopardy?"

"Sure, if we're talking about who was the forty-fourth president or the state bird for Minnesota," he argued. "But you're sensing when someone will die. That's pretty significant."

"We're all going to die," she murmured.

He gazed at her seriously, but Crystal leaned over the couch and draped her hair in Wes's face. He put a strand in his mouth.

"Mmm, tastes like you. Be careful or I'll eat you bald," he told her.

She rose, swinging her head back so her hair cascaded over the back of the couch.

"I didn't know they were death omens. I just figured…" She threw up her hands. "I'm not sure what I figured. Other people in my life have died and I never sensed a thing, didn't get a hint of anything and then… and then they died. I'm only saying it's not a useful gift. Not really. It's unpredictable and unreliable."

"It's also fascinating."

He sat up and leaned between Crystal's legs on the sofa, kissing her. "Tell me if you spot any shadows hovering around me. I want my last day on earth to be immersed in you."

Crystal cupped his face in her palms.

"I see nothing but light surrounding you," she whispered, nuzzling his cheek.

When he drew back, he wore a thoughtful expression.

"What?" she asked.

"I'm curious what your sister thought of me." He cringed as if expecting bad news.

Crystal smiled. "She liked you."

He cocked an eyebrow.

"Really? I get the feeling Bette is a little jaded about men," he said. "Is she?"

Crystal turned over on the couch, propping her legs on the back and hanging her head down by the floor. Wes reached a hand out and caressed her scalp, leaning over to kiss her temple.

"Bette's always had... sharp edges. That's what Lilith, our mom's best friend, called them. When we were younger, Lilith nicknamed Bette the porcupine and me the monkey. I'd walk up and climb into someone's lap five minutes after I met them. Bette would keep a safe distance, and if anyone approached, she'd glare at them until they backed away. She's had moments where she's let her guard down and it hasn't really gone well."

"How so?" he asked.

"Well, she fell in love her freshman year at college. His name was Elijah. I never met him. My dad loved him, apparently. He and Bette were both in anthropology classes together. They dated for about a year and then—"

"He broke up with her?" Wes asked.

Crystal shook her head.

The blood rushing into her face felt too hot, and she scrambled back up, remembering the dream she'd had on the opposite side of the country all those years ago.

Except it hadn't been a dream at all.

She'd been watching a car careen down a dark slippery road. Headlights splashed over the iron gates of a cemetery. It was as if she'd been looking out from the eyes of a bird perched in a tree. As she watched, the car came around the curve too fast; it left the road and smashed headlong into a tree.

The collision had detonated in Crystal's head, as she slept soundly in her bed in California. Crunching metal and splashing glass, and the beginning of a scream cut off before it had even begun.

She'd woken next to Neal, the man she'd been sleeping with in the previous weeks. She'd been drenched in sweat and shaking so badly she almost fell when she stepped from the bed.

Crystal had run to the phone on wobbly legs and called Bette. Bette had been in that car because that was Elijah's car. Crystal had never seen it, but she knew the car belonged to her sister's boyfriend.

Except, at four a.m. on the other side of the United States, Bette's groggy voice had come on the line. Crystal had stood in the kitchen, her sweat-slick feet glued to the warm linoleum floor, her breath gusting in terrified waves as her sister said "Hello? Hello?" And then there'd been a pause. "Crystal?" Bette had asked.

Crystal had set the phone in its cradle and walked to the little concrete porch that jutted out from the second-story apartment. She'd stood, naked except for Neal's tank top, and gazed at the dark expanse of sky, the glow of the city lights in the distance.

She had known that Bette's boyfriend was dead, but she'd been unable to say the words out loud.

All that dark morning and into the dawn, Crystal sat on the porch.

When the phone rang at noon, Crystal had known who was calling.

She'd let it ring a second time, staring at the yellow receiver with a heaviness that left her heart hanging sodden and weary in her chest.

The moment she picked it up, Bette's wails boomed through the phone. Her sister had cried so hard and so loud, Crystal feared for Bette's eyes and brain. Could those soft organs withstand such ferocious pressure as the sobs erupted into the world like gale-force winds?

Bette sobbed for more than two minutes without saying a

word. Every time she started, barely croaking out Elijah's name, a fresh peal of cries would overwhelm her.

"I'm here, I'm here," Crystal had reassured her until Bette's story finally poured forth.

Elijah had died the night before in a terrible car crash. He'd hit a tree going seventy miles an hour. But that hadn't been all, and when Bette revealed the next part, Crystal's stomach had clenched painfully.

Bette's best friend since high school, Heather Stewart, had been in the car with Elijah.

Both had died instantly.

Bette had no explanation for their being together. Elijah had told her he was going out of town to visit his grandmother. She'd called Heather the night before thinking they might catch a movie, but Heather had complained of a migraine and said she was staying in.

Now they were both dead, together in those final moments, leaving a grief-stricken Bette with a flurry of questions and a shattered heart.

Crystal told Wes an abbreviated version of the story, leaving out her dream.

When she finished, Wes hung his head. "Poor Bette. No wonder she's a porcupine."

Crystal pulled her legs close to her body and rested her chin on her knees. "Bette never really got over that. She goes out once in a while, but she's suspicious of men. She thinks you're too good to be true."

"Moi?" Wes pressed a hand against his chest.

He turned and fixed his stare on Crystal, and she felt a flutter in her belly. Looking into Wes's eyes left her breathless every time.

"But I know the truth," she murmured, sliding to the edge of the couch to pull him closer.

"Whatever I am," he whispered, "I'm yours."

19

Now

"Hi, are you Dan?" Bette asked the man who stood washing the Michigan Mayhem Tour Bus.

He turned and smiled, dropping a rag into a sudsy bucket.

A large German shepherd lay watching from the grass. It perked its ears as she approached.

"Dan I am," he said, wiping his wet hand on his surf shorts and holding it out.

Bette shook it.

Dan reminded Bette of more than a few guys Crystal had dated over the years. Tan, blond, and forever looking as if they'd just run out of the waves after a totally gnarly surf session.

Crystal had two types, sexy surfer dude and brooding artist. Bette feared the latter had been her undoing.

"I'm Bette Childs. Crystal Childs is my sister."

Recognition immediately flooded his face.

"Gosh, yeah. Nice to meet you, Bette. I called the police to let them know that Crystal came on the tour a few weeks ago. They said they might call back, but I haven't heard from them."

Bette frowned and bit back her complaints. The police weren't doing enough as far as she was concerned, and though she liked Officer Hart, it frustrated her that she was the first to hear Dan's story.

"Thanks for calling them," she said. "I'm sure they'll get back to you soon. In fact, I'm going to call them today and make sure they do. But I'd like to hear anything you have to say myself. Did everything seem okay with Crystal and Weston on that trip?"

Dan leaned against his van and then, as if remembering he'd just washed it, he stood and wiped at the spot his shoulder had touched.

"Nothing bizarre at first. They seemed pretty into each other. But on our last day, something weird happened at Pictured Rocks. We were kayaking around the cliffs. I wasn't paying them much attention. I had a few poodles on the trip and they always take ninety percent of my attention."

"I'm sorry, poodles?" Bette asked.

"Oh," he laughed and slapped his muscular thigh. "My brother and I nicknamed the higher maintenance guests poodles. They take up most of my time because they're out of shape, have a gazillion questions and want to stop at every fudge shop and viewing deck on the trip. Crystal and Weston were comfortable in the kayaks, so I wasn't watching them. They paddled off into one of the little caves under the cliffs. It's not a big deal. I've done it a thousand times, but something went down in there."

"What do you mean?" Bette asked.

Crystal had mentioned nothing out of sorts happening on the trip. She said they'd had an amazing time.

"Crystal tipped over," Dan admitted. "When I found her, she was in a full-on panic. She screamed before she went into the water too. I heard her from out in the lake. It was a scared scream, not like someone tipping over so much as someone being attacked."

Bette's eyes widened. "Are you saying Weston attacked her in the cave?"

Dan glanced at his van and then paused, tossing his hair as he caught his reflection in the window.

"I didn't see what happened. I can only tell you what I heard, and she sounded terrified. She also hit her head on the cave wall. She had a nasty bump on the right side of her head."

"Did you ask her what happened?"

Dan nodded. "She said she panicked from being in the small, dark space, which isn't unusual. That's why we don't lead people into those caves. They're safe enough, but a lot of people freak out. Put them in a dark little hole with a half mile of rock above their heads, and the buried fears start coming out."

"Crystal wasn't claustrophobic," Bette disagreed. "She's been spelunking in Missouri three times. When we played hide and seek as kids, she used to close herself in an old wooden chest in our attic. She doesn't have a claustrophobic bone in her body."

Dan shrugged. "She didn't strike me as the type who would panic in one of those caves, but that's what she said happened. I wasn't going to challenge her on it."

Bette sighed and looked at the dog, who had returned his head to his front paws.

"I need you to tell the cops that story," she said.

~

Bette stopped at a pay phone and called Officer Hart's direct line.

"This is Officer Hart," he said.

"Hart, it's Bette. Listen, I just talked to the tour guide who took Crystal and Wes into the Upper Peninsula a couple weeks ago. Her kayak got tipped, and she screamed like she was being attacked. The guy thought Wes attacked her."

"Okay, got it," Hart said, sounding distracted.

"Hello? Did you hear what I said? He attacked her! Are you sending someone to talk to him?"

Hart sighed.

"Yes. I've made a note of it here, but Bette, I'm on my way out the door. We've got a warrant to search Weston Meeks' house. That's our priority right now."

Bette clutched the pay phone and felt her hear skip in her chest.

"You're searching his house?"

"Yes, I've got to go. I'll be in touch."

He hung up before she could ask more.

20

Then

"Stop the car," Crystal shouted, grabbing the wheel and almost jerking them into oncoming traffic.

"Whoa, Jesus, Crystal. Are you trying to kill us?" Wes huffed, turning on his blinker and letting off the gas.

He pulled into the parking lot Crystal had been wildly waving at.

She jumped out of the car and ran around to Wes's door, pulling him out, and pointing eagerly at the sign.

He glanced at it and then back at Crystal's face as if she'd gone insane.

"You want a cheeseburger?" he asked. "We just had lunch."

She turned and saw the sign next door for Big Dean's Burgers and Fries.

"Not a burger," she laughed.

She pointed at the Michigan Mayhem sign. "They do tours

to the Upper Peninsula. Cliff jumping, rappelling, kayaking. Let's go! This weekend."

Wes glanced at the windows plastered with images of the Michigan outdoors.

Crystal looked as well, her chest ballooning at the sight of the brightly colored parachutes drifting over craggy cliffs.

"Crystal, I've got a meeting in Traverse City on Saturday. I can't—"

She pressed a hand over his mouth and moved close to him, quickly pulling her hand away and putting her lips in its place. As she crushed her mouth against his, the set of his body relaxed. He kissed her back, sinking his hands into her hair.

"Come on," she insisted, dragging him to the store.

As they pushed inside, the bell tinkled over the door. A young guy with shaggy brown hair looked up from the long counter.

"Hey," he said, his eyes lingering on Crystal. "You guys looking for some adventure?"

"Yes!" Crystal nodded, pulling Wes to the counter and marveling at the brochures.

"What's available this weekend?" she asked.

"Crystal, we can't—" Wes started.

"Bro," the guy drawled, fixing his gaze on Wes. "You've got a beautiful woman asking for a weekend of turquoise water and sandstone cliffs and you look like somebody just told you that you need your gallbladder removed."

Crystal laughed, seizing the brochure that boasted cliff jumping and kayaking.

"That's a bestseller," the guy told her, winking. "My brother Dan is the guide on that and he knows Presque Isle Park better than his own eyebrows."

"His own eyebrows?" Wes asked sarcastically

"Yeah, he's a plucker. It's weird, but anyway, he's the best. He started this company. Loves to take folks like yourselves into the Upper Peninsula to get lost for a few days."

Crystal's heart fluttered against her ribs. She'd been back in Michigan for two years, and though she'd had a few adventures, she wanted to have one with Wes. She wanted to float in the cool water of Lake Superior and see him looking down at her as he stepped to the edge of a cliff and jumped.

"We're in. How much?" she asked.

Wes took her shoulders and turned her to face him.

"Crystal, we can't go this weekend. I have to head back to Traverse City on Saturday. I've got a student meeting and—"

Crystal frowned, disappointed, but she'd already mentally committed. She was going.

"Okay," she turned back to the guy at the counter. "How much for one person?"

"No." Wes grabbed her elbow, but she didn't turn.

"Two hundred," he said. "That includes two nights in a yurt at Twelve Mile Beach, kayaking the Pictured Rocks, cliff jumping at Black Rocks, bonfires at night with hot dogs and hamburgers. It's amazing, you'll love it. Here, let me grab a waiver."

As he rifled in the cabinet behind him, Wes turned to Crystal.

"Crys, come on. The timing is all wrong for me this weekend."

Crystal cupped his face in her hands.

She thought of her image in the bathroom mirror that morning. She'd been groggy, hadn't even had a cup of coffee, and she wanted to pretend it was that simple. The skeletal face looking back at her, the sunken eyes, the teeth poking from yellowed flesh had been merely a sleepy hallucination, but when she'd opened her mouth to scream, a black shadow had poured forth. Crystal knew such shadows—or "omens" perhaps better described them.

"It's okay, Wes. It is. I'm not pressuring you. I want to go. I need to go and," she gestured to the air as if something existed there, which might explain her desire to go now, "when the moment arises, I grab it."

Unfortunately, she couldn't explain to him a lifetime of such whims. She lived on the cusp of the breath, awaiting the next inhale. The knowledge that death crept ever near lay always coiled in the back of her mind.

Crystal opened her purse and pulled out a wad of cash. She didn't have a bank account, which Bette told her was irresponsible, but she'd never claimed to be anything else.

"Two hundred," Crystal said, placing the bills on the counter.

Wes frowned but didn't argue.

She filled out the forms, paid the money, and took the glossy brochure with pictures of Lake Superior sparkling against a backdrop of rocky cliffs.

Wes was quiet as they walked back to the car and climbed in. When she looked at him, he seemed to be fighting tears.

"Hey," she grabbed his hand. "Don't be upset, Wes. It's okay if you can't go. We'll plan another one. I just have to do things when they come up. That's my nature. My reckless nature, according to Bette, but..." She paused and tried to choose her next words in a way that wouldn't alarm him. "We're not guaranteed tomorrow. You know? Remember when we first met, and I told you I try to live every day like it's my last? Well, I'm doing that. This is me doing that."

Wes nodded and climbed behind the wheel. He said nothing as he drove to her apartment..

"I'll see you next week, then?" she asked, her heart thundering in her chest.

His silence hadn't upset her at first, but as the minutes dragged on, she tensed.

"Wes?" she demanded when he didn't turn to look at her.

He shifted his eyes to hers. He looked devastated, as if a terrible tragedy had befallen them.

She blinked at him, startled. "Wes, I don't understand."

He swallowed and forced a smile.

"I'm good. Yeah, I'll see you next week." He leaned forward, not bothering to unlatch his seatbelt, and kissed her, catching only the corner of her mouth.

Crystal climbed from the car, and Wes didn't look at her as he pulled away from the curb.

~

Crystal packed a duffel bag, moving listlessly between her closet and dresser, throwing shorts, tank tops and a bathing suit in a pile on her bed.

She thought of Weston's eyes, the tight bud of his mouth. He hadn't been angry. No, it had been sorrow in his features, but why hadn't he spoken? The man with so many words, with words like a steadily moving stream, had said nothing. He'd left her on the sidewalk without even a parting glance.

She shoved the clothes in her bag and grabbed the brochure on the table beside her door.

On the inner flap, a couple kissed across their kayaks.

She frowned and shoved the pamphlet into her bag.

Her excitement at signing up for the adventure had dissipated with her thoughts of Weston.

She walked across the hall to Garret's apartment and knocked on the door.

He pulled it open, wearing a red button-down shirt open at the collar. Tight black jeans hugged his sinewy body.

"Crystal, my love, come in, come in. I just opened a bottle of Chardonnay. Have a glass."

Crystal followed Garret into his immaculate apartment. Garret didn't suffer dust or disarray. She heard his vacuum power on every morning at seven a.m., despite more than a few neighbors' complaints. The landlord would never reprimand a tenant for excessive cleaning.

"How's the new stud?" Garret asked. "I saw him leaving your apartment the other morning, sneaking out like a fox from the henhouse. My goodness, that luscious hair. I thought of inviting him over so I might run my fingers through it."

Crystal laughed and took her glass of wine, perching on one of Garret's bar stools.

"He is delicious, isn't he?" she asked.

She wanted to engage in the easy banter she and Garret usually shared about their various lovers, but a knot had formed in her stomach. The wine only seemed to send it roiling.

"I'm going out with Barry again tonight," Garret said, sitting on the other stool. "Don't ask me why. He's a terrible kisser, but he's funny. Best ab workout of my life just listening to him talk. My mother always said a man who makes you laugh is a keeper." Garret made a gagging face.

"I like Barry," Crystal said, thinking of the man Garret had brought home the week before.

He was not Garret's usual type. He stood a foot shorter than Garret and had a mop of curly blond hair, a nose splashed in freckles, and he'd been wearing corduroy pants. Clothes that Garret called the curse of heterosexual men.

But Barry wasn't heterosexual. and though he dressed badly, kissed badly, and didn't match the Calvin-Klein-men's-underwear model types Garret usually dated, he had a smile that turned angry dogs into puddles of mush at his feet. Really, Garret had seen it with his own eyes, and told Crystal all about it.

"I thought gay men were free from falling for the responsible, safe type," he complained. "Hear that, Grandma?" He looked skyward. "I'm gay. Even a respectable, kind, trustworthy man won't produce any Kasper babies."

Crystal grinned and took another sip of wine. Garret's joy sent the little knot unraveling, if only slightly.

"Don't dismiss him yet, Grandma Kasper," Crystal called. "There's always adoption."

Garret sighed and grabbed a bottle of vodka from the counter, taking a swig.

"I need a nip of the hard stuff to stomach that idea. But tell me, darling, Crystal. Where is your hunk on this Friday afternoon? Surely he hasn't left you to the company of your cats and a TV dinner?"

"I don't have cats," she snapped playfully, throwing an oven mitt at him.

He caught it and quickly returned it to the little hook beside the oven.

"He left," she sighed. "I booked a trip to the UP for the weekend to go kayaking and... he couldn't go."

Garret watched her for a moment and then leaned both elbows on the counter.

"Okay, spill your guts, Miss Childs. You're telling me you're taking a last-minute, carelessly romantic trip that includes waterfalls and heart-shaped cliffs and Dream Boat isn't joining you?"

Crystal stood and walked to the window. The street Wes had driven down only an hour before stood empty.

"Yeah, he said he had a meeting this weekend. I'm fine. I've been wanting to go. I've driven by that travel place a half dozen times and today was the right day, you know?"

"Oh yes, I know all about your spidey sense," he told her.

"So I made Wes stop, and we went in and I booked it. I thought we'd go together. I wanted to, but he said he had a meeting in Traverse City and he couldn't stay here through the weekend, which is fine. It is," she insisted at the look on Garret's face. "But then he was so quiet on our drive home and he barely kissed me goodbye. It felt... I don't know. Like I'd screwed something up. And since when do I think like that?" she demanded, spinning away from the window.

Garret smiled and shrugged, moving to the couch and patting the space beside him.

She sat down and snuggled into his armpit.

"Since you fell in love," he murmured.

Crystal sighed, leaning forward to set her glass on the table.

Garret moved faster than her and slid a coaster beneath it.

"Sorry," she mumbled.

"*Au contraire,* I fancy myself a coaster-wielding magician. I prefer to slip it in there before you even know it's happened," he chuckled. "That sounded far more sexual than I intended."

Crystal laughed and squeezed the cushion beneath her with both hands. "I feel like an adolescent girl with hurt feelings. And worse, that's what he acted like. A teenage boy sulking in the car."

Garret shifted to face her on the couch.

"Love does that, you know? Makes us crazy and stupid. But you're doing the very best thing. You're going off on a grand adventure without him. Leaving him pining for you this weekend, and by Monday he'll be ramming his head against your door and begging your forgiveness."

Crystal grinned.

"I hope not. I like his head. But I wish we'd had a better goodbye. You know? I feel conflicted now. I hate that. I wanted to go into the weekend clear. Instead, I'm all muddied in my head and…" she trailed off and placed a hand over her heart.

"Call him, then. It's a simple answer, Crystal. But you won't, right?" Garret challenged.

Crystal sighed and looked at her watch.

"I don't know. Maybe." She kissed Garret on the cheek and stood.

"I have to go. The bus for the UP leaves in an hour and I have to check in."

Garret stood and carried her glass to the sink.

"Call him, Crystal. And then have an amazing time. Don't give him another thought until that bus crosses the Mackinac Bridge on Sunday."

She smiled and nodded, backing through his door. They both knew it didn't work like that. If only you could wipe someone from your mind for a weekend.

21

Now

"Did you find anything?" Bette demanded before Hart had made it across the threshold into the house.

Homer popped into the hallway, face anxious. Lilith followed, holding Oolong in her arms.

"Yes," Hart admitted.

Bette froze, her breath catching.

"Not Crystal," Hart quickly assured them. "But I have a few questions."

Bette ground her teeth and walked into the kitchen, where Lilith had made spaghetti, baked cookies, and arranged fresh flowers in a clear vase on the dining room table. Lilith had always been good at that, making things seem okay, softening the sharp edges of tragedy.

None of them were hungry, but they were trying to do the responsible thing and eat.

"Can I get you something? Tea or—?" Homer asked. He reverted to host when in the home where he'd spent so much of his life.

Though Bette had lived in the house alone for over two years, when Homer returned, they unconsciously assumed their former roles as father and daughter. He'd never been much of a host, but he was better than Bette, who rarely remembered to offer guests a glass of water unless they were there for dinner.

"No. I'm fine. Thank you," Hart said.

Lilith set Oolong on the floor and offered Hart her hand.

"Hi, I'm Lilith Hawkins."

"Oh, sorry, yes," Homer said, sounding embarrassed. "Lilith was my wife's best friend. Lilith this is—"

"Officer Hart," the policeman told her before Homer finished.

He shook her hand.

"We can sit in the living room," Homer said, motioning toward the front room.

"Or you're welcome to join us for dinner." Lilith gestured at the table.

"No, thank you. I can't stay for long." The officer followed Homer into the living room and stood near the wall.

"What did you find?" Bette demanded, unable to sit.

She paced to the window, flicked open the curtains and watched a gray van drive by.

Homer sat but immediately started tapping his socked feet. Lilith sat opposite him on the couch and her eyes flicked to his bobbing toes.

"We found a pregnancy test," Hart told them. "It was positive, and Wes admitted it belonged to Crystal. She told him she was pregnant two days before she disappeared."

Bette gasped and yanked the curtain. The rod pulled from the holder and crashed to the floor, startling all four of them. She made no move to pick it up.

"She was pregnant?" Bette asked, unbelieving. "No, she would have told me. She tells me everything. She calls me if she stubs her toe."

Homer said nothing, but he folded his hands in his lap and stared at the gold band on his left finger. He'd never remarried after their mother died. He'd never gone on a date, as far as Bette knew.

Lilith stood and walked to Bette, putting a hand on her low back.

"Wes is married, and Crystal is pregnant…" Bette shook her head.

"Just breathe," Lilith murmured.

Hart knelt and grabbed the curtain, reaching up and replacing the bar in the holders, pushing the fabric to one side.

"What did he do to our Crystal? What did he do to my little girl?" Homer's voice caught. He touched the gold band and stared at the floor.

Hart shook his head. "We don't have evidence of foul play. If something happened to Crystal, I doubt it happened in Weston's house. His story, his newest story, is that Crystal visited him on Wednesday. They were only in the house for a few minutes when she told him she was pregnant. He was shocked and didn't say much, which seemed to upset her. She ran out the door and drove away. That was the last he spoke to her."

"What bullshit," Bette snarled. "And what was the story before? She stopped by to say hi and left. I knew he was fucking lying."

Homer pulled off his ring, slid it on his pinkie and started rotating it around and around.

"Where did you find the pregnancy test?" Lilith asked.

"In the master bedroom on his dresser."

"Did he try to deny it was Crystal's?" Bette demanded.

Hart shook his head. "No. He told us right away it was Crystal's. He said he reacted poorly when she showed him the test.

Not angry, but not happy. Later, he said he realized it would complicate things, but he was happy."

"Liar," Bette muttered.

"You searched his trash cans?" Homer asked. "His cupboards? Any place he could have hidden evidence of a crime?"

"Yes, but the trash goes out on Mondays, which means he could have taken stuff out already."

"God damn it!" Bette shrieked, pulling away from Lilith.

She stalked across the room, but there was nowhere to run.

"Was his house clean?" Homer asked. "Were any spaces unusually clean compared to the rest of the house?"

Again, Hart shook his head.

"We looked for that, but no. His place has an air of neglect. It's not dirty, just not very lived in. Like I said, he divides his time between East Lansing and Traverse City. Most of his stuff is up north. This house has a lot of textbooks, papers, but otherwise..." Hart shrugged. "He had framed poems and art on the wall, a guitar in the living room. We found one photograph in the whole place. It was a series of photobooth images he and Crystal had taken at a tourist shop when they went to the Upper Peninsula."

"Where he tried to kill her!" Bette shouted.

Her father winced.

"I sent an officer to Michigan Mayhem this afternoon to get the tour guide's story," Hart told Bette.

"Why doesn't he wear a wedding ring?" Homer asked, pulling his ring off his pinkie and returning it to his ring finger.

"He said he lost it a year after he got married," Hart offered.

"Yeah right," Bette spat.

"I'd better get going. I just wanted to let you guys know what we'd found," Hart told them.

"Thank you, Officer." Homer stood and extended his hand.

Hart shook it.

Bette followed him onto the porch.

"Hart," she said.

He turned back to her, clearly wanting to rush to his car and escape the despair oozing out from the Childs' home.

"Can we talk? Just for a minute?" She gestured toward the porch, where a rocking chair and a swing sat.

He wanted to say no. She saw it in his face, but he gave a tight nod and walked to the rocking chair.

He sat in the chair, both feet planted on the ground as if he preferred stability rather than the uneasy swaying of the chair.

Bette opted for the porch swing. It rocked forward and back — the cyclical movement, like everything - reminded Bette of her sister.

Crystal had spoken often of cycles, the in and out breath, the rise and fall of the sun, the highs and lows of emotion. Crystal loved the shift from one end to another, the ever-swinging pendulum.

Bette felt just the opposite. Crystal's disappearance had left no great rift in the fabric of the world. People carried on. Even those who loved Crystal continued to get up, put on their socks, drink their coffee and go off to work. Why hadn't the whole world slid to the edge alongside Bette?

How did everyone else do it? Even the tiniest thing, the in and out breath, had become near impossible.

"Do you think he killed her?" Bette asked.

He took a long time to answer.

"I don't know, Bette. And I'm not just saying that because I'm a cop and I'm not supposed to assume anything. Sometimes you meet a perpetrator and in your guts you're sure he's guilty. Other times, you think you've met the husband of the year only to find out he's been beating his wife for a decade, and strangled her a week ago, despite crying at press conferences and begging for her abductor to bring her home. People are unpredictable and if their own skin is on the line, they can become very convincing. I don't have a gut feeling about Weston as a killer. But everything we've found…" He trailed off.

"Makes him look like a killer," she finished.

"It doesn't look good. I'll say that," Hart agreed.

"Crystal's always been the brighter daughter," Bette began. "Not brains wise, though she is smart. But brighter in light. Her light has sometimes made me feel kind of small. Insignificant, maybe."

Bette touched a strand of her hair and then lifted it, gazing at the dark color, void of light.

"Do you think one daughter is always less compared to the other?" she wondered out loud. "All the things I've coveted in Crystal's life are phantoms. The beautiful men are ugly on the inside. The bright clothes wrinkle and fade with time. The feelings that ignite poetry die. All of it is temporary. Some of it is not even real at all."

Hart didn't look at Bette as she talked.

"I don't think one sister is always less," he said. "Different, but not less. I have three siblings, in some ways we're similar. In others, we're like aliens from different planets and that's good. Right? We're meant to be different. Snowflakes and all that."

"Snowflakes," Bette laughed, and the laughter cut deep because Crystal had loved snowflakes.

She'd gone through a phase somewhere in her teen years when she talked of snowflakes constantly. She studied them on the windowpanes. She lay in the yard on freezing cold days and watched them fall one after another and pillow on her long dark eyelashes.

Bette would run out, join her for half a minute and then race back inside to warm up.

She'd never had Crystal's devotion, her strength, her willingness. Crystal was all in. That's how Lilith had once described her. She was all in on life for every single hand.

"Are you going to arrest him?" Bette asked.

Hart stood and offered her a sympathetic smile. "Not yet, but I promise you'll be the first to know."

He said nothing more as he walked down the driveway and climbed into his car.

22

Then

"Great to meet you, Crystal. I'm Dan. Your dashing, daring and deviant tour guide for this Michigan Mayhem Adventure."

Dan grabbed Crystal's duffel bag and hoisted it into the back of the Michigan Mayhem van.

Dan was tall, six foot five at least, with tanned skin and sun-bleached hair that hung past his collar. He had big brown eyes, a wide smile and an energy toward which Crystal would have previously gravitated. He was just her type.

Instead, as he flirted, she thought of Weston.

A German shepherd jumped from the passenger seat of the tour van and ran over to lick Crystal's hand.

"Hey there, Willy, how are you today?" she asked, rubbing the dog's scruffy neck.

"Whoa, how d'you know his name?" Dan asked, holding his hand out for the dog to lick.

Crystal paused.

She'd simply known it. The dog's name was Willy after the character in Willy Wonka.

"Tags," she offered, tugging on the dog's collar. She had no idea if the dog had a nametag, but assumed so.

Four other people had signed up for the trip. Two middle-aged couples. The husbands worked together at a large insurance company downtown and their wives had been planning the trip for months.

"Why don't you ride up front with me?" Dan asked, flashing her his gorgeous lopsided smile.

She nodded, grabbing her notebook and climbing in to the seat.

Willy bounded in through the back, laying on the floor between them.

Dan closed the door and leapt into the driver's seat.

As he started to pull from the parking lot, Crystal jumped as a hand pounded on her passenger side window.

She turned to find Wes, hair messy, eyes gleaming, standing outside the van.

She didn't roll down the window. She pushed open the door and jumped into his arms.

"I cancelled everything. I signed up. I'm going," he announced.

He waved his ticket at Dan in the driver's seat.

Dan turned off the engine and climbed out, examining Wes's ticket.

"You guys know each other?" Dan asked, looking slightly crestfallen as he glanced back and forth between them.

Wes put an arm around Crystal's waist, lifting her.

"I'm sorry," he whispered in her ear.

She looked at him, his eyes telling her everything she needed to know.

"I love you," she murmured, realizing she had spoken the words after they'd already slipped out.

His eyes widened, and he leaned his forehead against hers.

"I love you too. I love you so much it hurts."

"Guess you guys are in the third row," Dan interrupted, pointing toward the back of the van. "Willy, you get to ride shotgun after all."

~

CRYSTAL HOISTED herself onto the cliff ledge, skipping across the hard, uneven surface. She paused at the edge, waiting for Wes to catch up.

When he climbed to the top of the cliff, he paused, craning his neck forward.

"I don't know," he murmured. "That cliff down there looked safer."

Dan climbed behind him, muscular and agile. He reached the edge in two long strides.

"Epic fall, baby," he said to Crystal as he stepped backwards to the ledge and jumped.

Crystal watched him fall, feet first, arms and legs straight. He shot into the water like a bullet.

She turned back to Wes, ready to talk him into the jump, but he took off, running head down toward the edge.

She gasped as he flung himself into the wide expanse of sky. He curled over and stretched his arms out, making the long dive, hands first into the water below.

Dan popped up and clapped as he watched Wes take the plunge. The ripples where Wes disappeared into the water spread out, creating an ever-widening circle in the calm lake.

Crystal watched, waiting, the smile slowly falling from her face. Her heart spasmed, and she saw Dan's own features far below warping into a grimace as he scanned the water for Wes.

She clenched her hands and stepped to the edge, still desperately searching for Wes, sure he'd hit the bottom, broken his arms, or worse, his neck.

Panicked, she jumped.

As she fell, Wes popped up, a few yards out, his wet hair a shade darker against the blue water.

He lifted a hand to wave, but she'd already leapt from the cliff. She flailed for a moment before sticking her legs together, falling fast, and slicing through the water feet first.

When she broke the surface, Wes paddled to her, grinning.

"Let's do it again," he beamed.

She smiled, heart crashing in her ears, as she wrapped her arms around his slick neck and hugged him.

THEY ATE hot dogs and marshmallows by the bonfire. Dan regaled them with spooky stories of a man-sized crow that stalked the Upper Peninsula woods feeding on the hearts of cruel men.

"I'm going to head back to the yurt," Weston whispered in her ear. "Wait five minutes and join me?"

"What are you up to?" she asked, nuzzling her face into his beard.

"Who, me?" he asked, feigning innocence. "I just want to be sure my beloved doesn't get eaten by the ten-foot crow if he's tucked into our bunk."

Crystal laughed. "Go on. I want to take a quick swim. Might be more like ten minutes than five."

His eyes flicked to the slope of the dune leading down to the beach.

"Alone? Are you sure? Maybe I should come with you."

She shook her head. "I've been doing things alone for many moons, Professor Meeks. Go slay the man-eating crow."

She kissed the tip of his nose and stood, bidding the others goodnight. Running down the sandy bluff to the water's edge, she slipped off her t-shirt and kicked her shorts away.

The nearly full moon cast the lake in a ghostly light.

As she stepped in, wading quickly to her waist, the icy water stole her breath. In the bright midday sun, distracted by the exhilaration of cliff jumping, she hadn't noticed the cold. Now it sank into her flesh like icy teeth.

She gathered her courage, sucked in a breath and dove forward, slicing through the frigid water. For several seconds, the cold jarred her. Gradually her body acclimated, and she swam deeper into the lake.

Rolling onto her back, she stretched her arms wide and floated, gazing at the velvet black sky adorned with a million stars. She tried to quiet her mind, calm the voice urging her back to Weston.

"Let me be here first," she murmured, a token phrase she'd used for years when she found her mind jumping to the future and threatening to miss the glory of the moment blossoming around her.

She breathed and floated, and marveled at the heavens, and she did not fear the end of her life, though she felt it looming, knocking quietly at a door in some faraway place.

Stilling her churning legs, she allowed her body to drift beneath the surface before sliding back out and swimming for the shore.

A shadow passed above her, and Crystal glanced up to see birds, hundreds of dark birds, swarming across the sky. They blotted out the moon and the stars, and for several seconds she didn't swim but watched them in awe.

Goosebumps lit her spine from nape to tailbone. As she reached shallow water, she stood and walked uncertainly toward the beach.

The birds, and more still coming, settled in droves in the trees. She heard their mad chittering and saw them nipping and rustling their feathers, but their numbers made the trees themselves appear like giants perched on the bluff.

As she approached the trail leading back through the dune grass, the crows, as if in unspoken agreement, hushed.

Their silence was more unnerving than their sound, and Crystal stopped, pulling on her shorts and t-shirt and looking down the beach, vaguely hopeful that Weston had followed her and she wouldn't have to walk beneath the gathering of birds alone.

Her mind hurdled to Dan's story of the man-sized crow and she shuddered, imagining the birds melting together, forming the monster that would devour her on the moon-washed beach.

Lifting one leg, she tried to step forward, but her other foot held firmly in place, half of her refusing to walk into the shadow of the sleek birds. She watched them watching her, pictured a thousand shiny black eyes studying her on the white sand.

A shadow broke from the trees, tall and man-shaped, and Crystal gasped and pedaled backwards as it fled down the sand toward her.

She threw up her hands and shrieked.

"Crystal?" a familiar voice called. Dan's voice.

She lowered her hands to find Dan standing before her, a wicked smile stretched across his face.

"Damn, I scared you, huh?" He laughed and shook his head. "I always get somebody with that old crow story." He clapped his hands together as if terribly pleased with himself, and Crystal offered a shaky smile in return.

"Thanks a lot, Dan. If someone throws a snake in your tent tonight, don't look at me," she told him, brushing past him to the walk up the dune.

"Oh, come on, your knight in shining armor would have

protected you from the crow man. And if he didn't, I'd swoop in to save the day," he yelled to her back as she trudged up the hill.

She offered a backward wave, and as she passed under the line of trees, she realized the birds had returned to their chittering.

The eerie silence had vanished.

When she peeled back the canvas door on the yurt, she saw Weston had lit white candles along the floor and sprinkled yellow rose petals across the bed.

"Too much?" he asked when she stepped in, barefoot and still wet.

Her hair dripped water in rivulets down her body. Wes sat on the edge of the bed, wearing only a pair of black boxer briefs. He watched her, his face glowing in the candlelight, his chest steadily rising and falling.

Crystal pulled her t-shirt off and lifted a hand to her bathing suit top, untying the strings and letting it fall to the floor. She kicked off her shorts and crossed the space between them, feeling his hands, warm and large, run up her clammy backside.

He pulled her into his lap, and she pressed her face into his shoulder.

"You're shaking," he whispered, kissing her temple.

"Cold water," she murmured, but it was the crows that rose into her thoughts.

~

THE FOLLOWING DAY, their group ate a light breakfast of fruit and granola bars before launching kayaks and paddling toward Pictured Rocks.

The huge sandstone cliffs rose from the water, revealing half a dozen layers of copper, cobalt, sand and cream.

"These cliffs were formed millions of years ago," Dan called as they drifted into the lake. "The colors originate from different minerals. Iron creates the red shades, manganese is responsible for the blues and blacks, limonite contributes to the whites and tans, and finally copper adds the green tones."

"The copper color isn't from copper?" Melanie, one of the two wives in the group, asked, lifting a disposable camera encased in a plastic Ziploc bag.

"Nope," Dan answered. "Ever worn copper jewelry? When copper interacts with the air, it leaves a green residue."

The tip of Melanie's kayak knocked against her husband's.

"Hey, now, bumper kayaks is not my idea of a good time," he complained, using his paddle to nudge her kayak away as he drifted toward the other husband in the group.

"Look at that," Crystal murmured, pointing to a heart-shaped cliff above them.

Wes tilted his head up.

"Wow," he breathed. "Can we jump off of that one?" Wes called to Dan, who had paddled over to Kristy, a fifty-something homemaker who hadn't been away from her three children since they were born. Her husband was yapping away to his colleague about insurance claims, oblivious that his wife was dangerously close to flipping.

"Ha, I'd lose my license for that. Some of those cliffs are two-hundred-feet high," Dan responded. "This is an adventure tour, not a suicide mission," he told them. "Kristy, I need you to you stay in the center of the kayak. Okay, doll? No rocking with the boat. Understand?"

The woman pursed her lips and nodded, holding still as she attempted to paddle further between the rocky outcroppings.

Her husband continued chattering on, and Wes shot Crystal an amused look.

"Come on," he told her, nodding toward an opening in the bottom of a cliff.

They kayaked over, Dan still trying to keep Kristy from tipping.

As they slid into the dark cavern, Crystal studied the slick rock walls.

Weston paddled ahead of her.

She glanced at the water. It had gone from green to black in the darkness.

Without warning, a fist seemed to grab hold of Crystal's heart and squeeze. She gasped, dropping her paddle, her hands flying to her constricted chest.

Weston hadn't realized she'd stopped. He was paddling on, moving deeper into the darkness.

Crystal was sure the moment had arrived: the point of her young and untimely death. She had thought there was still time. Time to leave notes, to tidy up the loose ends of her short life.

Her kayak thumped against the slimy black rock, and she struggled to pull air into her choked lungs.

A voice sounded behind her. Dan's voice calling out to them.

A shadow pushed from the darkness in the cave. A pale hand reached out, and she shrieked, pushing it away. The tumult rocked her kayak too far, and her head smacked the rock as she plunged sideways into the water.

The cold of the water shocked her and stole the meager breath she'd sucked in before going under.

It was black beneath the surface, the sun blocked by the yards of impossibly heavy rock overhead.

She thrashed her arms and legs trying to swim for the light, but she couldn't tell up from down. Her fingers scraped against rock.

Something grabbed her from behind, hard fingers snaked into her hair and pulled. She fought away from the grip and kicked back, her foot connecting with something soft like a stomach.

She swam forward, she saw the first glimmer of light and then a figure in front of her.

Dan.

He was blurry but recognizable. Her lungs screamed for air as he grabbed her arm and hauled her to the surface. She burst from the water, gasping and coughing.

Dan wrapped an arm around her waist.

"Where's Weston?" he shouted.

Crystal's eyes shot wide open. She'd forgotten about Wes.

"He's... He's..." She struggled to get the words out. Her throat burned when she spoke.

A head exploded through the water behind them.

"Wes!" she croaked.

He gasped and swam to Dan and Crystal.

"My God, are you okay? What happened?" he demanded. "I heard you flip. I tried to help you, but..."

Dan didn't wait for Wes's story.

"Throw us those life vests," he yelled to Kristie, whose kayak bobbed by Dan's.

She grabbed three life preservers and flung them across the water.

"Here," Dan thrust one to Wes.

He made sure Crystal had a life jacket clutched in her hands before he released her, and then he slid his arms into one, buckling the front as he floated on his back.

He helped Crystal fasten the buckle on hers and checked Weston's.

"You'll never get back in your kayaks in this deep water. Best if we just swim into shore," he told them.

Dan tied their kayaks to those of the other members in their group, and they began the slow swim to shore.

"What happened, Crystal? I heard you scream, but by the time I got there, you were flipping." Weston spoke in huffs as he did a wide breaststroke in the cold water.

Crystal closed her eyes and thought again of the pale hand coming from the darkness.

She shook her head. "I don't know, Wes. The darkness and the small space. I guess I panicked."

It wasn't entirely a lie. She didn't know what had happened. For those long, frightening seconds in the cave, she thought death had arrived to take her.

23

Now

Bette sat on Garrett's couch sipping her glass of wine and watching the tiny metal balls in his Newton's Cradle clink back and forth. She'd set it moving a moment earlier. It stood next to a large coffee-table book filled with glossy photographs by Ansel Adams.

Garret returned with a black date book.

"This is my bible. I'd forget to tie my shoes without this thing."

He sat next to Bette on the couch and flipped open to the week Crystal disappeared.

"So, two days before I last saw Crystal, I worked from nine to three, left early to get my teeth whitened. Hmm..." He mumbled a few things. "Oh, yeah, yes. I went bowling with my friend Jack. I invited Crystal, but when she opened her door, I saw Wes stretched out on her floor, a towel wrapped around his waist. I'm sure you can imagine what they were up to."

A knock sounded on the door and Bette jumped, managing not to spill her wine, which would have sent Garrett scrambling for a rag and carpet cleaner.

"Garret?" a voice called through the door.

Weston's voice.

Bette held a finger to her lips and pointed at Garret's bedroom door.

"Answer it. I want to hear what he says."

Garret cringed and shook his head, but Bette grabbed his arm and dug her fingers into his wrist.

"Yes," she hissed.

Bette slipped into Garret's bedroom, where she had a clear view of the couch and could easily listen to their conversation.

Garret opened the door.

"Hi Wes," Garret said, and Bette grimaced at the forced politeness in his tone. "Come on in."

Wes followed him into the apartment.

Garret glanced at Bette and quickly plastered on a smile when Wes faced him.

Bette eyed Wes, who looked haggard under the bright apartment lights. Dark grooves marred his forehead, and his cheeks were sunken and hollowed.

"How are you holding up, Wes?" Garret asked. "You look... tired."

Wes closed his eyes and teetered on his feet for a moment.

Garret grabbed his arm to steady him.

"Are you drunk?" Garret asked.

Wes shook his head. "I haven't slept in days, and I've been getting sick a lot. I'm having nightmares. My world is just... it's falling apart and Crystal..."

Garret directed a horrified expression at Bette as he guided Wes to the couch.

Bette wished she could feed him the hundred questions circling in her mind.

"Can I get you something? A cup of coffee or—?"

"Have anything hard?" Wes interrupted. "Vodka?"

Garret nodded. "Yeah, sure, vodka cranberry?"

"Just ice," Wes murmured.

He leaned back on the couch and closed his eyes, reopening them and gazing at the table where Bette's and Garret's glasses of wine sat.

"Do you have company?" Wes asked, glancing toward the cracked bedroom door just as Bette slipped away from the opening. He hadn't seen her.

"Umm… no." Garret walked back in holding Weston's drink. "I mean, not now, but I did earlier. My friend Mitch stopped by."

"They found Crystal's car," Wes muttered. "Did you know that?"

Garret nodded. "Of course. I was there for the search. I was surprised you weren't, Wes."

"They told me to stay away. The police. And…" He paused and sat up, downing the glass of vodka in one gulp. He set it on the table, not bothering with the coaster.

Bette saw Garret staring at the glass, fixated on the condensation gathering on the mahogany finish.

"I'm married. Did Bette tell you? They haven't printed it, but it's only a matter of time."

Garret nodded, leaned forward and picked up the glass, swiping the wetness with his palm, and putting a coaster beneath it.

Wes cringed. "Damn, I'm sorry, Garret. I know you keep your stuff nice. I'm such a fucking mess."

Garret peeked at Bette, who cracked the door open and mimed taking another drink. She pointed toward the kitchen and then back to Wes.

"You want another one?" Garret asked, grabbing the cup and standing.

"Yeah. Thanks."

Wes sat forward, elbows on his knees, hands pressed into his scalp.

Garret returned with the second glass.

This time Wes swallowed only half of it before returning it to the coaster.

"Bette told me you're married," Garret admitted, sitting stiffly on the edge of the sofa. "I was pretty angry and hurt too. I mean Crystal loves you so much…"

Wes screwed his eyes shut.

"I know," his voice sounded choked as he spoke, and when he opened his eyes, tears ran over his sunken cheeks. "I ruined everything."

"Why? Why did you date her to begin with when you're married?" Garret asked.

"People don't plan to start affairs," Weston said. "Everyone thinks so, but it's not true. They say they'd never do that. They say they love their husband, wife, children too much. They don't realize that affairs come like a blast of fate, a shooting star, a thousand little moments, choices, accidents, creating this meeting, this chemistry. And once you've gone, you can never go back. But you believe in those first hours, days, months, even, that it's casual, a one-time, two-time fling. And both of you are in on it. It's a secret. Neither of you wants a commitment, so it will be okay. You can have this indiscretion, this once-in-a lifetime thing, and keep your wife."

"It never seemed like a fling," Garret countered.

"No, it never was," Wes admitted. He picked up the glass and finished the vodka, allowing an ice cube to slide in his mouth. He crunched it loudly and swallowed.

"I fell in love. I fell in love with Crystal the instant I saw her in my class. I felt like someone had punched me in the gut. That's how powerful that moment was. It's insane. I went insane, maybe. I couldn't not be with her. And I knew if I told her about my wife, well, that would have been the end."

"Then why didn't you leave your wife?" Garret asked.

Wes blinked at Garret as if the thought had genuinely never occurred to him.

"I… she… she saved me. Hillary saved me when I was at the lowest point in my life. I'd been living like a vagabond for years, since my dad had died. I was addicted to heroin."

He looked away from Garret as he said the last part.

"They haven't printed that either, but it's only a matter of time. Oh, and Crystal's pregnant. Let's not forget that part. Have you ever heard of a more sensational story? And then what? My professional life is over, my marriage is over and Crystal…"

"Crystal, what? Wes, do you know what happened to Crystal?" Garret asked.

Wes shook his head. "I thought she took off. She has an aunt or something in Portland. She has friends all over the country. When Bette started saying she was missing, I kept thinking she'd just reappear, tell me to fuck off, and apologize to Bette for scaring her. But then she didn't. She kept not coming back, and I started to get scared because Crystal cares too much to hurt other people like that. She might have wanted to hurt me for being such a shit, but she'd never hurt Bette. And then they found her car…"

Garret shifted uncomfortably and snuck a look at Bette, who twirled her finger, encouraging Garret to keep him talking.

"I would never hurt Crystal, Garret. I would die for her."

Garret nodded, but looked unconvinced. "Do you still do drugs, Wes?"

Wes widened his eyes. "No. God, no. I haven't touched anything harder than booze in ten years. I quit cold turkey when I was twenty-one. I mean, that sounds like I did something, but it was Hillary. She's a nurse, and she locked me in a room. She hooked me to a saline bag to keep me hydrated. She got me sober. I owe her my life. That's why I didn't leave her when I met Crystal."

"But now she knows about Crystal?" Garret asked.

Wes nodded. "She knows."

"And she's angry?" Garret wondered.

Wes blinked at his hands, which he'd braced against his knees as if to keep himself upright.

"She's quiet. That's what happens when she gets angry, she goes eerily quiet. I spent a few days in Traverse City, but I had to teach, so I came back. The thought of returning…"

"Have you looked for Crystal, Wes? Do you have any idea what happened to her?"

"I keep going over it again and again in my mind," Wes said. "When they found her car, I wondered if she killed herself."

Garret sputtered and shook his head.

"I know, I know," Weston said, holding up his hands. "Crystal would never, but I couldn't think of any other explanation, especially because they found her car at Frasier Gorge, a place where we went together. I wondered if she was trying to tell me something, send me a message. But they didn't find her body…"

"The police believe foul play was involved," Garret said. "There's nothing in Crystal's life that points to suicide. Nothing."

Wes leaned back. "Thank god. If she did that, I couldn't live with myself."

Bette glanced at the window behind her, shuffling quietly across the room to look into the parking lot.

Weston's Wagoneer was parked in the middle of the lot.

Bette went back to the door.

"Keep him talking," she mouthed, and pointed toward the window. She mimed opening the window and jumping down to the ground. "Search his car," she mouthed and pointed at herself.

Garret shook his head, and when Wes focused on him, he turned his head to the side and patted his ear.

"Got some water in my ear in the shower earlier, darn stuff won't come out." He shook his head again and widened his eyes at Bette as if urging her not to do it. She ignored him.

She slipped to the window and undid the latch, sliding it up quietly.

Refusing to consider the height, she crawled out and held firmly to the ledge until she'd pushed her whole body through the window. She counted to three and let go, landing with a jolt on the grass. The impact reverberated up through her feet and into her knees, but she managed to stay upright.

Bette jogged to Wes's car and reached for the passenger door handle. Locked.

"Damn it," she cursed.

She hurried around to the driver's side and, to her amazement, she found the car unlocked.

24

Now

"YES," Bette hissed, pulling the door open and squatting down.

"Keep him talking, Garret," she whispered as she slid into the driver's seat, ducking her head low.

She popped open the glove compartment and rifled through Wes's stuff. A handbook for the car was inside, a pack of spearmint gum and a few CDs. Under the driver's seat, she found a Twix wrapper but nothing else.

Leaning over, she searched beneath the passenger seat, pausing when her finger brushed something hard. She wiggled it loose, recoiling when she realized she held the black handle of a sheathed knife.

"Shit." She dropped it. She shouldn't have touched it. Now her fingerprints were on the handle.

Bette pulled her shirt over her hand and picked up the knife a second time, sliding off the sheath.

It was a hunting blade, sharp with a serrated edge. A scary

knife, and just looking at it caused goose bumps along her forearms. She leaned closer, studying the blade, searching for stains.

"Wes, wait!"

The sound of Garret shouting startled her, and she dropped the knife. It clattered to the mat on the passenger's side.

She peeked over the dashboard and spotted Wes leaving the apartment building.

He paused and looked back at Garret, who was waving his arms, his face ashen.

"Oh, crap." Bette dipped her head, not bothering to cover her hands, and stuffed the knife back into the sheath before flinging it under the seat.

She slid out of the car and pressed the door closed. Peeking beneath the car, she watched Wes's shoes moving across the parking lot.

Bette crawled on hands and knees, concrete biting into her kneecaps, but not daring to stand. When she got behind a van, she stopped, shifting to a squat and listening as Wes climbed behind the wheel.

She waited until he pulled from the parking lot to emerge.

"Holy smokes, Bette," Garret breathed when he saw her. "Have you gone mad? He nearly caught you."

Bette didn't speak. Her heart was still racing. Her fingertips tingled where she'd touched the blade of the knife.

"Officer Hart," Bette called, trying to get his attention across the busy police station.

He stood next to the desk of another officer, both of them gazing at a sheet of paper.

"Hart," she tried again.

He didn't look up.

"He has a knife in his car!" she shrilled, attracting stares not only from Hart and the officer next to him, but from four or five additional cops.

Hart closed his eyes as if preparing to deal with another lunatic who'd stumbled in from the street.

Bette had a moment of embarrassment, immediately followed by a vision of her sister. The embarrassment vanished, and she marched towards Hart.

"Did you hear me?" she demanded.

"The sandwich shop across the street heard you," he retorted.

"Well, if you had looked at me, I wouldn't have screamed it," she snapped. "I said Weston has a knife in his car. You need to search his car. What if he used it to—?"

Hart held up a hand to silence her, shot an exasperated look at his colleague, and steered her to an empty room.

"How did you get access to his car, Bette? Please tell me he invited you to borrow it or take it for a ride, because if you broke in, we have a problem."

"I didn't break in," she exploded. "It was unlocked."

"I see. So, you consider an unlocked door an open invitation? If a man's walking down your street and turns the doorknob to your house and finds it unlocked, he's welcome to come inside and have a look around?" Hart asked.

Bette fumed. She planted her hands on her hips.

"If that man's sister is missing, and he has reason to believe I might be hiding her in my house, then hell, yes, come on in, man! Ransack the place. Why do I feel like Weston Meeks has more rights than the rest of us here? What about my sister? Who's worrying about Crystal's rights? It sure as hell isn't you guys. The supposed upholders of the law."

Hart stared at her incredulously.

"I've been working day and night on your sister's case. Day and night. But I'm a police officer," he said. "Bette, not only am I bound by a code of ethics and actual laws, any bending of those laws will almost guarantee that Weston Meeks is never held accountable if he did hurt Crystal.

"Don't you get it? If I search his car without a warrant, anything we find in it is inadmissible in court. We could find a knife covered in Crystal's blood and it's useless. The jury would never hear about it, and guess who decides if Weston Meeks is guilty? A jury. Yeah, so you're right, Bette, we're treading carefully around Meeks' rights because when it comes time to nail him, we need a rock-solid case. He has a wife with money, which means he's going to have a slippery lawyer who gets guys like Meeks off all day long. And once he's off, once he's acquitted, we can never try him again. He's free forever, and whatever happened to Crystal..." Hart shrugged and let the words hang between them.

Bette had been filling up with air as he spoke, gathering a storm of rage on which to fly her rebuttal. Instead, she sagged against the wall with a defeated sigh, the fight leaving her body.

"But—" she managed, shaking her head, still high on the discovery of the knife. Still convinced it was the smoking gun that would force Meeks to talk.

"I'll grab us some coffee and fill you in on the latest. Okay?" Hart said, his frustrated tone replaced by one of sympathy.

Bette nodded and sat down.

A mirror took up most of one wall - a one-way mirror investigators used to watch criminals squirm under the harsh fluorescent lights.

Bette wanted Weston Meeks in that room. She wanted to stand behind that glass and watch his eyes dart from floor to ceiling as sweat spread out in a halo beneath his armpits.

Hart returned a few minutes later holding cups of iced tea.

"Paulette, the receptionist, turned off the coffeepot and is forcing everyone to drink tea this afternoon." He shook his head. "Here, it's terrible."

Bette took it. It was unsweetened but flavored with fresh lemon.

Hart took a drink, stared at it, repulsed, and slid the cup away as if preferring to put distance between him and the tea.

"We interviewed Hillary Meeks," he said.

"And?" Bette slid to the edge of her seat.

"She was not very forthcoming."

"Okay…"

"She didn't know about the affair, but she didn't react in the typical way. She was rather—"

"What?" Bette demanded.

"She was rather frigid. My partner called her Siberian," Hart explained.

"Siberian?"

"Yeah, cold. I've told spouses about affairs more than once and, well, let's just say her reaction was unusual. Women often cry. Men get angry. She sat like a statue. When we finished, she said, 'Is that all?' and grabbed her purse like she might leave. I explained that no, it wasn't all. The woman Meeks was having an affair with was pregnant and had disappeared."

"And then what?" Bette pushed.

"And then nothing," Hart admitted. "She barely batted an eye. She said she'd never heard of Crystal, and that if Wes had an affair, it was something they'd handle at home, not in a police station."

"Did you ask about his behavior? If he'd ever been violent toward Hillary? And how about his alibi? I mean he said he was in Traverse City that day, right?"

Hart nodded. "Never violent. She sort of smiled when I asked that question. It was the most emotion I saw out of her that day. She said 'Wes gathers up mice in a little box and lets them out the back door when they get into the house.' He doesn't hit her. He doesn't even kill rodents, apparently. She also said he was in Traverse City the day Crystal vanished. He'd gotten sick the night before, and she believed he spent the day in bed. She was running errands and visiting a friend, so she can't confirm. He was home in bed when Hillary returned at 10 p.m."

"It's a three-hour drive from Traverse City to Lansing. If Wes took her, he wouldn't have had much time," Bette thought out loud.

"No, not really. And it's hard to believe someone wouldn't have seen him. We've got alerts out to other departments. Any officers working Highway 127 have been asked whether they spotted his car that day. He didn't get any infractions, so there's that."

"Has the Traverse City house been searched?" Bette asked.

Hart shook his head. "No. The house is in his wife's name, and we don't have probable cause to get a search warrant."

"Then he has unlimited time to destroy any proof that Crystal was there and there's nothing we can do about it?" Bette fumed.

"There's no evidence that he took Crystal to Traverse City. His wife was home on Thursday when he returned," Hart said. "I'm pretty sure she would have mentioned it if he brought his girlfriend with him."

"But what if all the evidence is in Traverse City? It might be our only chance—"

"We're doing the best we can, Bette. Right now, we can't search the Traverse City house."

25

Then

CRYSTAL LOOKED up from her coffee.

She'd covered the morning shift at Sacred Grounds, the coffee shop she'd worked at for the previous year, and then settled into a table to work on a research paper due the following day.

Across the cafe, a woman stood rifling through her purse.

"I'm so sorry. I know I put cash in here this morning," she said.

The woman set her purse on the counter and laid it on its side, revealing a hollow stuffed with a paperback book, lip balm, a notebook, a scarf and more. The paperback slid to the floor, and Crystal eyed a copy of *Rebecca* by Daphne De Maurier.

Crystal had read the book at least five times.

The woman huffed and searched for her wallet, returning an embarrassed gaze to the man behind the counter.

"I'm so sorry, I must have left it on my table. What an idiot. I won't be able to pay for this."

"Wait—" Crystal called, jumping from her chair and grabbing her purse. She pulled a ten-dollar bill from the inside pocket. "Here, let me," she insisted, handing the money to the barista, Rick.

"No, I couldn't," the woman started, her face red as she looked at Crystal.

"Don't give it a second thought," Crystal insisted. "I've been in the same situation more times than I'd care to admit. I'm covering this," she told Rick.

"Sure. Thanks, Crystal." He put the money in the register and handed her the change.

The woman continued to blush, pushing the contents of her purse back into the leather bag.

Crystal knelt and grabbed the copy of *Rebecca* from the floor.

"This is one of my favorite books," Crystal told her, handing her the book.

"Really?" the woman's face brightened. "Mine too. I've already read it, but that first line…" She sighed. "It gets me every time."

"'*Last night I dreamt I went to Manderley again*'," Crystal quoted.

The woman closed her eyes and nodded. "Such a great book."

"Would you like to join me?" Crystal asked, gesturing toward the table she'd been occupying near the window. The sun slanted through, casting a shining light on the metal chairs.

"You don't mind?" the woman asked, slinging her purse over one shoulder and picking up her sandwich and coffee. "I'm so embarrassed I forgot my money. This has been the day from hell for me."

"Tell me about it," Crystal said, leading her to the table. "I've been working on an assignment for my Environmental History class and my brain is about to quit on me."

The woman sat across from her.

She was older than Crystal, closer to thirty than twenty, with dark curls that looked odd against her pale face. Her eyes were light and her eyebrows too. Her hair should have been lighter, Crystal thought.

"Are you studying at Michigan State?" the woman asked, sipping her coffee, which she drank black.

Crystal nodded. "I'm majoring in English."

"To be a teacher?" the woman asked. "Or an MFA - something like that?"

Crystal chuckled and tucked a strand of hair behind her ear.

"I'm not sure yet. I love reading and writing. There are some wonderful poetry and creative writing instructors at Michigan State, and I'm inspired to follow in their footsteps. I love spending my days talking about the languages of love, the ways other people express themselves. It's such a lost art, writing. I wish there was more of it," Crystal admitted.

"Like what? Writing letters to our lovers?" the woman cocked a sharp pale eyebrow.

Crystal thought of Wes and her body grew warm.

"Exactly. And parents too. I started writing letters to my mother when I was twelve, the year after she died. I wrote her a letter every month. I told her about my days in school, the boys I had crushes on. I wrote her poems. I cried onto the pages. There was something liberating about knowing she'd never hold the paper in her hands. I'd never have to look her in the eye after I told her my secrets."

Crystal paused, surprised at how much she'd revealed to this perfect stranger in a matter of minutes. "I'm sorry," Crystal laughed. "Apparently, you're repaying me for the sandwich by pretending to be my therapist."

The woman laughed, throwing her head back and revealing her long delicate throat.

Crystal could see the sharp bones of her chest. She was beautiful in a cold, crystalline way, like a marble sculpture in a museum.

"I'm Greta," the woman told her, extending a hand.

Her hands were cold, her fingers narrow and bony.

"Crystal. I guess I should have at least introduced myself before I started revealing my deepest darkest secrets."

"Not at all," Greta told her. "There's no better person to divulge our secrets to than a stranger. My hair stylist knows more about me than my lovers ever will."

Crystal widened her eyes. "Well then. Pretend I'm her."

Greta laughed, took another swallow of her coffee, and leaned back in her chair.

"Well, for starters, I side-swiped someone this morning, and I didn't leave a note," Greta confessed.

"Yikes. That doesn't sound like fun."

"The asshole deserved it," Greta continued. "He blocked me into my parking spot at the pharmacy. I went into the store and looked for him, but he'd disappeared. I had to get out. I had to be to the bank by ten. I did my best, but unfortunately he paid for his carelessness with his passenger side mirror."

Crystal smiled and shook her head, lifting her own coffee and sipping the sweet milky drink. She'd never taken her coffee black. *Everything is improved by milk and sugar,* her mother used to say. Their father would sigh and moan about the milk and sugar added to tea, cereal, oatmeal, you name it. But Crystal and Bette lapped it up like kittens.

"Karma," Crystal told her. "Sometimes fate forgets and we're forced to bring the balance ourselves."

The woman studied her with a curious expression and then she bobbed her head in agreement.

Crystal sensed suddenly that Greta was angry, violently

angry about the man who'd blocked her in, despite her good-natured explanation.

"Karma, boy would I like to believe in that," Greta said. "I have a handful of people waiting to get what's coming to them."

Greta took a bite of her sandwich, shaking her head and swallowing. "Sorry, wow, now it's me who's going overboard. I don't mean to unload my anger." She replaced her scowl with a smile. "Like I said, I've had a day. I want to pay you back for the sandwich, though. Can you give me your address? I'll pop a check in the mail."

Crystal shook her head. "It's on me, okay? Maybe we can meet for lunch again sometime and you can pick up my sandwich. How does that sound?"

"It sounds great," Greta said.

"Do you go to the school?" Crystal asked.

Greta shook her head. "I'm a researcher. No specific title. I do research for a small publishing company. They work with writers who publish nonfiction and I'm in charge of collecting information, scouring newspapers, visiting old places — that kind of thing."

"That's neat. What's it like?"

Greta shrugged.

"Like any job. It has its ups and downs. It's flexible and I get to travel a lot, which is good for me. I don't enjoy working for other people."

"I get that," Crystal agreed. "I work for lots of other people, but I'd love a job with more freedom someday."

Greta finished her sandwich and stood up.

"I've got to run. I'm meeting with an author in twenty minutes, but can I get your phone number, Crystal? I'll call you for that lunch date."

Crystal wrote her phone number on a napkin and handed it to her.

She watched the woman leave and realized her entire body

had grown taut. Crystal took a deep breath and felt the tension slowly drain out.

Crystal hadn't picked up many little tidbits about the woman as she often did in first meetings. A May birthday, she thought, Taurus. What she most felt was the woman's anger, a hot boiling anger that seemed to flow beneath her skin.

26

Now

Bette sat down with the cardboard box Officer Hart had returned from Crystal's car. She'd looked at it a dozen times since he'd brought it over, but had not brought herself to look inside a second time.

"I can do this," she told no one.

She pulled out one of Crystal's journals, a flimsy notebook covered in little silver spirals. Headbands, a few CDs, a half-eaten bag of cashews, and a purple rain jacket. There was also a gift box with a little card in a red envelope taped to the front.

The envelope contained a card from Wes, which included a sappy love poem and more declarations of love. Bette trembled as she read it and tried not to rip it into a thousand pieces.

Inside the box, wrapped carefully in tissue paper, she found a framed picture.

It was a poem superimposed over a faded photograph. She leaned closer and realized it was a photograph of Bette and

Crystal perched in their mother's lap. It was the photo that sat beside Crystal's bed. Their mother had been sitting in the rocking chair that now stood on Bette's porch. The sisters were young. Bette probably four and Crystal two.

The poem over top of the image was Edgar Allen Poe's, *Dream Within a Dream*.

"What is it, honey?"

Bette looked up to find Lilith standing on the porch.

Bette held it out.

Lilith took the frame and smiled sadly.

"Your mother's favorite poem."

Bette nodded.

"Did Crystal make this for you?" Lilith asked.

Bette shook her head. "Weston must have given it to Crystal as a gift."

Lilith frowned. "Hard to believe that he could love her so much and still..." Lilith didn't finish the thought, but Bette did in her mind.

Murder her. Love her so much and still murder her.

They didn't know if he'd murdered her.

Bette continued to hang on to some shred of hope that he'd abducted her and hidden her somewhere, or she'd escaped but been injured and was hiding at some little cottage deep in the woods, where an old medicine man was nursing her back to health. Foolish fairy tales. Bette had never been keen on such stories, but now they were the only things keeping her going.

Lilith sat down. "It's strange that he kept the pregnancy test," she said.

Bette glanced at her profile. She still looked young, far younger than her sixty years, but her face had become drawn in the previous days.

"Yeah," Bette murmured. "I've wondered about that. Why didn't he throw it away?"

Wes had to know the police would search his house. Why on

earth did he choose to keep the very item that would most implicate him in Crystal's disappearance?

"Maybe he didn't hurt Crystal," Lilith puzzled. "What if it's not Weston at all, but some random guy who saw her pumping gas or buying a book and followed her?"

Bette shook her head, her obsessions with Weston's guilt churning rapidly in her head.

"He did it. He built a world of lies and with the pregnancy, it was going to implode. I think he kept it because he believes he's smarter than anyone else. He assumed they'd never get an actual warrant. I think they caught him off guard." Bette spat the words out, but the picture in her hands told another story.

Weston himself told another story.

"But I don't believe it," Bette hissed.

"Don't believe what, honey?" Lilith asked.

"Nothing, sorry," Bette grumbled.

The phone rang in the house.

"I'll get it," Lilith said, standing and walking inside. A moment later, her head peeked out. "It's for you, Bette."

Bette returned the picture to the box and walked in the house.

"Law Offices of Henderson and Kissinger," Lilith said, lifting an eyebrow and handing Bette the phone.

"This is Bette," she said, wondering why their father's attorney would be calling.

"Bette, hi, this is Marvin Kissinger. How are you?"

"Not great. Crystal is missing. Have you heard?" she muttered.

"Yes, actually that's why I'm calling. Could you come to the office? I wanted to talk about a few things."

Bette frowned, watching as Lilith sprayed and cleaned the kitchen sink.

"I'll leave right now," she said.

"Crystal didn't have much, but she wanted to put it in order. She visited me four weeks ago, Bette," Marvin explained.

Bette sat in the stiff leather chair that faced his enormous desk. A gold placard displayed the lawyer's name: Marvin Kissinger, LLM.

Bette leaned forward in her chair, clutching her knees and studying the dizzying weave of red and blue carpet beneath her flats.

"Wait, no. Crystal created a will four weeks ago?" she asked trying to look at him.

He was older than their father, pushing seventy, but his lined face was tan and he still had a head of thick dark hair.

Marvin nodded.

"But why? Why would she do that?" Bette demanded.

Bette's thoughts spun in her head. Crystal was not a planner. If someone had asked, Bette would bet on her sister never putting a penny into a retirement account, never writing a will, never even signing up for health insurance.

Their father had sometimes referred to her as the invisible girl when they were young because she floated through life seemingly unscathed. While Bette suffered broken bones, sobbed over failed tests and obsessed about college transcripts, Crystal drifted as if on a rainbow that always delivered her to the pot of gold, to the perfect man, school, job — whatever.

"Did she say why, Marvin? Was Crystal sick?"

Marvin shook his head.

"She didn't mention an illness. She just popped in one day, no appointment, and chatted with our secretary, Hollie, for a few minutes before coming back here and asking me to draw up a will. I did ask her why, and she just said she was trying to be more responsible. She didn't offer more, and I didn't ask. I wish now that I had."

"Have you told the police?" Bette asked.

Marvin looked surprised.

"No. For starters, the police haven't visited me. But you understand Bette, I'd be obligated to share that information. And she mentioned a life insurance policy as well."

Bette felt as if the wind had been knocked out of her.

"Life insurance?" she asked.

"She'd set up a policy that morning. One hundred thousand payable to you."

Bette left the office on paper legs. She collapsed inside her car and rested her head on the steering wheel.

She didn't cry. Not yet, not in a public parking lot where people would see the red blotches on her cheeks and the snot rushing from her nose. And grief wasn't there yet. Shock was.

Why had her sister visited the office?

Could it have been merely a coincidence?

Crystal wasn't suicidal. Her sister had never been depressed a day in her life; well, save for the three days leading up to her period. She hadn't looked sick.

The secrets were piling on, and Bette wasn't sure how much more she could take.

~

BETTE RETURNED HOME to find her father on the phone.

She waited in the kitchen, the news still swirling in her mind, making the world feel off-kilter. Her own house looked alien.

Homer hung up.

"Lilith went to the grocery store," he explained. He nodded at the phone. "That was Crystal's friend, Jenny. They graduated together. Calling to offer her assistance. Lot of good any of it does." He frowned, studying Bette's face. "What? Did you hear something?"

"Crystal bought a life insurance policy. She created a will," Bette told her father. "I just left Marvin Kissinger's office."

Homer's mouth turned down.

"Crystal?" He shook his head as if he didn't believe it. "A will? But why? What did Marvin say?"

"He didn't know why, Dad. She walked into his office four weeks ago and asked him to draft a will."

"That's not like Crystal. She couldn't have been ill. Right, Bette?"

Bette wanted to say no. She and Crystal shared everything, their deepest secrets, their most troubling thoughts, but Crystal had created a will, bought life insurance. Crystal had been pregnant.

Crystal had known something that Bette hadn't, and she'd never said a word about it.

27

Then

CRYSTAL SAT in the wicker chair by her window, willing herself to be lulled by the gentle swaying. It didn't work its usual magic. She stared out the window as the daughter of another tenant in the apartment building ran around the courtyard, pulling a wooden duck whose mouth opened and closed with the revolutions of its wheels.

"Long enough," she whispered, standing and walking into the bathroom. Her hands tingled, and she rubbed them down her thighs as if that might calm them down.

She stopped in the doorway and looked toward the little plastic stick balanced on the edge of the sink. It was an inconsequential object, cheap and flimsy. She could crush it beneath a tennis shoe, and it would cease to exist.

Stepping into the bathroom, the tile cool against her bare feet, Crystal stared down at the pregnancy test.

Parallel pink lines met her eyes. A harmless symbol if

encountered anywhere else in the world, but there, on that white plastic stem, they held a Godlike power. The power of life and death. The power of a magnificent shift that the receiver was hopeless to avoid.

Pregnant.

Crystal's hands shook as she picked up the test and held it closer to her face. People suffered from double vision all the time. If she were Bette, she'd march back to the store and buy two more to confirm, but she wasn't.

Her body had revealed its secret that morning when she'd risen slowly from the abyss of her dreams to find her hand resting on her belly and the unshakable sense that another being lived within it.

Crystal studied her face in the mirror. No shadow lingered behind her, no gaunt face transformed her rosy cheeks, but the truth of her imminent death still hovered somewhere, somewhere in the space between body and spirit, where knowledge that the mind couldn't access slithered and slipped at the corner of one's eye.

She grabbed her purse and tucked the pregnancy test inside, slid on her sandals, and left the apartment to meet Weston.

~

CRYSTAL SAT on the low brick wall at the Michigan State University campus and looked at the clock tower.

She'd loved the structure since girlhood, when she'd visited the university with her parents. She and Bette would play in the bowl of grass at the base of the clock tower. Crystal would imagine racing up the stairs all the way to the room at the top. It would be filled with gears and dials, a room always in movement, tiny constant shifting and clicking, reminding the world that a second, now a minute, had elapsed. That moment was gone, this one was here, and now this one too had passed.

Bette had been less interested in the clocks and much more interested in the library, which they were rarely allowed to enter. It was for students of the college and professors like their father. Like Homer, Bette could pass hours between the stacks. Crystal loved to read as well, but her tastes tended toward fiction and poetry.

"Crystal," Wes jogged out of the library, smiling.

She stood and he grabbed her hand, pulling her into a dense bracket of trees. He wrapped his arms around her waist and picked her up, kissing her.

"Ugh, you feel so good. I thought this day would never end," he told her.

She laughed and breathed deep, smelling gardenias and the sun-warmed grass.

"My place?" he whispered, kissing her closed eyes and then her cheeks and finally her mouth.

"I'll meet you there," she promised.

They'd gotten more relaxed about their affection for one another.

In the first month, Wes had been adamant they keep it a secret. They still hid their romance, showing no outright affection on campus, but they touched each other in little ways now. Anyone looking closely could have seen they were in love.

Wes owned a house in Lansing, outside the high real estate prices of East Lansing, not to mention the watchful eyes of the other professors, but Crystal seldom joined him there. They mostly stayed at her apartment.

She parked on the street, leaving room for him to pull into his driveway.

As she waited, she tapped her fingers on the wheel, which reminded her of Bette and her father. They were terrible fidgeters. On road trips, one of them would drum the wheel while the other clicked a pen open and closed, until Crystal insisted they turn up the radio to drown out the sound of their constant fiddling.

The little white stick poked from an interior pocket in her purse. She didn't know why she'd brought it. Surely, Wes wouldn't demand proof. It had been a combination of excitement and anxiety. The part of her that was unsure how he'd react compelled her to bring something concrete to show him.

Crystal knew Wes had secrets. Mysteries that he'd almost revealed a dozen times in their few months together, but each time he pulled back from those secrets before letting them loose.

Wes parked his Jeep Wagoneer, complete with wood siding, in the driveway and hopped out. He trotted over and opened Crystal's door.

"I stopped by the party store and grabbed a bottle of wine. It's not the good stuff, but I've had it before. It's drinkable." He grabbed her hand and helped her out, kissing her on the mouth.

"Great," she murmured, reaching back in to grab her purse before following him inside.

He stood at the counter, uncorking the wine, while Crystal wandered to the glass sliding doors that opened onto his little back porch. He neglected his yard. The overgrown grass nearly reached the top step of the porch.

It was the curse of living two lives, he'd once said, no time to mow. His statement had unnerved her. Teaching in Traverse City and Lansing was hardly living two lives, but when she'd probed the subject, he'd shifted the conversation.

He paid a neighbor kid to mow the lawn every couple of weeks, but in the interval it always turned unruly, and he started to get annoyed looks from the old woman who lived across the street. The woman, whose name Crystal had learned was Henrietta, kept her lawn pristine. Every time Crystal had spent the night with Wes, she'd spotted the woman in her yard stalking the weeds with garden gloves and a trowel.

Wes handed her a glass of red wine.

Crystal smelled it, started to take a sip and felt her stomach clench. Saliva filled her mouth.

Wes noticed as she pulled away.

"What? Smells funky?" he asked, sniffing his own wine.

"Wes," Crystal said, her stomach continuing to churn as she set her glass on the table.

He studied her, his eyes shifting to the glass and back to her face.

"What is it, love?" he asked, taking her hand and kissing her palm.

"I'm pregnant," she blurted.

She'd intended a more eloquent delivery, but her mouth had jumped ahead.

As the words floated in the quiet kitchen, Crystal realized it was the first time she'd spoken them out loud. She'd thought it a thousand times in the previous two hours. Now the truth seemed larger, more alive.

Wes's eyes were wide, his mouth parted. When he swallowed, she watched the slow bob of his Adam's apple. He set his wine down next to hers.

He glanced at her stomach.

"Are you sure?" he asked.

Before she answered, he picked up his glass of wine and drained the red liquid in a single gulp.

"A baby?" he said in a detached voice.

She could see the revelation had knocked him off-kilter, and he hadn't quite grasped it.

Crystal walked to her purse and opened it. She extracted the small plastic stick, wondering if this is how she'd expected it to go. Wondering if she was disappointed and had hoped he'd smile and laugh and jump in the air. She didn't know. She hadn't considered how he might react.

He took the little stick. Two narrow pink lines.

He pulled out a chair and sat down heavily.

"Holy…" but he didn't finish. He just sat and stared at the test.

Crystal's eyes welled with tears.

A single drop slipped off her chin. It seemed to fall in slow motion and splash on the table.

Wes looked up, startled.

"I'm sorry," he stammered. "I'm doing this all wrong."

Crystal wiped her cheek and shook her head.

"No, it's okay," she backed away from him. "Just… take some time. Okay?"

She didn't wait for him to respond.

She walked out the door and climbed into her car. As she turned the key, she looked at the front door, hoping, wondering if he'd follow her, but the door didn't fly open.

Weston didn't run across the lawn and insist she come back inside.

Crystal started her car and drove away.

28

1970

Joseph Claude

JOSEPH SAW the black man leaving the dance hall. He wore a powder-blue tuxedo and walked confidently, as if he owned the street, the whole damn world.

A throb pulsed behind Joseph's eyes. The steady pulse of a hunger that lived within him but outside him as well. He appeased not only his needs but the needs of the land, of the forest, of the chamber.

He pulled alongside the man and rolled his window down.

"Care to make ten dollars?" he called.

The man looked at him with happy, drunken eyes.

"Ten dollars?" he exclaimed. "Sure would." The smile fell from his face as he looked down at his clean tux. "Best if I go on home and change first. I'm staying two blocks from here." He gestured down the dark road.

"Hop in and I'll give you a ride," Joseph told him.

"What do you need help with, sir?" the man asked, settling into the deep bucket seat and resting his hands on his knees.

"Can you grab my pen there?" Joseph asked, gesturing to the pen he'd deliberately knocked to the passenger floor.

As the man bent down, Joseph glanced in the rear-view mirror before lifting the iron bar he'd held tucked against his leg. He brought it down on the back of the man's head. A sickening crunch rang out as the bar connected with his skull.

People believed skulls were powerful, unbreakable even, but Joseph had seen how easily they cracked and caved. It took much less force than one imagined.

The man slumped forward. He hadn't let out a single cry.

As Joseph drove into the dark trees around the asylum, the pulsing grew in intensity. He parked on the hidden trail behind his house and pulled open his passenger door, grabbing the man beneath the armpits and hauling him from the car.

He slumped over in the dirt.

Blood had pooled on the floor of the car, but Joseph had come prepared with throwaway floor mats and, beneath those, two dark towels.

He didn't bother with the cleanup yet. He grabbed the man and dragged him into the house.

From her bedroom window, Greta watched the black man in the powder-blue tuxedo. The suit near his neck was stained dark, and she knew he was leaking blood, though she couldn't see the wound in his head.

She listened as her father threw open the back door and dragged the man through the front hall, pausing to open the basement door.

Thump-thump-thump went the man's head as her father dragged him down.

29

Now

Bette slipped on a pair of soft leather gloves. She usually wore them in winter. In June they looked ridiculous, but she stuffed her hands into the pockets of her shorts as she left her car and crept down the dark sidewalk.

It was an older neighborhood, and streetlights illuminated the corners but left the spaces between mostly in shadow. Weston's house was dark except for a small light over the garage door.

She pulled the key from her pocket.

The black "W" marked on the silver key could have stood for anything. A key for one of Crystal's many jobs, but when Bette discovered the key tucked into the interior pouch of her sister's purple rain jacket, she knew it belonged to Weston Meeks' house.

She slipped behind the house and took the two cement steps

that led to the back door. The key slid into the lock, but stuck halfway.

"No," she breathed, resting her head against the door and trying to wiggle it in further. The key didn't move.

When she tried to pull it out, the key remained stuck. Bette pulled off her gloves and stuffed them in her back pockets. She cursed silently as she shook the key. Finally, it jerked free.

As she retreated from the stoop, Bette missed the bottom stair. She flung her arms out to break her fall and landed with a crack on hands and knees. The key flew from her grasp as both palms smacked the cement walkway.

She winced at the pain and fought back her tears, leaning forward and searching gingerly for the bit of metal that would allow passage into Weston's home.

"Shit... shit... shit," she murmured, pausing and lifting one of her scraped palms.

The tears didn't stay put. They flowed down her cheeks as she pressed her lips to her tender skin.

Through her tears, she spotted a glint of metal on the path in front of her.

"Yes, thank you," she gasped, standing and hurrying over to the silver key.

She picked it up, hugging the house to stay in shadow, and moved to the front porch. She crept up the wooden stairs, glancing toward the house across the street, hoping whoever lived inside wasn't watching her too.

Bette opened the screen door and propped it on her hip as she slipped the key into the lock. It pushed in all the way and when she turned her hand, the lock slid open with a quiet click.

"Yes," she whispered, pushing into the dark foyer. She kept one hand on the screen door and eased it shut before shuffling in and firmly closing the door behind her.

As Bette crept down the hallway, pitch black as if the shades in every room had been drawn closed, she realized she hadn't brought a flashlight. Not even a lighter or a book of matches.

"I'm a terrible sleuth," she murmured.

She squinted into each room, frustrated as her eyes took ages to adjust to the shapes of the various pieces of furniture.

A sliver of light snaked beneath a curtain at the window over the kitchen sink. She walked in, nearly bumped into the table, and made her way to the counter. She peeled back the curtain, allowing the scant light to filter across the blue linoleum.

She opened drawers and pushed aside silverware, cooking utensils with plastic ladles and spatulas before finding the jumbled drawer of miscellaneous junk.

Bette bit her lip and sifted through the drawer, leaning her head close to it, which only blocked the sliver of light.

"Ugh," she hissed, squeezing her hand into a fist against her lips.

She pushed around guitar picks, dozens of poems scrawled on napkins, and twenty or more pencils.

"Where's the flashlight?" she demanded, but there was no flashlight.

She slammed the drawer shut, too hard.

Without light, she couldn't search for anything. What good would it do to stumble through a black house?

She leaned her back against the counter, panic rising as if her nervous system had only just gotten wind of what she was up to. The slender cut of light grew dark as her vision narrowed. Her lungs seemed to shrivel and collapse behind her ribs, and she opened her mouth, gulping for a breath. She gasped and pressed a hand to her chest.

She'd lose consciousness. Weston Meeks would find her on his kitchen floor and then he'd dispose of her just as he had disposed of Crystal.

Bette hadn't told her father where she was going. She'd

parked several blocks away. How long would it take for the police to find her car?

Her knees trembled as she sank to the floor, her mind kicking into overdrive, the terrified what-if thoughts drowning her.

"Three things," she croaked, reciting one of the many calming techniques she'd learned from Crystal to quell panic attacks. Focus on three objects in front of her.

She spotted Weston's phone and then her eyes slid down to a nail poking from the wall. A small blue flashlight hung from the nail.

She stared at the flashlight and pulled in a shaky breath.

"Oh, thank god," she croaked.

She started counting by threes, practicing another of the many coping mechanisms she usually forgot when a panic attack took hold.

"Three, six, nine, twelve, fifteen, eighteen..." Bette continued until she reached sixty and then forced herself up.

She swallowed, gulped two more deep breaths, and walked to the flashlight, pulling it from the nail.

During attacks, the sounds of the world grew muted, blocked by the rush of blood between her ears. Now she strained to hear any sounds, but nothing stirred in the dark house.

She walked from room to room, letting the small halo of light drift over furniture. Poetry and paintings of musicians hung from the walls. In the sitting room, piles of books sat on the coffee and side tables that butted against matching brown-leather furniture.

Bette walked up the stairs, coming first to a large bedroom with a queen bed covered in a black and white checked comforter. Draped across the foot of the bed was a fluffy orange blanket. Bette recognized it immediately. It was Crystal's blanket, and if she were to unfold it, she'd see a smiling sun with yellow and red rays streaming from its perimeter.

A dresser revealed a few stacks of clean laundry separated into jeans and shirts. More of Crystal appeared in the bathroom. Long red hairs in a black brush. Two tubes of vanilla lip gloss, Crystal's favorite, lay inside the medicine cabinet.

Only one other room stood on the second floor. It was a study with a cheap particle-board desk in the room's corner — the kind of furniture her father hated. It had multiple heights with space for files, a desktop computer and plenty of room that Weston filled with books and stacks of student papers.

Bette swung her light over the papers before she slid into the rolling ergonomic chair.

She opened drawers, shifting around pens and more papers.

Nothing offered any clues to Crystal's whereabouts.

Bette's foot kicked something tucked beneath the desk. She squatted and groped in the darkness until her hands found a hard suitcase, propped on its edge.

She pulled out the suitcase and laid it on its back, flipping open the fake gold clasps.

The suitcase was a jumble of stuff: photographs, letters in envelopes, old concert tickets. She lifted out a single pearl earring, frowning at the tiny piece of jewelry lost in the mass of stuff.

A shrill ring cut across the silence, and Bette gasped. Her heart pounded as she listened to the rings.

Downstairs, the message machine kicked on. Bette dropped the earring and stood, sprinting from the room and down the stairs.

"Hi, you've reached the phone of Weston Meeks. I'm currently unavailable. Please leave your name and phone number, and I'll call you at my earliest convenience."

"Hi, this is Eliza Sanders returning your call, Mr. Meeks. As I'm sure you're aware, my days at Sunny Angels are not terribly busy, but you caught me during a nap. Feel free to return my call when it suits you. I'm happy to answer any questions you have about Joseph Claude and the Northern Michigan Asylum."

The call ended and silence fell once more.

Unsure of the caller's purpose, Bette walked to the phone stand and scribbled the woman's information on a slip of paper, tearing it from the pad and stuffing it in her pocket.

30

Now

Homer hadn't moved from the picture window where he stood, staring at the street as if he expected the next clue might be somewhere in the yard, like an I Spy game with a pair of eyeglasses neatly tucked into a bush or a shovel lengthwise against the post of a mailbox.

The muted television played in the background.

"I have to fly home today," Lilith announced. "Irina has been covering the shop while I'm gone, but she's got her own work. I promised I'd only be gone for a couple days, and it's been nearly five."

She carried her suitcase down from her room upstairs

Bette hugged Lilith hard.

"Thank you for coming, Lil."

Lilith nodded, her eyes swimming with tears.

"I hate to go..." She glanced at Homer, who hadn't moved and seemed like a statue at the window.

"It's okay. I'll call you the minute we find out anything," Bette promised.

She wanted to say the minute we find *her*, but more than a week had passed. Finding her now meant something very different than it had in those first days.

Bette glanced at the television and saw Weston Meeks, hounded by reporters as he walked away from the East Lansing Police Station

"It's Meeks," she shouted, diving for the remote and jamming her finger on the volume button.

Weston ducked his head and shielded his face as a reporter snapped his photograph. The flash of the bulb was followed by voices as several other reporters ran up to him.

"Is it true you were having an affair with the missing woman?" one man yelled, thrusting a microphone in Wes's face.

"Was Crystal Childs pregnant with your baby, Professor Meeks?" a woman shouted.

Bette watched, frozen by the sheer terror on Wes's face. He looked like a little boy who'd stumbled into a room full of monsters. No one appeared to help him, no lawyer or officer or friend shielded Wes or ran with him to his car. He ran alone, his face a shade of gray that matched the sidewalk beneath him.

He climbed into his jeep and pulled from the curb, sending a plume of stones back toward the reporters. More bulbs flashed as they caught his desperate escape.

"That was him?" Lilith murmured.

Homer, too, had turned away from the window, eyes glued to the screen.

His cheek twitched, and for several more seconds he stared at the television.

A photograph of Crystal appeared on the screen.

"Crystal Childs is a twenty-two-year-old co-ed at Michigan State University," a man's voice announced. "She was last seen on the morning of Friday, June fourteenth. If you have any information about Crystal, please call the number at the bottom of the screen."

A reporter standing at Frasier Gorge replaced Crystal's image. The woman was young, not much older than Crystal and Bette, with curly blond hair and fashionable black glasses perched on her strong nose.

"Crystal Childs' pale blue Volkswagen Beetle was discovered at the bottom of this gorge eight days ago. The car was driven off the cliff behind me and landed in the woods below. Although search-and-rescue teams scoured the woods for more than two days, no trace of Crystal has been found. Police suspect foul play and have named Weston Meeks, a poetry and writing professor at Michigan State University, a person of interest in this case."

"Yeah," Bette said as the news shifted to the weather report. "That was Weston Meeks."

Lilith put a hand on Homer's shoulder. "I'm flying home today, Homer, but I'm only a call away. Don't hesitate."

He dragged his eyes from the television and looked at Lilith, nodding as if slowly comprehending her words.

"Home," he murmured. "Thanks so much for coming, Lilith."

He hugged her, but his eyes had taken on the distant glaze they had often held in the weeks and months after their mother's death.

At the beginning of Joanna's sickness, Homer had gone into fix-it mode. He drove all over the country buying mushrooms, tinctures and oils to save his ailing wife.

When the cancer progressed, despite his best efforts, Homer began to shut down. In the final days of her life, he rarely left the chair by her bed. He didn't shower or eat unless Lilith forced him to.

It took years for Homer to emerge from that dark place, and Bette was terrified he might slip into it once more.

"Dad." Bette stood directly in front of her father. "I'm going to Traverse City. I want to talk to Weston's wife and see if I can't find out more about that girl who disappeared a couple of years ago."

"I'll come with you," he said.

"No." She shook her head.

"You've got to keep the pressure on the police. Plus, that reporter from the Lansing State Journal wants an interview. I should be back in time, but if I'm not, you've got to talk to him."

Homer's face remained rigid. He blinked and nodded. "Okay. Call me, though. I want to know everything you find out."

"Of course." She hugged her dad. "Lilith needs a ride to the airport."

Bette kissed Lilith on the cheek and headed for her car.

31

Now

HILLARY MEEKS' white-blond hair framed her angular face. She was pretty in a sterile way, all sharp edges and narrow features. She wore sunglasses and walked with her chin lifted as if she were a movie star, and the paparazzi might descend at any moment.

And they might, Bette thought, to question her about her husband's mistress.

"Hillary! Hillary Meeks?" Bette shouted, hurrying to catch up with the woman as she walked briskly to her car.

The woman didn't acknowledge her. She pulled open her door, as Bette caught up with her, and dropped into the front seat. Bette grabbed the door.

Hillary's eyes flicked to her hand and Bette saw she intended to wrench the car door closed on it. Bette winced, preparing for the pain.

Another nurse from the hospital walked to a green pickup

truck parked next to Hillary's car. Bette saw the woman's eyes narrow at her co-worker. Hillary released the handle of her car, apparently not comfortable crushing Bette's fingers with a witness present.

"Please, I'm not a reporter," Bette whispered loudly. "My name is Bette Childs. I'm Crystal Childs' sister. Please talk to me."

Hillary's lips flattened into a line, and she threw Bette a withering, almost hateful look. After a moment, the look slid away, and she smiled coolly.

"I'm sorry for your situation, Bette, but I've already spoken with the police. I'm sure I can't help you."

"Please," Bette said again, still holding the door.

Hillary stared straight ahead through her windshield, putting both hands on the steering wheel and squeezing.

"Fine. There's a park on Union Street. You can follow me there."

Bette ran to her car and jumped in. Hillary was already pulling from the parking lot, and Bette had to jam the gas pedal to catch up with her. The woman drove fast and barely paused at stop signs, slamming on her breaks when a lady walking her dog stepped off the curb in front of her.

Bette found the whole experience unsettling. The woman was clearly angry, and Bette tried to approach the situation in the way Crystal would have, finding compassion for the scorned wife. Instead, she felt her own mixture of emotion: anger, but also fear.

Hillary whipped her car down a side street and pulled to the curb. She stepped out, and walked down a steep hill toward a slow-moving river. She perched on a bench at a picnic table, her eyes trained on the dark water.

Bette followed her, glancing both ways. It was a cloudy June day in the middle of the week and not another soul occupied the park.

Bette sat across from Hillary at the picnic table. She felt as if the woman's steely gaze passed right through her.

"I just want to know about Weston. The police said you provided his alibi," Bette explained.

Hillary Meeks said nothing. She continued to stare through Bette with cruel indifference.

Finally, she shifted her eyes to Bette's face.

"I told the police Weston returned home on Thursday June thirteenth. He became ill. I saw him the following morning, Friday the fourteenth. He was still vomiting in the morning. I visited a friend further up north and returned in the late evening. Weston was still in bed. What he did in the interim, I can't say."

"How long were you gone?" Bette asked.

Hillary shrugged. "I left around eight a.m. and didn't get home until after ten that night. I have a sick friend in Petoskey who I spent a good deal of the day with. Since Weston had been violently ill the night before, I assumed he slept most of the day."

"Did you have any idea that—"

"He was having an affair?" Hillary asked, her mouth turning down. She shook her head. "No, not a clue. He's a clever man. He knows how to tell a story. Writers usually do."

Bette swallowed. "Do you think he did something to Crystal? To hide the affair?"

Hillary rubbed her eyes. She looked tired, suddenly. Bette noticed small lines fanning like spiderwebs from the corners of her eyes.

"I found out a few years ago I can't have children," Hillary confessed. "Weston loves children. I think that hurt him. Sometimes I wondered if he'd stay, but I never really believed he would, except for the money, that is. Men never veer far from that."

"Wes doesn't have his own money?" Bette asked.

Hillary sneered.

"Oh sure, his salary at the university, but it's not the money he's become accustomed to." Hillary sighed, and her shoulders slumped forward. She put her elbows on the table and rested her head in her hands, pushing her fingers into her delicate, pale hair.

Bette almost touched her, some show of empathy, but instead kept her hands close to her own body. The woman probably wouldn't appreciate comfort from the sister of her husband's mistress.

"Do you think he killed her, Hillary? Do you think Wes murdered my sister?"

Hillary didn't look at her. She trained her eyes on the picnic table, and after a moment they filled with tears.

"I hope not. I truly hope not."

"Are you going to leave him?" Bette asked.

The woman looked up sharply and for an instant, her face contorted with rage. The expression turned her instantly ugly, her thin lips pulled away from a snarling mouth.

She looked away from Bette, seemed to compose herself, and turned back.

"That's all the time I have, Bette. Best of luck."

She stood and stalked back to her car, not giving Bette a second glance.

~

BETTE STEPPED into the Traverse City Library and smiled at the woman behind the desk.

She was a square woman with glossy dark hair parted in the middle. Her shoulders were broad and almost gave her the appearance of wearing pads under her dark blouse.

"Hi, I'd like to look at old newspapers. Can I do that without a library card?" Bette asked.

The woman smiled. "Sure can. I'll need to hold on to your driver's license, but I can set you up in the computer lab. We have the microfilm in there."

Bette followed the librarian, Julie by her nametag, to a little room with three desktop computers.

"I'd like the years 1989 and 1990, please."

Julie loaded the microfilm into the machine and left Bette alone in the room.

Bette scrolled down, reading headlines.

She found the story of Weston Meeks' former assistant on the front page of the Traverse City News from May tenth, 1989: *Woman Vanishes from NMU Campus.*

Bette read the article. The girl's name was Tara Lyons, and she'd disappeared from the NMU where she worked as a teaching assistant for Professor Meeks, who taught poetry and prose classes. Tara was working towards an associate's degree in English. The girl had last been seen in the student lunchroom, purchasing a bottle of lemonade and a bag of chips.

Bette studied Tara's photo. She had long dark hair pulled over one shoulder. Her head was tilted as she smiled at the camera. She was pretty and wholesome-looking, with big dark eyes.

Tara was originally from Farmington Hills and had moved to Traverse City with a girlfriend after they'd graduated from high school. Her family was offering a reward of ten thousand dollars for any information that led to their daughter's whereabouts.

The next page made a brief reference to the missing nineteen-year-old. The paper a day later had nothing about Tara.

The following week, on page two, Bette found a short article: *No New Leads in the Case of Missing Student, Tara Lyons.*

After that, the paper went dark regarding Lyons until a front-page article on the one-year anniversary of the disappearance. The reward had been raised to fifty thousand dollars.

The article outlined the handful of hopeful leads that had come in over the previous year, including a tennis shoe found in the Boardman River believed to be Tara's, which later turned out not to be hers. The police had identified one person of interest. He had a criminal history involving aggravated rape, but produced an alibi for the day in question.

None, except the first article, mentioned Weston Meeks.

Bette wanted more information, but didn't know where to turn. She scanned the original article where Tara's best friend, the girl she'd moved to Traverse City with, had been quoted.

"Tara's one of the most reliable people I've ever met. When she didn't show up for dinner at Mo's, I knew something was wrong right away. My boyfriend and I drove to the school, but we never found her. Tara wouldn't just leave. Plus, her car was there. She obviously didn't run away without her car."

The girlfriend's name was listed as Molly Ward.

Bette grabbed a phone book and searched, finding three numbers in Grand Traverse County for Molly Ward.

Bette jotted all three numbers down, thanked the librarian, and walked outside to use the payphone.

Bette dialed the first number, but received a notice that it had been disconnected. On the second call, a man picked up.

"Hello," he said.

"Hi, my name's Bette. I'm trying to reach the Molly Ward who was friends with Tara Lyons."

"Molly's my wife," the man said. "She's at the store and I can't tell ya if she's friends with a Tara Lyons."

The man sounded older, in his fifties at least, too old to be married to the now-twenty-one-year-old Molly Lyons.

"Can you tell me how old your wife is, sir?" Bette asked.

"Not unless I want a swift kick in the ass," the man laughed.

"I understand. Can you just tell me if she's twenty-one?"

The man guffawed as if Bette had told the joke of the century.

"If she is, she has not aged well." He continued laughing.

"Okay, thank you. Wrong Molly," she told him, hanging up the phone.

She dialed the third number and a younger woman with a small, squeaky voice answered.

"Hello."

"Hi, is this Molly Ward?" Bette asked.

"Yes, it is," she said.

"The Molly Ward who was friends with Tara Lyons?"

The woman didn't respond for several seconds, and Bette worried she'd hung up.

"Yes, this is her," she responded, slightly breathless. "Have you found Tara?"

"No, I'm sorry," Bette admitted. "I'm calling because my sister has gone missing. Crystal Childs is her name. We live downstate."

"Oh, I'm so sorry to hear that," Molly said, and she sounded genuinely sorry.

"Molly, could you tell me about Tara's relationship with Weston Meeks?"

Again, the pause.

"Were they involved?" Bette continued. "As more than teacher and assistant?"

"No, not technically," Molly said. "Tara… well, Tara had a bit of a crush on him, but I don't think he ever reciprocated."

"So, as far as you know, they weren't having an affair?"

"No."

"Do you think Weston was involved in her disappearance?"

Bette heard a small grinding sound and wondered if Molly had begun to chew her nails.

"Not Weston, no," Molly admitted, "but… and I shouldn't say this because my parents' attorney told me not to, but it's been two years. Two god-damned years, and nothing."

Bette waited.

"I think Weston's wife had something to do with it," she said.

"Hillary Meeks?"

"Yes. Right before Tara disappeared, she'd found out some disturbing shit about Hillary. She didn't tell me what, only that she was afraid for Weston. She thought he didn't have a clue who he was married to."

"You have no idea what she found out?"

"No. I tried to figure it out after she disappeared, but I ran into a brick wall trying to get any information about Hillary. People are tight-lipped about her. Money and power and all that crap."

"But she's a nurse. Where's the money and power coming from?"

"Beats me," Molly admitted.

"Any clue where Tara might have discovered something about Hillary?" Bette asked.

"Kind of. Tara went to visit her cousin in Marquette the week before she disappeared. She came back all keyed up, like she'd stumbled on something that really freaked her out, something that had to do with Weston's wife."

"Did you tell the police all this when Tara vanished?"

"Oh yeah, absolutely. But word around town was that the police were on Hillary's side. She has connections there, maybe. I don't really know. I was in way over my head, and when I started insisting they look at Hillary, someone contacted my parents' lawyer and told them I'd be getting sued if I kept slandering her. I'm pretty sure they threatened my dad's job too. He works for the Road Commission. My parents told me to stop talking about it."

"Molly, do you have contact information for Tara's cousin in the UP?"

"Yeah. Her cousin's name is Whitney. I still talk to her every couple of months. Staying connected to each other helps us feel closer to Tara. Hold on just a second, and I'll grab her number."

Bette wrote down Tara's number and promised to call her if she discovered anything.

Whitney's boyfriend answered the phone when Bette called. He explained that Whitney was working at a pub in downtown Marquette and wouldn't get off her shift until late that night.

"What's the name of the pub?" Bette asked.

"Maury's," he offered.

Bette hung up and looked at her watch. It was just before noon. Whitney worked for another eight hours; the drive to Marquette would take five. Bette hadn't intended to drive further north or to stay overnight, but once the thought popped into her head, she couldn't shake it.

She dialed her dad.

The phone rang and clicked to voicemail after several rings.

"Dad, it's Bette. I'm chasing some leads up here. I've decided to drive to Marquette so I'm not going to make it home until tomorrow—"

"Hello, Bette. Hello?" Her dad picked up mid-way through her message. "Sorry, I was outside. My neighbor just brought Teddy over, and wouldn't you know, he chased Chai outside and up a damn tree. I've been out there for a half hour trying to coax her down. My shoulder looks like I've been attacked by a jungle cat."

"Oh Dad, I'm sorry. I forgot all about Teddy."

"No, it's okay," he insisted. "My neighbor's wife is having some kind of gall-bladder episode and he had to bring him over, but we'll be fine. It's good to have him. Even the animal fights are a nice distraction."

"Good. I'm happy you've got some company. Dad, I'm heading to Marquette. I want to talk to the cousin of the girl who went missing up here."

"Okay, sure, yeah. Do you think it's related, Bette? Did Weston Meeks do something to that girl?"

"I don't know yet. But I'll call tonight, okay?"

32

1972

Joseph Claude

JOSEPH STARED straight ahead as his daughter drove on the dark road, searching for the opportunity that always appeared.

Greta's hands were white on the steering wheel, her body tense. It wasn't the impending murder that scared her, but driving.

He almost smiled at the thought, but in the road before them a man stepped out.

Joseph pulled back and slammed his foot down as if to depress the brake that wasn't there. His eyes bulged as the black man in the blue tuxedo slipped into view.

The car slammed into the man, but no sound emerged.

The man in the blue tuxedo slid up over the hood, his face

pressed against the windshield, his dark eyes filled with accusations as they locked onto Joseph's.

Joseph pressed his hands against the dashboard and let out a bellow of shock and fear as the man continued to glide over the glass and disappear into the night.

Greta slammed on the brakes, pitching both of them forward in their seats.

She looked wildly through the windows and then at Joseph.

"What? What did you see?" she asked.

Joseph's mouth hung open, his eyes still staring at the spot where the dead man's face had been.

He rubbed his eyes and finally turned to look at his daughter.

"Did you see him?" He pointed at the windshield. "The man in the blue tuxedo?"

Greta frowned and squinted toward the windshield.

"No, Dad. You buried him months ago."

33

Now

By the time Bette reached Marquette, her butt ached from sitting, and she'd gone over every scenario of what might have happened to Crystal.

She drew in a grateful breath when she climbed out of the car, bending her legs and stretching her arms overhead.

Maury's Pub occupied the lower floor of an aged brick building across the street from a sprawling Lake Superior ore dock.

People sat in stools along the curved mahogany counter.

Bette stopped at the host stand.

A young woman with dark blond hair piled on her head, beamed at her. "Hi there!" The hostess grabbed a menu. "Seat for one?"

Bette shook her head. "I'm actually looking for Whitney Lyons." As she said the words, Bette's eye drifted to the girl's nametag.

"Whitney," the black letters read.

Whitney's smile widened. "You've found her."

"Great. That was easy." Bette sighed. "Listen, my name's Bette Childs. Do you have a few minutes to answer questions about your cousin, Tara?"

The enormous smiled faded. "Did they find her?"

Bette shook her head. "No. I'm sorry. My sister's missing and I think her disappearance could be connected to Tara's."

Whitney frowned. "How?"

"Whit, table six needs their drinks," the bartender called, pointing at several beers lining the counter.

"Shoot," she whispered. "Have a seat over there." Whitney motioned to an empty booth by the window. "I can get another waitress to cover me for ten minutes."

Bette walked to the table.

Whitney bustled to the bar and grabbed the drinks. She delivered them to a table of guys who eyed her appreciatively, as much for her good looks as for their beers, probably.

Whitney stopped next to an older woman wearing the same uniform. The woman glanced at Bette and nodded, giving Whitney a sympathetic pat on the back.

"Are you from Traverse City?" Whitney asked, sliding into the booth.

Bette shook her head. "The Lansing area, actually. My sister's name is Crystal, and she's been seeing Weston Meeks."

"The professor? He got divorced, then?"

"No, he didn't. He was having an affair."

Whitney scowled. "Yikes. And now she's missing?"

Bette nodded. "I spoke with Molly Ward, and she said Tara visited you the weekend before she disappeared. Molly was convinced she found out something about Weston's wife when she was here."

"She didn't tell me if she did. She talked a little about Hillary, but mostly just mentioned she got a bad vibe from her,"

Whitney offered. "She talked about Weston a lot. How brilliant he was, about the amazing poetry he wrote. She clearly had feelings for him, but he was married, and Tara is not a homewrecker."

Whitney's face blanched. "Not that your sister is-"

Bette held up a hand. "It's okay. My sister had no idea Weston was married. He never told her."

"What a rat," Whitney exclaimed.

"Yeah, exactly. But I'm more curious about his wife, Hillary. Do you have any idea where Tara might have discovered something about Hillary Meeks?"

"No. I can't imagine where she stumbled across something. It's not like we spent a lot of time talking to people that weekend. She left early the last day. She ran into town to get a newspaper and some donuts, and when she came back, she was in a big rush to leave. She didn't say why. She packed her stuff and hit the road."

"Where did she get her paper and donuts?" Bette asked.

"A bakery called The Bread Box. It's a block away from here on Washington Street."

"Hmm... okay. I'm going to check it out. Thanks, Whitney."

Bette stood and Whitney grabbed her hand.

"Hold on one second," Whitney pleaded. She ducked behind the bar, emerging a moment later with a slip of paper. "I wrote my name and phone number. Will you call me if you find anything? I think about her every day. I pray every night. Our family needs to know what happened to Tara."

Bette took the card and promised she'd call.

She walked down the street, glancing in store windows at souvenirs and sweatshirts with slogans like "Yooper's Rock."

The Bread Box was a small shop with a fluffy pink cupcake painted on the front window.

Bette walked in to the aroma of chocolate-chip cookies.

"Fresh out of the oven!" a woman said, grinning at Bette. She held a cookie sheet with a purple oven mitt and used her other hand to scoop cookies into a display case.

"They smell amazing. I'm actually here about something else, but I think I'll take a cookie to go," Bette told her.

"Oh no," the woman shook her head, gray curls bobbing. "You have to eat one hot; it's a special treat to walk in at the precise moment I've taken them from the oven. My grandmother called that heavenly timing. If you ignore heavenly timing once, it won't come again for you."

Bette smiled. She definitely could use some heavenly timing, and the cookies did smell good. Her stomach rumbled in compliance. Her head had been ignoring her belly lately, but the lady was convincing her to override it.

Bette accepted the cookie the woman handed her and took a bite.

The texture was soft and warm; the chocolate oozed richly against her tongue.

"It's delicious," she admitted.

The woman winked at her.

"It's all in the timing, my dear. Now, what can I help ya with? Birthday cake order? Or" —the woman smiled conspiratorially — "a wedding cake, perhaps?"

Bette sighed and shook her head.

"I wish it was something happy like that. I'm wondering if you were working the morning Tara Lyons came in. She's the girl who-"

The woman interrupted before she could finish.

"Yes," she frowned. "This is my bakery. I was here the morning Tara came in. Her family visited me a few days later, hoping I could offer some clue as to her state of mind that day. Unfortunately, it was a Sunday morning at nine a.m. Probably the busiest time of the whole week for me. I sold her a dozen donuts. She was very sweet, but we didn't chat. I regret that now. I should have spoken to her more, taken the time..."

"Did she buy anything other than donuts?"

The woman nodded and pointed to a stack of newspapers by the door.

"A dozen glazed donuts and a copy of *The Mining Journal*. That's our daily paper."

~

BETTE WALKED into the Marquette library.

The librarian, a plump middle-aged woman in a blue blouse spotted with little gray mice, sat at a large circulation desk swiping a stack of books across the magnetic strip that would make a buzzer sound if they were carried out of the building.

"Hi," Bette said, pausing in front of her. Can you direct me to old newspapers? *The Mining Journal* in particular, from 1989."

"It would be my pleasure," the woman said, standing from her chair with a groan. "That chair gets my sciatica flaring up like gasoline on a fire. I keep telling Mrs. Nelson, our director, that we need decent chairs in this library, but every year it's stripped off the budget. I might get me one of those little cushions you sit on. They're on the home shopping network every other week and come with a lifetime guarantee."

The woman chattered on about her sciatica, arthritis and indigestion as they walked deeper into the library. She stopped at a square room with floor-to-ceiling shelves containing boxes of newspapers.

"We keep old copies of newspapers in this room," the woman said. "*The Mining Journal* goes back five years, but we also have microfiche for older versions. They're arranged by year, starting with January. Don't hesitate to call out if you need me. This place is one big echo chamber. I'll hear you fine if you need some help."

"Thanks," Bette told her.

The woman paused as if she wanted to see what story Bette sought.

Bette wandered away, slowly scanning years until the librarian left.

She grabbed the box that contained the newspapers from 1989. Flipping through until May, she found Sunday the twenty-first, 1989.

"Questions Linger as Anniversary of Murder Approaches," announced the front-page headline. The photograph depicted a handsome teenage boy with long shaggy hair brushing the collar of his varsity jacket.

Bette read the article, which outlined the case of seventeen-year-old Matt Kelly, found slain in Bishop Park in 1974. The brutal murder had remained unsolved for fifteen years.

It continued on page three, where a full spread was devoted to the details of the case and included several more pictures of Matt Kelly.

Bette examined the images, and her eyes caught on a prom picture of Matt. His date, a young woman with pale-blond hair, looked familiar. Bette studied the woman's face, the sharp angular cheekbones and thin pale lips. Most startling of all were her harsh gray eyes. The eyes of Hillary Meeks.

Bette read the caption below the image: *"Matt Kelly at the senior prom with his date and girlfriend, Greta Claude."*

"Claude?" she asked the empty room, eyeing the name for several more seconds. She'd heard it before.

And then it came to her.

The name "Claude" had been spoken by the woman who'd left a phone message for Weston Meeks. Bette had written down the woman's name and the place where she lived, Sunny Angels.

Bette photocopied the article and examined the shelves. One wall contained yearbooks from the Marquette High School. She pulled the 1974 book down and searched the book for Greta Claude. Sure enough, she was listed as a junior.

She flipped to Greta's photo and stared at the young woman. It was, without a doubt, Hillary Meeks. Her hair was cut short in a boyish style that barely went past her ears, but her piercing gray eyes were unmistakable.

34

Then

"THANKS, Rick. I'm digging the new t-shirt," Crystal told the barista at Sacred Grounds.

He grinned and looked down at the shirt, which stated "Smells Like Teen Spirit" in red dripping letters.

"Thanks, Crys." He handed her a cup of decaf coffee, arching an eyebrow. "Since when are you into decaf?"

She shrugged and took the cup. "Cutting back on stimulants. You know the drill."

As she walked toward the door, a hand reached out and snatched the hem of her shirt.

"Hey girl," the woman said, releasing her shirt and gesturing at her table.

It took Crystal a moment to remember her name.

"Greta!" she said, smiling. "How are you?"

Greta flitted her hands, gesturing at the stream of papers spread across the table.

"Busy like a wasp," she muttered.

"I think the saying is like a bumblebee," Crystal chuckled sipping her milk-heavy coffee.

"They're too fuzzy for my tastes," Greta retorted. "Sit and have a chat." She pointed at the empty chair.

Crystal glanced at the door, tempted to offer an excuse. A book and a nap sounded infinitely more appealing, but Greta's hopeful expression got the best of her.

"Sure okay."

"Crystal!"

Crystal looked up to see Greta hurrying down the street toward her.

She held up Crystal's wallet.

"You forgot it at the coffee shop," she said.

Crystal slapped herself on the forehead. "Wow, thank you. I would have been screwed. My rent is in there."

"Fancy an adventure?" Greta asked, eyes sparkling.

Crystal took her wallet and tucked it into her purse, puzzling at how it could have fallen out.

"Well, I'm curious, that's for sure. I rarely say no to an adventure. What are we talking about?" Crystal asked, though her earlier desire to go home and crawl into bed had only heightened in the previous half hour.

It was the anniversary of her mother's death. She was pregnant with the child of a man who was keeping secrets, and every time she looked in the mirror, she searched for the shadow of death she was sure hid somewhere behind her.

Weston had called several times, and she hadn't answered or returned his calls. She wanted to tell Bette about the baby. She should have told her sister first.

That night, when they marked the anniversary of their

mother's death, Crystal planned to come clean about everything. Once she'd gotten Bette's insight, she'd be more ready to face Weston.

"I've been hired to research old houses for an author," Greta explained. "There's an abandoned house out on old Highway 27. It's tucked way back in the woods. No one has entered it in forty years, but I," she held up a small silver object, "got a key."

"Wow, really?" Crystal eyed the small key.

Bette and her father had more of a penchant for old houses, but Crystal couldn't deny they held a certain allure. Plus, she wasn't meeting Bette until five, which meant seven more hours of filling the time and thinking about Wes and the baby.

"Okay," Crystal agreed. "But I have to meet my sister at five."

"Not a problem," Greta assured her. "I'm parked down the block. Why don't you ride with me?"

~

A RUSTED GATE plastered with "No Trespassing" signs barred their entrance to the weedy driveway. It was overgrown and sheltered by trees. From the road, you wouldn't assume a house lay in the gloomy depths at all.

The old farmhouse was large, the windows not boarded but void of glass. Black holes in the bleached face of the monster. And look like a monster it did.

Moss coated the sagging roof. Trees, bushes and vines crowded around the crumbling structure, snaking through the empty windows. More vegetation swarmed across the porch.

Crystal shivered and wrapped her arms over her chest.

"Coming?" Greta asked, climbing out of the car and grabbing a camera bag from the backseat.

Greta took out her camera and started snapping pictures,

walking around the exterior of the house and taking shots of the derelict structure.

Crystal took a final sip of the bottled water, Greta had given her, before she stepped from the car.

The quiet in the forest was thick. It coiled around Crystal, and a sense of menace rose through her feet as if it were a message from the poisonous ground beneath her.

"Poisonous?" she murmured, wondering where such a thought had originated.

The ground looked healthy; overgrown to be sure but, if anything, that signaled good health, not bad.

"Ready?" Greta asked.

She stood on the porch, her smile glowing in the shadow of the rotted eaves.

Crystal considered staying in the car, or rather walking out of there, following the wooded pathway from the house and waiting for Greta at the road.

The dread seemed baseless, foolish, but Crystal had always followed her instincts.

She stepped back toward the car.

Greta peeked inside the half-open door and gasped.

"You've got to see the stone hearth in this place. Unreal," she called, disappearing through the doorway.

Crystal swallowed her fear and followed Greta into the house.

The stone hearth was grand, rising to the ceiling and built from huge boulders, pudding stones and Petoskeys.

"Wow," Crystal breathed, walking to the fireplace and putting a hand on one of the Petoskey stones. "I've never seen one so big. Whose house was this?"

Greta took a picture and the flash illuminated black mold streaking up the walls.

"A psychiatrist at the Northern Michigan Asylum," Greta said. "He's dead and gone now, but apparently he lived here before he moved up north onto the asylum grounds. He never sold this place, and after he died it just sat…"

"He didn't have children that wanted it?" Crystal wondered.

Greta's face was pressed into the camera, but she pulled it away.

"They all died, right here, in fact. Murdered. Two daughters, a son, and his wife. Good old Ralph died at the asylum. He was nearly ninety when he passed, but a few of the doctors still went to him for advice."

Crystal stared at Greta horror-struck.

"Who murdered them?"

Greta took a photograph of the black mold. It looked like billions of tiny spiders scurrying up the walls.

"Unsolved," Greta said, and then laughed at Crystal's expression. "I guess I should have mentioned that. This is research for a true crime writer. I've always been fascinated by old places, by the things that live in the rotted walls, the memories, the dark things."

"Dark things?" Crystal touched the bannister leading up the narrow staircase.

"Oh, you know. What's left behind. In murder houses, plague houses. They're different. As if the house remembers."

Crystal blinked at the rotted floorboards of the staircase. The lowest board seemed to move, pulsing up and down. Crystal blinked at Greta, the room behind her tilting and then steadying again.

"I don't feel so well," she murmured.

"That's how I met him, you know?" Greta muttered. "The love of my life. He was living in an abandoned building in Detroit. He and two musician buddies, all three so doped up on heroin they barely lifted their heads when I walked in. I still have the pictures. A little leverage if I ever need it, which I haven't because he's been completely devoted to me for…" — Greta shrugged— "going on ten years."

Crystal tried to follow her words. Doped up and leverage, but the room spun, a slow whirling like a carousel just starting up. The light bulbs would flash, and the ugly smiles of the painted horses would spin by.

Crystal put a hand to the bannister to steady herself. The knobby top broke off, and she fell to one knee. The impact hurt, but seemed to occur in a body further away from her own, as if she, Crystal, had stepped through a veil into another dimension. She could sense herself there in the old house, but her conscious mind was walking away, retreating.

Greta loomed in front of her. Her usually gray eyes were almost black, and her smile was hard and bitter.

"Until you came along. He was totally devoted to me until you."

Crystal fell onto her hands and watched the floor fade to black.

35

1973
The Northern Michigan Asylum

Greta Claude

GRETA HELD her father's hand as he hunched forward in his chair, eyes clenched shut. Every few minutes he'd lift his head slightly. His eyes darted around and then bulged. He closed his eyes and commenced to rocking back and forth.

"It's the man in the blue tuxedo," he whispered. It's him, he's here."

"Shh..." Greta murmured, though she knew all the doctors and patients had heard Joseph Claude ranting about the man in the blue tuxedo, the man he'd murdered six months before.

They didn't know that part, of course.

They didn't know the man's body lay in the unmarked graveyard deep in the woods, on a hill overlooking the secret chamber. There had been a raised mound of dirt in the days after the burial, but over time Joseph and Greta stamped the earth down and spread out the soil. The rain and wind did the rest.

Days before, Greta had noticed flowers had popped up on the grave. Bright yellow dandelions.

A nurse paused behind Joseph. She rested a hand on his shoulder.

"Time for your medicine, Joseph," the nurse told him kindly. "And how are you, Greta?" she asked.

Greta blinked at the woman, at her sunny, maddening smile and her stiff gray hair clinging to her head like a helmet.

"I'm fine," Greta said, standing and walking from the room, Joseph's mumbled words echoing behind her.

36

Now

Bette didn't have to look in the phone book for the number of someone connected to Matt Kelly.

When Bette mentioned to the librarian that she wanted to speak to a family member of Matt Kelly, the woman pointed to a flier hanging from the large glass-covered bulletin board in the lobby of the library.

"The number on that flier is for Matt's sister, Lisa."

The librarian even offered to let Bette use the library telephone to call, a polite enough gesture, though Bette sensed the woman mostly wanted to eavesdrop on the call.

"Hello, Lisa speaking."

"Lisa, my name's Bette Childs. I'd like to speak to you about your brother, Matt."

"Matt?" The woman's voice dropped lower. "Are you a journalist?"

Lisa did not sound hostile. Instead, it was hope that tinged her voice.

"No, I'm not. My sister is missing, but I'd prefer not to explain over the phone."

She felt the librarian stiffen behind her.

"Can we meet in person?"

"Okay, sure. Just come by my house."

Lisa rattled off her address and Bette wrote it down.

BETTE CLIMBED the porch and knocked on the front door.

A petite woman with dark blond hair pulled into a ponytail answered the door. She was probably approaching thirty, though her size made her appear younger. She couldn't have stood over five feet tall. She wore no make-up and a mismatched jogging suit with gray pants and a purple zip-up shirt.

"Bette?" the woman asked.

"Yes, hi. Thank you for meeting me."

"I'm happy to do it. Come on in." Lisa opened the door wide.

Bette stepped into a short hallway. Family photographs decorated the cornflower blue walls.

"Can I get you a cup of coffee?" she asked.

"No, thanks. I had some on my drive up," Bette explained, following her into a tidy living room with couches and chairs striped in blue and white. A corner of the room held a small kids' table scattered with crayons and coloring books.

Lisa sat on a couch and pulled a scruffy-looking stuffed bunny into her lap.

"It belongs to my daughter," she explained.

Bette opted for a chair in a matching pattern.

"You said on the phone you had questions about Matt and Greta Claude. I've always wondered what became of her," Lisa murmured. "A part of me hoped she'd met some untimely and painful end."

Bette's eyes widened, and Lisa laughed.

"That sounds cruel," Lisa said, though she didn't take the words back.

"Can you tell me why you've hoped for that?" Bette asked.

Lisa crossed her legs and lit a cigarette.

"Because Greta Claude murdered my brother." Lisa didn't blink as she said the words.

"She murdered him?" Bette breathed, remembering one of the several newspaper headlines: *Boy's Throat Slashed.*

Lisa took a shaky breath. "Matt was my older brother. I just adored him. So did my younger brother, Gary. Matt was such a good person. I know everyone says that about their family, but in Matt's case it was absolutely true. Matt used to bring home injured animals: birds, raccoons, an opossum once. My dad called him the bleeding heart.

"'*Bring all the hurt animals home you want, just don't vote Democrat*'," Lisa drawled in a deep, masculine voice.

Bette laughed.

"He probably would have voted Democrat," Lisa murmured. "Shit, he could have voted for Scooby Doo for all I care. But he never made it to his eighteenth birthday."

She tapped the ash of her cigarette into a lumpy clay dish painted in shades of purple and pink.

"My daughter made this." The woman smiled. "She's five and goes to this great pre-school. The owner has a kiln in her house, and once a month the kids get to make ashtrays or coffee mugs. It's so sweet. Matt would have loved my little girl. I named her Matilda. If she'd been a boy, I would have named her Matt."

"Lisa, what makes you think Greta killed Matt?"

Lisa looked out the window toward the wooden swing set in her backyard. A jumble of toys lay in the grass around the little play area.

"Matt was stabbed to death in Bishop Park," Lisa explained. "Back then, a lot of teens hung out there, in a spot with a circle of boulders and a firepit in the middle. They went out to smoke and drink, make bonfires. I never went. By the time I was old enough, Matt had been killed there, and the town had demolished the site. It took a lot of work, bulldozers and stuff. No one made an outcry like they normally would. Protect the trees and all that. Everyone wanted it gone. They removed those big boulders and threw them in Lake Superior. They ripped the trees down and leveled out the land. A woman's group planted a garden but a few years later, they demolished the whole park and built a shopping center. Small towns have long memories. No one was sad to see that park go."

"That's terrible," Bette said. "Was there evidence that Greta did it?"

Lisa shook her head and took a final drag on her cigarette before snuffing it out in the ashtray. She crossed her arms over her chest.

"Not really. No knife, no fingerprints. Matt didn't put up much of a fight, but he didn't have a chance. Someone walked up behind him and slit his throat while he was sitting on a rock. He bled to death. She stabbed him in the back thirty-two times. The cut to his throat would have killed him. But she kept on going."

Lisa's story terrified Bette. Each new revelation made Bette heart shrivel and slip deeper into her body as if preparing for the inevitable blow that would soon come.

Bette rubbed her eyes. The long day crept up on her. She yawned and covered her mouth. "Sorry, I haven't slept well lately. I will take you up on that coffee."

Lisa offered a sympathetic smile and stood. She returned with two cups of coffee.

"Milk or sugar?" she asked.

"No, black is great. Thanks."

"Me too," Lisa admitted, returning to her seat and automatically running a hand over the stuffed bunny. "I used to add globs of sugar and cream, but after I had Matilda, I could never shake the extra ten pounds. Out went the cream and the sugar."

"You look great," Bette told her, though the compliment felt flat and irrelevant in the midst of Lisa's story.

"The police didn't fail in their investigation," Lisa went on. "They didn't leave a stone unturned. The sheriff is the father of Matt's best friend, Nate. That man was obsessed. Still is. He calls me a couple times a year with updates. Unfortunately, most of the tips dried up years ago. Every lead was a dead end."

"And Matt was dating Greta?"

Lisa pursed her lips and nodded.

"You didn't like her?" Bette asked.

"No, I didn't. She was a bitch, and I have no problem saying that. It's true. She was the exact opposite of Matt. I never understood what he saw in her. I couldn't find a single redeeming quality in that girl. She was attractive. Slim and blonde, but she rarely smiled or laughed. She walked like she had a two-foot pole shoved in her ass."

"How did they meet?" Bette asked.

Lisa shrugged. "At school. Greta was the new girl in town. She moved here in 1973 to live with her aunt and uncle out at this dingy trailer park east of town. The place was a dump! Matt took a liking to her. She had that stray-kitten-needs-to-be-saved look about her, and Matt loved to rescue strays."

"She wasn't from here, then?"

"Nope, she came from Traverse City. Matt told me she lived in an asylum down there. Creepy! But both her parents died and there was nobody to take her, so they shipped her up here. She was fifteen."

"She lived in a mental institution?" Bette shuddered.

"On the property, I guess. Her father was the caretaker or something. No wonder she was nuts."

"Did the police ever officially name her as a suspect?"

"Not publicly." Lisa scowled. "But the sheriff started considering her and then one day, poof, some rich guy in a fancy car pulled into town and whisked Greta Claude away. Just like that, she was gone."

Bette widened her eyes. "So, wait. She lived up here in a trailer and then suddenly someone with money came and took her away?"

Lisa nodded. "Pretty much. I spoke to the sheriff a few months after she left. He tried to track her down. He wanted her to take a polygraph test, but lawyers protected her; not a lawyer, but plural lawyers. He couldn't get anywhere near her. She was still a minor, so that only complicated things more."

Bette frowned. "Why did the sheriff suspect her?"

"More than a few of Matt's friends mentioned her name. She isolated Matt. For a while, she had total control over him. He quit the football team, stopped hanging out with his friends. If she said jump, he asked how high.

"But his senior year, he changed. He was graduating in the summer, and he'd gotten into Michigan State. My parents planned to take him to East Lansing early. We had an uncle who lived down there for him to stay with. My parents claimed they wanted him to have extra time to get acclimated, but you know what? They wanted to get him away from Greta. She was wicked and everyone knew it.

"By the spring, he'd started to pull away from her. I heard them fighting on the phone a few times. She showed up at our house in the middle of the night more than once. They'd be screaming at each other on the lawn, and then they'd be in his car, windows all fogged up."

Lisa shook her head.

"Talk about a dysfunctional relationship," she continued. "It was an abusive relationship but the typical roles were reversed. Greta was the abuser. She held all the power, except she was losing it. He was leaving her. Two weeks before he was scheduled to move, she murdered him."

"What about Greta's aunt and uncle? What are they like?" Bette asked.

"Well, her uncle is dead. He died six months after Greta moved in with them."

"You're kidding me. How?"

"Fell off the cliffs at Presque Isle Park."

Bette gave a little start at the park's name.

"What?" Lisa asked.

"My sister visited Presque Isle Park a few weeks ago. Just... odd coincidence I guess," Bette murmured.

"Greta's uncle was a drunk," Lisa went on. "Apparently, he went out there to fish and just fell right off the cliff. They didn't find his body for a week. His wife called the police after he never came home. Later they spotted his truck at the trailhead for the Black Rock cliffs. One strange thing, the cops found his fishing gear in the bed of his pickup. He didn't take any of it up there with him."

"Where was Greta?"

Lisa shook her head. "No idea. I'm sure they questioned her, but everyone, cops included, assumed he fell. Peter wasn't exactly a model citizen. He'd spent a few nights in jail for drunk and disordelies."

"Did Greta like him? Or her aunt?" Bette asked.

"No, definitely not. She hated them, and she hated living in the trailer park. I'm pretty sure the aunt hated her too, though I don't know for sure. I only heard one side of the story, when she'd complain to Matt about them."

"Two deaths in less than two years. That's pretty crazy," Bette said.

"Yeah, tell me about it. You should talk to Sheriff Montgomery, Bette. He's been working the case for the last seventeen years. I am curious, though, what does Matt's death have to do with your sister's disappearance?"

Bette finished her coffee and set it on a magazine on the glass-topped side table.

"My sister was having an affair with Greta Claude's husband."

37

1973

Greta Claude

Greta bit back a scream when the social worker slid the key into the padlock she'd placed in the old caretaker's house.

She felt her blood rushing hot into her ears, pulsing in her head and behind her eyes. She expected the trees to split open and black mist to roll from the forest and wrap around her. Surely the land would not let her go – would not allow Greta to simply climb into this stranger's car and drive away.

But no black fog arrived to claim her.

Greta carried her hard little suitcase packed with her best clothes, her diary and the few personal items worth keeping, or so the woman said. Greta would get all new things when she moved in with her aunt and uncle. She'd get proper things and go to a proper school and become a proper young woman.

As they drove from the grounds, the asylum faded behind them. She twisted around in her seat and watched the tall windows reflecting the midday sun. She wondered if her father watched the car disappear down the winding road.

Greta's aunt and uncle resided in a rusted double-wide trailer situated between equally dilapidated trailers in the Upper Peninsula. The metal porch was rusted, looking like the bolts might fall away at any moment and send the structure collapsing into the weedy yard.

"Home sweet home," her aunt said dryly.

She parked the pickup truck in a patch of dirt and shoved her door open.

Greta's Uncle Peter, whom she'd only met once, walked onto the porch and watched the girl climb out of the truck.

His eyes slid over her body in an appraising, sickly way that made Greta's skin crawl beneath her stuffy cotton dress.

"Wasn't expectin' no kids," her aunt grumbled. "But I emptied half of my sewing room, and we put up a twin bed and dresser. It'll have to do. In another year you can drive, and then you're free to go if you want," her aunt continued as she walked to the trailer, Greta close behind her.

"Good to see you again, Greta," Peter said, rubbing a hand along her arm slowly and nearly touching her breast. She managed to cringe away before his fingers, nails dirty, brushed against her.

When her aunt left her alone in the room, the small space stuffed with boxes waist high, Greta almost let out a sob. It was sorrow — but more than that it was anger, hatred.

She hated her Uncle Peter and her Aunt Dolly. She wanted to shove them both down the basement stairs in the old farmhouse and listen to the thumps and groans as her father prepared them for the forest.

That night, when she tried to lock the door to the cramped

little room, she found only a hole where the knob should have been.

She slept fitfully, waking at every creak.

When the sun rose and she heard her aunt making coffee, she finally slept, grateful to have survived the first night in the trailer and convinced that her uncle would not arrive to assault her.

She soon learned that he'd merely waited for Dolly to leave for her shift at the Shell Gas Station.

Greta opened her eyes around ten to find Peter filling the doorway, his shoulders so wide they touched the frame on either side. He held a belt in his hand, and she could see the bulge in his dirty sweatpants.

For the first week she fought him. She screamed and kicked and clawed at his face. He beat her senseless and raped her when she was too exhausted to fight back.

By week two, she'd learned to lie still. It was over faster and it hurt less if she didn't resist him.

She'd never been a nighttime dreamer. For most of her young life, she closed her eyes and fell into a black void, waking in the morning with no more memories than an occasional jaunt to the bathroom.

Maribelle had dreamed. She'd whisper her dreams to Greta while she brushed her teeth. Dreams of flying on the backs of winged cats or of swimming deep into the sea and finding jewels and glowing flowers. Sometimes Greta thought Maribelle lied about the dreams. How could they be real? Then she heard patients in the asylum talking of their vivid, sometimes fantastical dreams and she started to wonder if Maribelle was insane like the people locked in the buildings.

But when she moved into her aunt and uncle's trailer, Greta started to dream.

She dreamed every night of the asylum grounds. She dreamed of the field filled with bodies and the blood-spattered basement floor. She dreamed that the land was breathing, rising and falling beneath thick grass or heavy snow.

When it rained, the earth cracked open, gulping, but it wasn't water that fell from the swollen gray clouds.

It was blood.

38

Then

"Where am I?" Crystal asked.

She'd come to in a dark room, strapped to a wooden chair.

The floor beneath her bare feet was dirty. A single dark candle in a silver base sat on a rickety table missing one of its legs.

Crystal couldn't see Greta but sensed her nearby, watching.

Dark tattered curtains hung over the windows, but along their edges Crystal could see night had fallen. She struggled to make sense of the room, at first assuming she'd awoken in the abandoned house in the woods, but this house seemed… more intact. No mold crawled up the walls. Gone were the rotted floorboards and sagging walls replaced by a simple farmhouse kitchen.

"Where are we?" Crystal murmured.

Her head seemed heavy and waterlogged. It took enormous effort to hold it up. She feared if she let it fall forward, her neck would snap and her head would roll across the dusty floor. It was a crazy thought, but one she couldn't shake.

The woman still didn't answer. Crystal sensed she stood behind her to the right.

"Left to the ghosts," Greta said, stepping from a corner and walking along the kitchen counter, her finger trailing through a layer of silty dust. She held the finger close to her face and licked it off. "That's what a reporter wrote when they shuttered the asylum last year. It's all been left to the ghosts. And, boy, are there a lot of those." Greta laughed, and the sound fell empty in the room.

"I grew up in this house," Greta confessed. "My father was the caretaker at the Northern Michigan Asylum. God how they cowered when Joseph Claude walked into the ward. Even after he'd lost his mind, they feared him."

Crystal steadied her eyes on the woman, but she slid in and out of the shadows like vapor, and Crystal's eyelids kept tumbling closed.

She leaned her head back and gazed at the cracked plaster ceiling.

"I'm a nurse," Greta said. "Did I ever tell you that?" She let out a harsh laugh. "Nurses today have access to drugs my father would have murdered someone for."

Greta grabbed a chair and spun it around, straddling it and balancing her chin on the back.

Her dark curls were gone, replaced by limp silver-blond hair that stuck to her sweaty cheeks.

"Not that he was a drug addict. Not at all. But drugs would have made everything easier, cleaner. God knows it has for me. You can't avoid the blood, of course. But there are so many ways to drain blood from a human body. Cleaner ways."

Crystal trembled in her chair. The warmth of the room drifted near her, but didn't penetrate her body. Her bones felt cold. Her teeth began to chatter loudly.

Greta studied her.

"You're coming down from the anesthesia," Greta explained. "But don't worry, I've prepared your room, Crystal. I'm sure you'll love it here."

~

CRYSTAL WOKE AND FOR ONE, two, three seconds, she didn't remember. Her first thought was that she needed to pick up flowers for her mother's grave.

And then she opened her eyes.

She sat up with a jolt, and pain shot through her numb hands and wrists. They'd been bound behind her back, and she must have rolled, crushing them beneath her body. Her hands prickled, and she flexed and unflexed her fingers, gazing around the nearly empty room.

It was an old house, the same house she'd been in the night before. Gray wood floors and faded beige wallpaper gave the room a drab, colorless appearance. The bed Crystal had slept on had an iron frame painted black with a thin twin mattress. A wool blanket lay crumpled on the floor as if Crystal had kicked it off in the night.

As feeling returned to her hands, Crystal scooted her legs off the bed and planted them on the floor. She wasn't groggy anymore. The drugs had worn off, but her head ached, and her mouth felt fuzzy and dry.

She stood and walked to the single curtainless window. Someone had covered the glass in the exterior with opaque plastic. The window revealed only a blurred image of what lay outside. Grass and trees, and the sunlit blue of sky.

She returned to the bed and sat, concentrating on the squeeze and release of her lungs.

Fear sat beside her, his shadow long and threatening. He wanted to get closer, climb inside, but she refused him.

"Just breathe and trust. Breathe and trust." She repeated the words, and the sound of her voice soothed her.

She thought of the day before, struggled to piece it all together and slowly she remembered Greta's words. She'd been talking about a man who had loved her until Crystal came along.

"Weston," she murmured.

Greta was Weston's secret.

IT WAS LATE AFTERNOON, the sun in the western sky when Greta unlocked Crystal's door.

"Drink," she said, holding a glass of water to Crystal's lips.

Crystal slurped the lukewarm water and her stomach clenched painfully.

She wouldn't throw it up; couldn't throw it up. She closed her eyes as the nausea swam through her.

"Time for fresh air," Greta told her, smiling strangely.

She grabbed Crystal's bicep hard and pulled her up, forcing Crystal ahead of her as they walked down a shadowy hallway to a flight of wood stairs.

The old farmhouse was mostly empty, but it was not derelict. The walls and floors were in good but worn shape.

Crystal followed Greta into the woods. Beneath the dense trees, the high grass and vegetation thinned out. They started up a high hill, the ground soft and poked by huge gnarled roots.

She wanted to run. She could turn and throw herself down the hill, but her hands were bound with zip ties, and Greta had drugged her water. The drug already seemed to be streaming along the blood pathways in her body, distorting the world around her.

They came to the top of the hill and walked through an opening in the trees to a grassy field.

The ground looked oddly bumpy. Crystal's eyes fell upon the raised mounds, grass covered, some flecked with flowers, and she frowned.

Though no tombstones marked the graves, Crystal saw the place as Greta had as a young girl. A place to hide bodies.

"It's a graveyard," Crystal breathed.

"Daddy marked them with a single rock," Greta murmured. "Even Maribelle's. But I added to hers over the years."

Greta led Crystal to a raised mound, long overgrown and swallowed by the earth, barely a lump anymore. A pile of stones stood at one end. The rocks were small and gray, with bursts like ashen fireworks on the hard surfaces. Petoskey stones.

Crystal thought of Bette and her father discussing the stones during their various summer trips to Lake Michigan. *Just found another three-hundred and fifty-million-year-old fossil,* Bette would call out each time she found a Petoskey stone.

Greta stared blankly at the grave and walked on, looking back sharply to let Crystal know she expected her to follow. Crystal considered running again, fleeing into the woods, and letting the steep hill tumble her down.

Instead, she followed Greta through another thicket of forest that opened onto a grassy mantel.

Far below them, Crystal gazed at huge white buildings with peaked roofs topped by sharp dark points. Beyond the buildings, Crystal could see all the way to a small city and beyond that, a large body of water.

"Where are we?" she mumbled.

Nothing in East Lansing looked like this place. Of that she was sure.

Greta stopped beside her, staring at the buildings below.

"The Northern Michigan Asylum."

Crystal searched for the place in her mind.

Traverse City. It was the mental institution in Traverse City. The other city where Weston lived.

"It's fading, this place," Greta said, and anguish filled her voice.

"The asylum?" Crystal asked.

Greta didn't answer.

Just above the treeline, the blue sky, cloudless, lay across the world like the watchful eye of the mother. The mother of the world, but Crystal saw her own mother in that sky. So close.

She lifted her face and closed her eyes, imagining the sun as her mother's hand caressing her cheek.

A wave of nausea rose through her belly, and Crystal's mouth filed with saliva. She tried to fight it away, but her resistance only intensified the sensation. She stumbled forward, too close to the edge. Her foot slipped, and she started to fall.

Greta's hand closed on her hair.

A sharp jolt of pain ripped across the back of her skull as the woman yanked her back.

Crystal's eyes watered, and she fell to her knees. She threw up on the grass, her stomach spasming. The nausea came again. She puked a second time. Whatever was in the water had made it into her bloodstream, but not all of it.

"I used to watch them," Greta said, as if Crystal hadn't just gotten sick. The woman's stormy gray eyes gazed toward the asylum. "The men in their black suits and the doctors in their white coats. They came at night. The brotherhood. They brought patients right down that hill into that black hole, the mouth of the forest. Sometimes I hid in the trees and saw the patients. Sometimes the patients saw me. Not with their eyes. Never with their eyes."

Crystal didn't understand what Greta was referring to. She lay with her face in the grass, her hands resting on her back as she struggled to calm her churning belly.

"The caretaker knows everything," Greta continued. "That's the way with these places. The doctors didn't hide the brotherhood from Daddy. He knew more about the origin of this land than any of them ever would. They were merely servants to that darkness, and my father was a steward, a keeper of the balance of things. If too many months went by without a meeting, my father brought a sacrifice of his own to the forest. A nobody, a drifter or a prostitute. Someone the world was better off without."

Sweat coated Crystal's forehead. She felt feverish and wanted to sleep. She couldn't imagine standing and trekking back through the forest and up the stairs of that old house.

Greta grabbed her arm and jerked her up.

"Better move quick," she muttered. "Fall asleep out here and the ground will swallow you up."

39

Now

"SHERIFF MONTGOMERY?" Bette asked when a silver-haired man appeared in the small lobby of the police station.

"Yes. How can I help ya?" He spoke with a slight accent; one the locals called it a Yooper dialect.

"I'm Bette Childs," Bette offered, holding out her hand.

He shook it and waited for her to explain her reason for being there.

"I wondered if you had some time to talk about Matt Kelly and Peter Budd?" she went on.

The sheriff raised both eyebrows. "Sure do. Follow me."

He turned and walked down a narrow hallway, stepping into a little office.

The sheriff kept his office clean. His desk was mostly clear, except for a coffee mug that read "If Dad Says No, Ask Grandpa."

The sheriff sat down and picked up the mug, finding it empty.

"Wouldn't be gentlemanlike if I didn't offer you a cup of joe. Need a refill myself. Cream and sugar?"

"No coffee for me," Bette said. The coffee at Lisa's had her nerves bouncing and jostling.

The sheriff left.

Bette heard a woman stop in the hallway.

They spoke briefly and the man let out a chuckle.

He returned several minutes later with a cup of coffee and a plate of cookies.

"Oatmeal chocolate chip?" he asked, pushing the plate toward her. "Chloe, wife of one of my deputies, has made it her life's mission to fatten us up." He laughed and bit into a cookie.

Despite the woman's efforts, Sheriff Montgomery was anything but fat. Probably approaching sixty, he looked like he'd still outrun most teenagers. Long and lean, the man moved like an athlete.

Bette took a cookie and nibbled the edge.

"You caught me off guard, Bette. Did you know Matt?"

Bette shook her head. "I didn't know Matt or Peter. I'm from downstate, the Lansing area, and my sister disappeared ten days ago."

The sheriff nodded and took a sip of his coffee.

"Not of her own accord?"

"No. Something happened to her. Something terrible, I'm afraid," Bette confided.

"And somehow you've linked her disappearance to Matt Kelly and Peter Budd?"

"Greta Claude."

A stormy look passed over Montgomery's features, and he didn't bother hiding it.

"You suspect she hurt your sister?"

Bette set her cookie down and threaded her fingers together.

She thought of her conversation with Hillary and the torment in the woman's face. She hadn't thought so, no. She'd assumed Weston Meeks had hurt Crystal, but the more she uncovered about Hillary or Greta Claude, the more convoluted the whole story became.

"Crystal, my sister, was having an affair with Greta Claude's husband. Greta's name is Hillary Meeks now. A few days before Crystal vanished, she found out she was pregnant."

The sheriff blew out a breath and shook his head.

"That's one woman I wouldn't want to cross, I'll tell you that. But Bette, I never found an ounce of evidence that Greta murdered Matt or Peter."

"But your instincts told you she was involved?"

He planted his hands on the table and shook his head. "I can't say that. I'd rather not say it. People are allowed to share their theories, but without evidence it's only gossip and I make it a point never to gossip."

"But you looked into her? You considered her a possibility?" Bette demanded.

"I understand why you want me to confirm your fears," Montgomery told her. "When someone disappears, we're desperate to make the puzzle pieces fit. It's always strange when one person has so many dark things happen in their life. Two people very close to Greta Claude died while she lived here in Marquette. I can't say what other tragedies surrounded her in the years before she came here and the years after she left, but I know that coincidences exist. I've met people who seem forever in the hurricane's eye through no fault of their own. I looked into Greta because she was Matt's girlfriend. We always consider the significant other in cases of violent crime."

"And did she have an alibi?"

The sheriff cocked his head. "Sort of. A high school boy threw a big house party in town, not three blocks from Bishop Park. Greta showed up at the party. People saw her, but there was a lot of drinking. She might have slipped away for a half hour. Her alibi didn't clear her. But she got a ride home from the party, and Matt's murder was…"

He paused and put both palms together as if in prayer. "Messy. I can't imagine how she could have returned to that party without a speck of blood on her. I mean, we're talking about a sixteen-year-old girl, not a seasoned killer. A boy drove her home. He said she seemed perfectly normal. Cool, kind of distant, but that was her nature."

"Matt's sister, Lisa, told me they found him in a hangout spot, a fire pit area. Why was he there that night?" Bette questioned.

The sheriff spread his palms out. "That's one of the many pieces we've never fit into the puzzle. Nobody knows why he went there. No one said they had plans to meet him. Everyone figured he'd be at the house party down the road. A few of the kids figured he was planning to head there after he met someone at the bonfire.

"A lot of rumors circulated. Some people thought he might be seeing a girl on the sly, maybe somebody with a boyfriend and her boyfriend showed up that night. Matt's friends, my son Nate included, swore up and down that wasn't the case. He was still dating Greta, although he intended to break it off. Matt didn't have a disloyal bone in his body. He wouldn't run around, especially with another guy's girl."

Montgomery picked up another cookie and picked a chocolate chip off the top, sliding it into his mouth.

"What about Peter Budd?" Bette asked.

"The coroner classified his death as an accidental fall."

"But you didn't believe it?"

He laughed. "I notice how you keep putting words in my mouth."

"I'm sorry. I don't mean to presume."

"It's okay, you're presuming right," Montgomery confirmed.

"I didn't believe it. One, because not a single person had ever heard of Peter Budd going up to that cliff. Not his wife, his buddies, nobody. The man was lazier than a toad. He had to hike a mile up a rocky path in the woods to get to that cliff. Nature enthusiasts and teenagers are the only people who hike up there. It's beautiful.

"But Peter wasn't exactly a man who appreciated nature. He rarely veered far from his trailer and his refrigerator of beer. When he did go out, he frequented a pub within walking distance of his trailer. When he fished, he went to the river a few miles from his place. I found it odd that he'd go to Black Rocks, even odder that he'd get close enough to the edge to fall. Odder still that he left all his fishing gear in the truck."

"Did you investigate his death?"

"Sure, absolutely. I prodded the coroner to do a thorough autopsy including a toxicology screen. I wondered if someone had drugged him. He wasn't a loved guy, so I had more than a few people to consider if murder had been the cause of his death, but the coroner came up empty.

"A couple saw him on the trail that day and said he was alone. He was struggling up the hill, panting. One funny thing is they saw a blanket laid out on that cliff edge. They passed it before Peter, so he couldn't have taken it with him unless he'd gone up and back down. Anyhow, they didn't see anyone else around, but when they passed the area twenty minutes later, the blanket and Peter were gone. They had no idea he'd gone over the cliff. They didn't hear a scuffle, a scream. They figured the man they'd seen had walked back down the hill. They saw his truck when they left the park.

"The couple spotted his picture in the newspaper a few days later. His body had washed up on the beach about a mile from the park. Once they came forward, we found his truck and got a better idea of how he died."

"How do you know he fell off the cliff?" Bette challenged.

"Our guys searched the whole park and the cliffs. We had a deputy who rappelled out there on the regular and found one of Peter's shoes lodged between two of the rocks at the bottom of the cliff. Seemed likely that he'd fallen on the rocks. His foot had been stuck, but the water eventually pulled his body out, leaving the shoe behind. The coroner also suspected a fall based on the damage to his body."

"Did he have life insurance?"

The sheriff shook his head. "Nope, didn't leave a penny to his wife."

"Was she a suspect at all?"

Again, Montgomery shook his head. "She worked full time at the plant. She'd clocked in that morning and worked on the line until five that evening."

"How about Greta?"

"Well, she was harder to pinpoint. Greta attended school that day and claimed she returned to the trailer that night. There was no one to verify her whereabouts that evening, but you've got to remember Greta was a teenage girl. How did she lure him up there? How did she push him off? It seemed like an unlikely scenario and one I gave zero thought to until Matt died."

"And then you wondered if Greta was behind it?"

Montgomery shrugged.

"I mulled it over a bit. I asked around about Greta and Peter's relationship. It sounded tense. A few of the residents in the trailer park thought Peter had a thing for the girl. I wouldn't have put it passed him to act on those urges, but if he did, she never told anyone. At least no one who came forward and reported it."

~

Bette checked into a hotel overlooking Lake Superior. The

wind had picked up throughout the day, causing the water to churn and crash. She watched it smash against the dark rocks jutting from the surf.

Bette wondered if the woman she met could have done the things people believed. Slit her boyfriend's throat? It didn't seem plausible. The girl had only been sixteen. The grown Greta was thin. The sixteen-year-old version had probably weighed a hundred pounds.

And then there was Peter Budd. Montgomery had described him as big and paunchy. He probably outweighed Greta by more than a hundred pounds. Greta's boyfriend, Matt, played football and in their photos Matt stood a foot taller than his lanky girlfriend. How could she have killed them both?

Bette had stopped at a convenience store and bought a nightshirt, toothbrush, toothpaste, a comb and a bottle of wine. She pulled the wine from the bag and dropped the other items on the bed, walking to the window.

"Where are you, Crystal?" she whispered, leaning her forehead against the glass.

She uncorked the bottle of Cabernet and started to pour a glass.

A knock sounded on Bette's door and she jumped, nearly spilling the dark liquid onto the beige carpet. She set the wine on the table and walked to her door, peeking through the viewing hole.

40

Then

CRYSTAL LISTENED as Greta paced outside her room. Up and down the hall, the sharp slap of her shoes on the wood floor. The woman sometimes said things as if she were speaking to someone else.

"Of course," Greta suddenly shouted. "But I'll kill her when I'm ready!"

Crystal curled into a tight ball and imagined a white light swirling around her, protecting her and the baby. She'd done the little visualizations for years, any time she was injured or someone was ill. She imagined they were wrapped in a ball of white light. It was a light so strong that evil, hatred, darkness could not enter.

When Greta finally flung the door open, Crystal cringed, sure she'd streak into the room with a knife and start sinking the blade into Crystal's back.

Her hands had been bound again while she slept, this time in front of her. She'd tried to work them free, but the zip ties were so tight they bit into her wrists. She stopped her rocking as Greta paused at her bedside.

"I saw in the newspaper that you have a sister," Greta said, sitting on the bed and smoothing the hair away from Crystal's face. "I have a sister too."

"Bette?" Crystal whispered.

She tried to imagine Bette at that moment. Bette didn't handle stress well. She would be going crazy trying to find Crystal.

"Bette. She's desperate to find her sister. She'll do anything." Greta laughed. "People are so naive. As if appealing to a captor on television will help. Most people are dead within hours of being abducted. Can you imagine how many days, years, of people's lives are wasted hoping their sister or their mother or their daughter will come home? Wake up, people!" Greta shouted. "They're never coming home."

Crystal's eyes filled with tears. They slipped over her cheeks and soaked the mattress.

"We're going to take a little trip today," Greta announced, pulling on Crystal's bound hands until she stood.

Her legs felt weak, but she stepped into the hall in front of Greta, recoiling when she saw a single wood chair at the end. A child-sized doll sat in the chair with long dark hair braided into pigtails. The doll watched them with glassy blue eye. Bits of plastic had flaked off her chin and one cheek. She wore an ugly gray dress with black stitching.

Greta didn't address the doll as they passed it, but Crystal was sure she was the object Greta had been ranting to minutes before.

~

CRYSTAL WATCHED the sprawling brick buildings topped by

sharp spires. As they walked closer, Crystal's heart galloped in her chest. Her muscles grew taught beneath her skin, and she wondered whether she'd ever be found if she died in one of the abandoned buildings.

Bette and her father would never know what became of her. Weston would never know. She'd be a mystery, a hindrance to all their future happiness.

The mere thought of her sister made her knees go weak. She stumbled and almost fell, but Greta grabbed a handful of her hair and jerked her up. Crystal cried out and lifted her bound hands toward her head, wincing.

"If it hurts, then don't fall," Greta snapped.

Greta stopped at a brown metal door and pulled a ring of keys from her pocket. She inserted one into the lock, shimmied her hand and shoved the door open. A long dark corridor lay empty before them. Crystal felt the nearness of those who had left, the jumble of nurses, doctors and administrators filtering through the doors as a wave. The sadness, despair and fear of the patients shuffled out. Some of them wanted to leave and leapt for joy when they fled the building. Others grabbed at the doorframes, clung to the orderlies and sobbed like children.

Crystal's head throbbed with the onslaught of feelings that overwhelmed her as Greta forced her into the hallway. The walls were brick, the floors carpeted but worn thin.

Tall windows had already been shattered by stones thrown by teenagers. Broken glass speckled on the dirty carpet. Wheelchairs, desks, file cabinets, and clothes lay scattered in the halls and rooms. The building looked as if the occupants had barely bothered to take their coats as they left.

"This was the children's ward," Greta said, waving her hand at a mural of the Seven Dwarves. "And Maribelle stayed in this room."

"Maribelle is your doll?" Crystal asked, though she knew that wasn't quite right. Maribelle was the doll, but she'd once been... "Your sister," Crystal breathed as the realization came to her.

A yellowed cot stripped of its bedding leaned against one wall. Another cot stood tall next to its frame. A plush yellow Big Bird, its arm torn off to reveal a plume of white stuffing, rested among scattered drawings and broken crayons.

"What happened to your sister?" Crystal asked.

Greta kicked the Big Bird. It tumbled into the dark crack beneath the bed.

"Loose lips sink ships," she murmured.

She knelt and picked up half of a red crayon. She walked to the wall and scrawled the words on the brick — *LOOSE LIPS SINK SHIPS* — in the big broken letters of a child's handwriting.

"Someone killed her?" Crystal asked.

"Oh no," Greta took on a small girl's voice and shook her head adamantly. "She fell and hit her head."

Greta didn't look at Crystal, and Crystal suddenly thought the chance to run was upon her; but the moment she lifted her foot, Greta snatched her arm, sinking her sharp nails into Crystal's bicep.

~

THEY RETURNED to the mammoth asylum building at night, Crystal's arms pinned to her sides, her legs free.

Greta held a small flashlight. They went in through a different doorway this time. No carpet stretched down the long hallway. The floors were cement, the walls a formidable brick that seemed to close in on them. File cabinets crowded the corridors and papers littered the floor.

"Hi-ho, Hi-ho, it's to the tunnels we go," Greta sang under breath.

"What are the tunnels?" Crystal asked.

Greta didn't answer. She didn't answer most of Crystal's

questions, but Crystal asked them anyway, unable to stand the silence broken only by the clap of their feet on the hard floor.

Greta stopped at another door and pulled out her keys.

"Time to go down… down… down… down," Greta sang again in a deep, creepy voice that made Crystal want to scream.

Crystal spun around and ran through the dark corridor, quiet, holding her breath, heart racing. She barreled sideways into a door marked "Stairs," nearly tripped, fell into the darkness and then found her balance. She clamored up, legs pumping, arms stuck to her sides.

Greta didn't yell out, she didn't threaten Crystal, but she pursued her. Crystal heard the double slap of the other woman's footfalls, and she saw the beam of light as Greta burst into the stairwell behind her.

Crystal dove through another doorway and then slowed, trying to move quietly as a whisper, tiptoeing down the hall. She could barely see. Her shin struck the sharp edge of an object sitting on the floor, and the flash of pain in her leg momentarily blinded her.

Crystal pressed her back against the wall and shuffled until she came to an opening. She slipped inside and crouched low into a corner.

She heard Greta's footsteps walking down the hall, slow, deliberate. She was not hurrying, not afraid that Crystal had escaped.

"One, two, three, four, five," Greta called out in a sing-song voice. "Ready or not, here I come." She released a loud, shrill laugh.

The yellow glow from Greta's flashlight swept down the hall. The beam paused at the doorway, and Crystal held her breath.

It swept through and then back out again. She sighed and sagged against the wall.

If Greta walked further into the asylum, Crystal could double back, retrace her steps and escape.

She waited, listening to Greta's footsteps get further away.

"Come out, come out, wherever you are," Greta called.

Crystal used the wall to stand up. Holding her breath, she crept back to the hall and started down the stairs, unnerved by the blinding darkness and a haunted chill. She moved painstakingly slow, pressing each foot gingerly to avoid tripping.

When she was halfway down the stairs, she heard a sound beneath her and froze.

Before her, a light flicked on.

Greta stood at the bottom of the stairs, the flashlight beneath her chin, a diabolical grin on her pale face.

"Gottcha," she snarled, pulling her lips away from her teeth.

Crystal tried to turn and run, but she'd barely taken two steps when Greta's hand sank into her hair and jerked her. She fell backward, but the woman shoved her forward into the cement steps.

Crystal couldn't put her arms out to protect herself. Her knees and her chin cracked against the unyielding stairs.

"Oh-h," she cried out, as her head snapped back painfully.

Crystal had little time to register the pain as Greta wrenched her to her feet.

She pressed something cold and smooth against the side of Crystal's neck.

"Feel that?" Greta whispered. "Run from me again, and I'll drag the blade across your throat. Slow. You'll feel it slice through skin and fascia, then muscle, the carotid artery and the jugular vein, all the way to the spine. It's not as hard as you'd think to decapitate someone."

Greta's breath was hot against Crystal's neck.

"Walk," the woman hissed, and Crystal did as she was told.

41

Now

Bette half expected to see Hillary's piercing gray eyes staring back at her from the hotel hallway.

Instead, Matt's sister, Lisa stood in the corridor.

Bette pulled open the door.

"Hi," Lisa said, smiling apologetically. "I tried to call, but the front desk was busy."

"No, that's totally fine. Is everything okay?"

Tears shone in Lisa's eyes but she nodded. "After you left, I dug around in the attic and found this box. It has... well it's my Matt box. Yearbooks and photos and also newspaper clippings from after his death. I thought you might like to look through it. I'll need it back."

"Yes, absolutely. Thank you, Lisa. Listen, I'm going to go downstairs and grab a bite to eat—"

"Oh, I'm sorry," Lisa apologized. "I left my daughter with my neighbor to drop this by. But if you'd like to call and ask questions or talk about anything, I'd love that."

"Sure, thanks Lisa."

Bette took the box and closed the door, returning to sip her wine, before investigating its contents.

Inside the box, she saw photo albums and yearbooks.

Her stomach growled, and she realized she hadn't eaten a meal all day.

She'd seen a restaurant and bar in the lobby of the hotel.

Bette took another sip of her wine and gathered up two of the albums before slipping into the hallway. The hotel was nearly empty on a Monday evening. The thick carpet muted her footsteps as she walked to the elevator. A song too low to hear came from the scratchy speaker in the elevator, and she watched the numbers light up as it dropped from the fourth to the first floor.

She found the lobby as empty as the hallway had been.

When she stepped into the dimly lit restaurant, she noticed two men at the bar, but all the tables were empty.

"Sit where you like," the bartender, a slim thirtyish woman with short dark hair, said.

Bette opted for a little a booth near a window looking out onto the lake.

The sun had set, but tall light posts at the water's edge illuminated a rush of turbulent waves.

"What can I get ya?" the bartender asked, stopping near the table.

"Umm... I'd like a glass of Cabernet and an ice water, please? And a menu for food."

"Sure, hon. Just need to see some ID."

Bette pulled out her driver's license. She regularly got carded, but sometimes the idea seemed absurd. What person trying to sneak a drink would order a glass of wine?

The bartender glanced at her driver's license.

"A lower peninsula girl. What brings you way up here?"

The woman had a kind smile and interested blue eyes.

"Doing some sightseeing," Bette lied. "And I think I'll just have the cheeseburger with coleslaw," she added, pointing to the chalkboard listing the specials.

"Sure thing," the bartender, whose nametag said Frannie, told her. "And if you haven't been yet, Presque Isle Park is the place with the best views."

Bette looked at her, startled.

The park where Peter Budd had fallen to his death. The park Weston and Crystal had visited so recently.

"Is that far from here?"

Frannie shook her head. "Less than a ten-minute drive. Follow the coast road and it ends right there at the park. Some beautiful hikes, but make sure to wear comfortable shoes."

"Thanks," Bette told her.

After Frannie returned to the bar, Bette flipped open an album. The first page revealed a five by eight photo of Matt Kelly. It looked like a senior picture. Matt wore a collared shirt, and his shaggy hair had been tamed and tucked behind his ears.

The boy bore an even more striking resemblance to Weston Meeks in the large picture. It wasn't the same man, not at all. Matt was young and fresh faced with bright green eyes. But his wavy blond-brown hair looked similar to Wes's. They had similar strong square jaws and wide smiles that revealed slightly imperfect teeth. Matt had a small gap between his two front teeth. Weston didn't share that trait.

Beneath the picture, printed in bold letters on white, it said: *Matt's Senior Picture — 1974.*

Bette flipped to the next page. She saw Matt straddling a motorbike. His younger sister, Lisa, sat in front of him. More pictures followed. Matt wedged between his two parents as an adolescent, holding a very serious-looking puppy covered in brown and black spots in his arms. Bette saw pictures of Matt lying on the floor as his younger brother and sister crawled over him. Pictures of Christmases, Easters, Fourths of July with Matt holding up sparklers and wearing a blue, red and white t-shirt that matched his younger siblings'.

Halfway through, she came to dance and prom photos. The last one in the book included a young Greta Claude. Her hair was short, a pixie-style cut that highlighted her large gray eyes and sharp, bony face. It was an odd hairstyle for the 1970s, when most girls had kept their hair long and straight. Other pictures of Matt's friends revealed as much. Greta wore a long black dress that hugged her narrow frame. It made her pale skin look ashen and her light hair almost white.

The next page included Matt, Greta and their school friends. Again, Bette noted the contrast between Greta and the other girls. Greta's peers wore long pastel dresses, some with fuller skirts or shoulders. Their hair hung long, and a few of the girls sported the puffy curls that would appear in heaps during the eighties.

Matt's all-American boy appearance only added to the strangeness of Greta. He wore a white tuxedo and a mischievous smile. Greta's mouth was set in a thin line, and she narrowed her eyes at the camera.

Bette wondered if the person behind the lens felt unnerved by the intensity of her glare.

She flipped through the rest of the book and started on the second album. This one included newspaper clippings carefully pressed behind the clear pages.

The first showed a grainy picture of a forest trail. The headline, *Local Boy Slain in Bishop Park,* jumped out in black block letters.

"I remember that."

Bette looked up, startled at the sound of Frannie's voice.

"Sorry to be nosy," Frannie apologized, sliding Bette's food onto the table.

"Did you know him?" Bette asked.

Frannie nodded.

"We weren't friends. Matt was a jock. You know how teenagers love their labels." Frannie rolled her eyes. "I was in the band and took art classes. Lot of good those talents did me." Frannie laughed, gesturing at the bar.

"Such a waste of life… I don't have kids myself, but I have two nephews and I love them more than my dogs, and damn if I don't love those little fleabags something fierce. I can't imagine what his parents went through. They were on the news a lot the first couple of years. His mother could barely speak. It was just terrible."

"What did kids at school think happened?" Bette asked.

Frannie frowned and touched the article, shaking her head.

"I heard a lot of rumors. A few kids said he'd gotten involved with drug dealers and they murdered him over a debt. For a while, people were saying maybe he was seeing some other guy's girl, and the boyfriend killed him out of jealousy."

"But he had a girlfriend, right?"

Frannie scowled and nodded.

"Frannie, I need another Bud when you get a second," a man at the bar called.

"Give me a minute," Frannie told Bette, hurrying over to the bar, pulling out two glass bottles and setting them on the counter in front of the guys.

When she returned, she again looked at the clipping.

"The third theory, and the most popular, was that his crazy girlfriend murdered him because he broke up with her," Frannie continued. "After his death, Matt's best friends insisted he planned to dump her."

"Did that seem realistic, though? His girlfriend murdering him?"

Frannie croaked a laugh. "Not for most sixteen-year-old

girls, but the one Matt Kelly was involved with would have been my first choice. Greta Claude had a mean streak."

"What makes you say that?" Bette asked.

"I took the same art class as Matt and Greta. We painted landscapes one year, and I remember Matt complimented another girl's painting. Penny's. The next day we came into the class and Penny's painting was shredded on the floor. Greta did it. I know she did. Penny was just devastated. Her mother had cancer, and Penny had told everyone the day before she wanted to give the painting to her mother as a birthday gift. Instead, it ended up in the trash bin."

"What makes you think Greta did it?"

Frannie rubbed her neck and looked toward the lake through the window. "I saw her. I didn't know it at the time, and I never came forward. I regret that now. It might not have mattered, but… Anyway, I was outside practicing the trombone after school, and I saw somebody in the classroom. I figured it was Mrs. Lincoln, the art teacher. I walked over to say hello. I peeked in and spotted Greta. She was standing at the front of the room, staring at everyone's paintings. Mrs. Lincoln had hung them to dry. I ducked before she noticed me, but the minute I saw Penny's painting torn up the next day, I knew Greta had done it."

Bette frowned, trying to imagine a teenage girl shredding the painting meant for another student's sick mother. It made her think of her own mother and Crystal.

A trickle of despair slipped down her throat.

"Order up," a man called from the kitchen.

"Duty calls," Frannie told her. "Need anything with your burger?"

Bette swallowed her grief and shook her head.

"No, I'm all set. Thank you."

She pushed the album aside and pulled her plate toward her, but couldn't find any desire to consume the food. After half-heartedly eating a few French fries, she returned to the photobook.

Each page contained another article.

Within two months of the killing, the headlines grew smaller and started to appear on page six or page nine. They detailed little in the way of new leads, and not a single one identified a suspect or person of interest.

A few heated editorials had been clipped — angry citizens demanding justice for Matt Kelly.

Nate Montgomery, Matt's best friend, had written an editorial. He practically accused Greta outright, not using her name but mentioning how most murders were committed by the significant other of the deceased, and pointing out that Matt's girlfriend had fled Marquette within weeks of his murder. He demanded to know if they all could expect to commit murder and move away to avoid justice.

Bette wondered how Sheriff Montgomery had felt about the letter, considering his own son had written it.

42

1973

Greta Claude

"WHAT'S THAT?" Peter's voice froze Greta as she sat at the little scratched kitchen table that wobbled every time she moved.

"A project for school," Greta lied, shoving the notebook beneath her chemistry textbook.

She'd started in the public school the month before, and she hated it. The kids looked at her strangely, and she was behind in nearly all the courses. She stayed after most days for additional help, committed to reaching her age group before the semester break. She had to get her high school diploma as fast as possible. She had to escape from the trailer.

Peter tugged on a strand of her pale hair. It was long, nearly to her butt. Her father didn't permit either of his daughters to cut their hair. They were girls, and they'd look like girls, he'd snapped when Maribelle once insisted she wanted to cut her hair in the same style as the sisters from *The Parent Trap*.

Greta had also liked the actresses' hair, short and blond. Hair that wouldn't be tipped in blood if you spent the morning scrubbing the basement floor. Hair that didn't have to be brushed ten times a day and braided or secured in some bun to keep it from tangling in the night.

Now, as Peter touched her hair, Greta rose, sending her chair crashing to the floor.

His face contorted and he started to raise his hand, but Dolly's pickup truck spluttered at the end of the street. She'd pull in and catch him. Greta doubted her Aunt Dolly would leave her husband for beating and assaulting Greta, but she wasn't a woman to mess with. She'd probably smack him with a frying pan and force him to sleep beneath the porch for a week. She held all the power, and Peter knew it.

He pulled his lips away from his yellowed teeth and lowered his hand.

"You'll get yours," he hissed before stomping towards the back of the trailer and slamming the door to the master bedroom.

Greta shoved her books and notebook into her bag and wrenched open a kitchen drawer. She pulled out the silver-handled shears and stuffed them into her bag.

When she burst onto the porch, Dolly was just climbing out of her truck. She held a small brown sack in her hands. Cigarettes, probably, and a loaf of bread to make bologna sandwiches. The meal they ate five out of seven nights every week.

Dolly narrowed her eyes at Greta before she brushed past her toward the door. She didn't ask how Greta's day had been or where she was going. The screen door swung shut without a word from her.

Greta walked the cracked road out of the trailer park and

turned onto Highway 41. It was the major thoroughfare into Marquette.

Cars passed. A pickup truck filled with guys honked. One of the men, scraggly and unshaved, leaned out the passenger window and whistled.

Greta ignored them, her legs propelled by the rage bubbling in her abdomen.

She wanted to hurt someone.

Peter.

She wanted to hurt Peter. Lift the scissors and stab him over and over until he was unrecognizable, until he was a heap of blood-soaked meat.

An orange Ford Pinto pulled onto the shoulder of the road before her.

Greta stopped and watched the driver's door open.

A young guy hopped out. His sandy hair brushed his shoulders, and he wore ripped jeans and a blue Aerosmith t-shirt.

"Greta? Hey." He lifted a hand, his big smile faltering when she didn't return the greeting. "Do you need a ride or something? I'm just heading into town."

Greta studied him for several more seconds. Her anger had caused her vision to blur and go black at the edges. She struggled to place him.

His name slowly drifted up from the red coiling mass in her head.

Matt Kelly from Mrs. Lincoln's Art Class. Matt was the star of the class. He drew elaborate pictures of comic book figures, but he excelled in all of their subjects.

The week before, Mrs. Lincoln had asked her students to paint watercolor flowers. Most of the class had produced prints that looked like colorful blobs. Matt had painted a tree filled with different flowers: roses, daisies, and orchids. It looked like something in a gallery.

"Yeah, sure," she said, staring at the ground as she walked to his car.

Matt ran around the car and pulled open the passenger door. He grabbed a stack of textbooks from the seat and shoved them in the back.

Greta slid into the car, balancing her bag on her knees.

Matt climbed behind the wheel, brushing a hand through his wavy hair. He smiled at her, and she saw a dimple near his mouth. His eyes were big and brown. They reminded Greta of an orderly from the asylum that many of the patients affectionately called Colantha after the asylum's prize-winning heifer, who'd been buried on the grounds in 1932. It was partially the orderly's size that earned him the nickname, but mostly it was his soft brown eyes — cow eyes.

"Is this your car?" Greta asked.

Matt shook his head. "I wish. I just turned sixteen last spring. I'm saving up for a car but I've got a ways to go. This is my mom's car, but she lets me drive it if I run errands when I'm out."

Greta gazed through the windshield, watching the oncoming cars approach and then whiz by.

"So, umm… how are you liking Marquette?" he asked.

Greta didn't look at him but tightened her hold on her bag, thinking again of the scissors tucked inside.

"It's fine."

"Fine? Really?" He chuckled. "It's like the most isolated town on the planet. Most of the kids here are dying to get out."

"Are you?" she asked, turning to look at him. "Dying to get out?"

He blushed and shrugged. "Kind of. I want to go to Michigan State when I graduate. Ever been there?"

Greta shook her head.

She'd barely left Traverse City, barely left the grounds of the

Northern Michigan Asylum before that long desolate drive to Marquette.

"My dad teaches at Northern. Both my parents want me to stay here, but..." He shook his head. "Nah, I want to see the world, you know? Like in *Easy Rider*. I want to do that for a year. Get a bike and ride all over, maybe see Arizona and California."

"On a bicycle?" she asked skeptically.

Matt laughed and slapped the wheel. "On a motorcycle. You've really never seen *Easy Rider*? That's wild. What movies do you like?"

Greta thought of the movies she'd seen in her life. She could count them on two hands. They didn't have a television in the house at the asylum. She'd caught glimpses of TVs in town. Once or twice a year, Mrs. Martel would convince their father to let her take Greta and Maribelle to the state theater in town. *The Parent Trap, The Sound of Music, Mary Poppins, My Fair Lady*... The movies were all wholesome, and capped with happy endings.

Greta had often sat in the theater, trying to make sense of the films. Why did they try to paint the world in a golden light when it was filled with darkness? She'd watch other people munching popcorn, smiling and laughing, but she'd felt numb to the love stories, the heart-warming moments. Who could believe such lies?

Matt was still looking at her.

"I like *The Parent Trap*," she said.

She had liked it. She'd liked it more in the years after Maribelle died.

Sometimes Greta gazed in the mirror and pretended Maribelle stared back at her. In death, Maribelle had assumed the role of Greta's twin, always gazing out through the looking glass.

"*The Parent Trap*?" he asked, smiling as if she'd made a joke.

When she said nothing, he nodded. "Yeah. That was a good one. My sister loved it."

As they drove into town, Greta watched the people walking up and down the sidewalks. The girls wore bright clothes and had long feathery hair. The boys mostly had shoulder-length hair like Matt. The stores sold everything from candy to shoes.

She'd only passed through town on the school bus, and she'd barely noticed what went on behind the window displays. Now she could see people talking and laughing, filling their baskets. It reminded her of the movies, strange fake worlds — when at home people screamed and hit, raped and murdered.

"Where are you headed? I've got to run into a few stores in town. We could grab a burger if you'd like? On me."

Greta looked at Matt and wondered if he was joking.

"Why?" she asked.

He laughed uncomfortably and looked away. "In case you're hungry. I'm hungry and you're new in school, so..."

Greta flung open the car door while it was still rolling down the street.

"Whoa. Hold on." He pulled the little car to the curb as Greta jumped out.

She didn't look back. She ran down the sidewalk, attracting the startled looks of a mother and her young child when she nearly collided with them.

Tracing the route her school bus took every morning, she turned down another street and ran until she'd reached the little park that edged the high school.

She was relieved to find it empty, except for an elderly man watching the trees through a pair of binoculars. A little notebook rested in his lap.

Greta slowed to a walk and turned onto a trail. She'd been to the park in gym class. Once a week the class walked to the park to jog on the trails.

She found the place where a tall oak tree had been split by

lightning. Half the tree lay toppled over, the other half reaching its sharp, serrated trunk toward the blue sky. Behind the oak, deeper into the forest growth, stood a clearing.

In the glade, someone had arranged five large boulders in a circle. In their center was the charred remains of a fire and two blackened beer cans.

Greta had found the spot two weeks before, after veering off the path during her run to throw up. Peter had raped her that morning before school, and he'd punched her in the stomach when she'd resisted. Running had caused her stomach to cramp and seize. She didn't want the boys and girls running behind her to see her vomiting, so she'd slipped into the trees to hide.

When she'd come upon the rocks, she'd felt instantly at ease. The space reminded her of the asylum field, the secret spot held by the surrounding forest.

She sat on a rock and unzipped her backpack. She pulled out the shears and gazed at them in the sunlight. The light glinted off the blades. They were dull and dirty. She could see the smudges of whatever her aunt had chopped most recently. Probably something disgusting like the slimy bologna she and Peter lived on as if the modern world provided no greater variety. Her father would have slapped Greta if she ever used scissors and returned them to the drawer without cleaning them first.

She'd gone from an immaculate, simple house to a filthy trailer with a pedophile and television addict. The transition had left her reeling. She existed in a state of suspension, able to do little more than wake up, push through the day, and fall asleep each night.

But then there were the dreams. Dreams so powerful the land of the asylum seemed to call out to her, as if it were reaching through an alternative dimension to summon her home.

Greta pulled out a handful of her long, silver-blonde hair

and opened the scissors. She squeezed the handles, hacking when the blades struggled to cut through the strands. She chopped and cut until a pile of pale locks coated the rock she sat on and lay in a heap on the grass at her feet.

When she reached a hand to her scalp, her hair stuck out in sharp tufts. In some places, she'd cut so close to her head only a bit of fuzz remained. As she cut, her heartbeat had grown faster, her rage bigger. The end of her hair did not abate the feelings.

She dropped to her knees and plunged the scissors into the dirt. They sank in the soft ground. She did it a second time and a third, not realizing she'd started screaming until something moved at the corner of her eye.

The old man she'd noticed on the bench watched her from the trees, his eyes wide with shock.

"Are you okay, miss?" he asked uneasily.

When she looked at him, the fury and hatred palpable in the small space she occupied, he took an involuntary step back.

She saw the fear in his ugly and weak face, and she wanted to lunge at him and sink the scissors into his chest. She wanted to give the earth beneath her its due. But before she could spring to her feet, the man blinked and backed away.

"I'm sorry to have bothered you," he murmured.

He turned and hurried from the woods.

She could have caught him, dragged him back into the clearing, but she was not a fool. Her hair was everywhere. They'd catch her that very day.

Greta slumped against the rock, exhaustion overtaking her like a sudden storm.

She nodded off and when she woke, the sun had begun its westerly descent. The forest was lit with the orange-gold light of a day's end.

Her arms ached, and some of her cut hair stuck to the side of her wet cheek. She plucked it off and stared at the hair. She thought of gathering it in her bag and taking it with her. Instead, she left it.

She hated the hair.

Peter had sunk his hands into the hair, used her hair to wrench her head back. She wanted it gone almost as much as she wanted him gone.

43

Then

"WESTON BOUGHT THIS FOR YOU," Greta told Crystal, pulling out an opal ring. "But I slipped it out of his pocket. What could he say? 'Where's the ring I bought for my mistress?'"

Crystal watched Greta tilt the ring back and forth, trying to catch the sun. She had a distant, sad look in her eyes, but when she shifted back to Crystal, she'd replaced it with stony indifference.

"You're one of many. Did you know that? Probably five at least, maybe more. He's one of those weak men who fall for their students. Some men aren't cut out to be teachers; they have no heart, just that thing between their legs. You probably thought it was love, that you were his soulmate. I know Wes. I know the stories he tells, the words... black magic. They seduce you, blind you to the truth. The truth..." Greta paused and leaned in so close, Crystal smelled the coffee she'd drunk that morning, "is that Weston was a heroin addict, a user, a lowlife. He ever tell you that?"

The smell made Crystal's stomach turn, and though she tried to quell it, the instant oatmeal Greta had fed her spewed out and onto Greta's black trousers.

The woman looked at the vomit, studying it. Rather than disgusted, she seemed curious.

"That's twice now." She held up one, then two fingers. "Tick-tock."

She frowned and looked at Crystal's stomach.

Crystal tried not to follow her gaze.

"I get sick when I'm scared," Crystal lied.

Greta cocked her head to the side.

"Bungee jumping, cliff diving. You're lying to me, Crystal Childs. The question is why?"

~

CRYSTAL SAW the bucket inside the toilet and stopped abruptly.

"I'm okay, I don't have to go."

"Go," Greta hissed, shoving her into the little bathroom.

Crystal stopped, digging her heels into the hard tile floor. They slid as Greta pushed her. It took effort, but she forced her bladder to release. The warmth of her pee washed down the insides of her thighs and over her feet. Greta had dressed her in a skirt without underwear to make using the bathroom easier.

The urine pooled on the tile beneath her.

Greta snarled and knocked Crystal into the wall. Hands bound behind her, Crystal nearly slipped in her urine, but maintained her balance, hitting the wall with a shoulder and steadying herself.

Greta stared at the pee and back at Crystal.

"You think you're clever," she laughed.

Greta left the room and returned a moment later with a plastic folder. She pressed it on the floor next to the dark yellow urine which revealed that Crystal was dehydrated. The urine gradually flowed onto the folder. She bent the edges of the folder to keep it from spilling out and poured it into a plastic Dixie cup.

"Let's see if you do that again, shall we?" Greta smirked.

Greta stood, pulled the bathroom door closed and shut off the light.

Crystal didn't move.

The warmth of the urine had turned cold and sticky on her inner thighs. It had smeared her skirt too, mostly the hem.

Slowly her eyes adjusted. The room was nearly black, but Crystal slowed her breath and took small shuffling steps until she reached the corner. She pressed her back into the corner and slid down the wall, pulling her legs in and resting her chin on her knees.

~

HOURS LATER, Greta returned.

When she opened the door, Crystal grimaced and tucked her head down, clenching her eyes shut. The light stabbed her aching head.

"Funny thing in the paper today when I went to buy a pregnancy test," Greta told her. "*Mistress Pregnant with Married Man's Baby!* Oh, the scandal. I almost wasted twenty dollars on a pregnancy test. Things are not looking good for Mr. Meeks. The police have officially named him a suspect in your disappearance."

Crystal shivered.

A chill had come over her sometime in the previous hours. She had a fever. Heat radiated beneath her skin even as her teeth chattered.

"Ugh, you stink," Greta muttered.

She pushed Crystal aside with her foot and turned on the shower.

"There's water, but it's not hot," Greta said. "I'm sure you won't mind. It's summer after all."

Greta dragged Crystal into the bathtub.

Crystal gasped in shock when the icy water struck her. Her shivers turned into convulsions.

Greta stripped off Crystal's skirt, making a gagging face, and flung it to the floor.

She scrubbed Crystal's flesh with a coarse sponge that made her skin feel raw.

When the icy shower finally ended, Crystal panted on her knees, her head swimming. It took all her effort to keep from slumping over in the tub.

Greta toweled her dry and pushed her toward the room.

Crystal collapsed onto the bed pulling her knees into her chest.

Greta left the room.

Crystal stared at the open door, but her entire body shook. She couldn't stand, let alone run.

When Greta returned, she carried a lethal-looking knife. The long blade glinted in the light through the window.

Crystal closed her eyes, but the woman did not stab her. She reached behind Crystal's back and cut the zip ties. Crystal's arms were numb. She didn't have the strength to draw them from their position.

Greta wrenched Crystal's hands toward the front of her body. She lifted a wrist and let it drop. It flopped on the mattress, but Crystal barely registered it.

"Poor Crystal and Weston," Greta smirked. "Karma is cruel."

44

Now

After another fitful night of sleep, this one plagued by nightmares of a young Greta Claude stalking Bette through a dark forest, Bette woke to gray light seeping between the curtains.

She brewed coffee in her room, threw on the previous day's clothes, and called her dad.

He answered on the first ring.

"Any news?" they asked simultaneously.

Homer chuckled.

"Kind of," Bette admitted. "Not good news, though. Weston Meeks' wife is a total pyscho. Her name used to be Greta Claude, and they suspected her of murdering her boyfriend in Marquette over a decade ago. The murder is still unsolved."

"Dear Lord," Homer huffed. "That makes me feel half sick. Is it true?"

Bette rubbed her eyes and yawned. She drained the last of her coffee and refilled the cup.

"I don't want to believe it, but I do. Everyone in town seems to think so, and she left mysteriously right after he died. I'm going to track down one more person this morning and then I'm driving home. Any developments on Crystal?"

Homer sighed. "I spoke with the Lansing State Journal. They're running Crystal's story on the front page today. Officer Hart called to tell me that Weston Meeks is scheduled to take a lie detector test at the end of the week. Apparently, he's gone back to Traverse City but promised to return by Friday."

Bette flared slightly at the news, but her heart wasn't in it. She was no longer sure that Weston had a hand in her sister's disappearance.

Bette said goodbye to her dad, gathered up her few things, and rode the elevator down to the lobby.

She stopped at the front desk where a young, heavily made-up woman stood bobbing her head to the song on a little portable radio. When she saw Bette, she blushed and turned the volume all the way down.

"Don't mind me," Bette told her. "I like Bon Jovi. I do have a quick question, though, and this may be a long shot. Do you know Nate Montgomery?"

The girl nodded enthusiastically. "He owns The Rebel Music Store right downtown."

"The Rebel Music Store?" Bette asked, wondering at the name. The man's father was the sheriff, and he owned a business called the Rebel Music Store?

"Yeah, it's great. You should check it out while you're in town. It's not just music. He has books and concert tickets and instruments. It's the coolest place in town. You can walk there from here," the girl went on. "It's like two blocks that way." She pointed at the road that sloped up the hill into downtown.

"Great, thanks."

The Rebel Music Store occupied a large corner space in an

old redbrick building. It was butted on one side by a resale store and across the street from an ice cream and candy shop.

When Bette pushed open the door, a bell didn't tinkle. Instead, a plastic cartoon cat meowed loudly and flicked its tail.

The store was dimly lit. Twinkle lights ran along the tops of bookshelves. Waist-high racks stood in rows down the center, filled with CDs and records. Books and musical instruments lined the tall shelves against the walls.

Between shelves, squat, timeworn chairs offered patrons a spot to relax.

Bette eyed a young guy wearing earphones and sitting in a shabby purple velvet chair. His head bounced to the music in his head.

Bette recognized the song playing on the store speakers. "Black Magic Woman" by Fleetwood Mac.

She walked down the center of the store, finding a circular wood counter at the back. No one stood behind it.

Bette noticed a taped sign that said "Buzz for Service" next to a bullfrog with a red button protruding from its plastic back. She pressed the button expecting a croak. Instead, a comical Pee-Wee Herman voice announced, "Be Right Out!"

Almost immediately, a door behind the counter swung open, and a man popped his head out.

He smiled and waved a hand.

"Be with you in two shakes. Trying to cut the damned twine off these newspapers I just got delivered, as if reading the news isn't punishment enough." He disappeared back through the door, and Bette wandered to a table stacked with fliers, post-card-sized ads for various CDs, and posters for concerts and other music events.

The man walked out, a hefty stack of newspapers clutched to his chest.

Nate was not a conventionally handsome guy; his face was long, his hair longer and pulled into a ponytail draped over one shoulder. A carefully trimmed goatee covered the lower half of his face, surrounding large lips. Golden eyes gazed from beneath bushy eyebrows. He smiled a genuine, kind smile that travelled to his eyes. He looked nothing like the clean-cut guy in the prom photo, but Bette recognized him just the same.

"Welcome to the Rebel Music Store, young lady. How can I assist you?"

He plopped the newspaper copies on the desk, and she saw they were not local but called *The Upper Underground.*

"All your anti-establishment news north of the Mackinac Bridge," he told her, tapping the paper.

"Are you the sheriff's son?" she asked, suddenly wondering if he was not Nathan Montgomery after all.

The man showed the dazzling smile a second time and nodded.

"That's not a greeting I hear much these days. But yes, you've found the sheriff's son. One of three, I might add. I'm Nathan, Nate if you buy me a beer."

Bette smiled and shook his outstretched hand.

"I'm Bette and actually I'm on my way out of town, but—"

"It was a joke, no beer necessary to call me Nate."

Bette nodded and thought again of Nate's editorial. Nearly twenty years had passed since the death of his friend, Matt. He probably wouldn't be smiling much when she mentioned his name.

"Nate, I'm actually wondering if you'd be willing to talk to me about Matt Kelly."

Nate's smile faltered and then, as she suspected it would, dissolved.

"Are you a reporter, Bette?"

She shook her head. "I'm a research assistant for an anthropology professor. My sister disappeared a week and a half ago and I've been..." She searched for the explanation that took her from Crystal's disappearance to the murder of this stranger's friend nearly two decades before. "I've been following every possible clue."

"And somehow you've ended up in the Rebel Music Store asking about Matt Kelly," Nate murmured in wonderment. "Man, I haven't had a conversation about Matt in months."

"Months?" she asked, surprised. She would have suspected years.

"Yeah. I feel guilty right now, realizing it's been so long. I try to bring him up at every opportunity, but the summer around here gets crazy, and I've neglected my responsibilities to my friend." He sighed. "Let's sit over there. That's my gathering space. I've told Matt's story a hundred times or more from that armchair."

Bette followed him to a circle of well loved couches and chairs that surrounded a coffee table fashioned from a worn leather suitcase on wooden legs. Magazines lay strewn across the surface.

"Who have you told his story to?" Bette asked, settling into a cracked red leather chair.

"Anyone who will listen. Tourists, bands who visit the store, newspaper reporters, psychics. I've had two of those come in."

"Psychics. Really?"

He laughed. "Well, that's the question isn't it? They didn't tell me who killed Matt, but I'm a believer. I'm more of a prove-it's-not-real kind of guy. Our government likes to keep everything in a tidy little cafe while in the kitchen they're testing biological weapons and dropping atom bombs. I'll trust the psychics over the news most days."

Bette sighed.

She didn't believe in psychics. And though she didn't explicitly trust the government, she'd never had much patience for conspiracy theories.

"Did they say anything of value?" she asked.

Nate nodded. "The second one did. The first woman was

writing a book. She wanted to break open a case for publicity, but she couldn't tell me a thing about Matt. She was either full of shit or really off her game that weekend. The second woman came in out of the blue. She didn't do readings for a living or anything like that. She'd stopped into Blackbird Coffee. It's a little place with coffee and scones in a shopping center where Bishop Park used to be. She was sitting at a table and saw a vision of Matt in that same spot, bleeding to death."

Bette balled her hands in her lap, listening dubiously.

"She asked the owner of the coffee shop if someone had been murdered there. Pretty weird question, right? Anyway, the woman told her about Matt and the park that used to be there. Then she mentioned me. So the psychic walked into town and showed up here. She told me Matt knew his killer, and she had a strong sense that the murderer was a woman. She couldn't give me any more details than that. It wasn't groundbreaking news. I've known all along who murdered Matt. But it was a pretty amazing insight, considering she'd never heard of Matt and was just here for the weekend photographing the lakeshore."

"You believe Greta Claude killed Matt?"

Nate nodded. "Yeah. Greta Claude. And I'm not afraid to say it either. No journalist has ever printed it because she came into some serious money back in the day, but she murdered him. I'd bet my life on it. So, tell me, Miss Bette, how is your sister connected to Matt Kelly?"

Bette sighed and leaned her head back on the sofa.

"My sister was having an affair with Greta Claude's husband."

45

Then

"Why I am still alive?" Crystal mumbled.

She'd woken to find Greta sitting on the bed beside her, brushing her long hair. It flowed over the pillow in a plume of red. Her hands were still zip-tied in front of her, her ankles secured to the bed frame.

"That sounds like an existential question," Greta said, continuing to slide the brush through the strands.

Near the door, a stiff-looking gray dress hung.

The fever had passed, but Crystal's arms and legs still felt heavy and weak.

"Why haven't you killed me?" Crystal asked.

"I grew up in this house," Greta said ignoring the question. "People thought my father worked for the asylum, but he worked for the monster in the woods." She chuckled. "That's what we called it when we were little, my sister and I, the monster in the woods. The insatiable monster who fed on blood and fear and suffering."

Greta stood and walked to the wall, running a hand over the fading wallpaper.

"Only when I got older did I realize the monster was the land itself."

"What happened if you didn't feed it?" Crystal asked.

"Bad things. Our people died, my mother, my sister. My father went insane. You learned not to test its power, not to question its reach."

"Those things happened when you didn't feed it?" The questions were ridiculous.

Greta was insane, but Crystal wanted her to open up; she clearly longed to tell the stories, and there were stories to tell. Crystal sensed them swirling within the woman, a thousand angry shadows leaping for her attention.

"I spilled the blood once," Greta said, walking to the blurred window. "It was February. I must have been ten or eleven and my hands were frozen with cold. I had gloves on, but it didn't matter. They'd gone numb within minutes of walking away from the house. I started losing the sensation in my fingers, but I trudged on, my father in front of me. And suddenly one of the buckets just fell out of my hand. It splashed across the snow. There was so much blood, and the snow was so white. The snow made the blood look vivid, scarlet."

She lifted a hand to the windowpane and moved close, as if she were watching the scene unfold before her.

"My father turned back and saw it. He cursed and stomped over to me, setting his own buckets down. Taking mine, too, before he whacked me on the side of the head. My ear rang for days after."

Greta put a hand to her right ear and winced.

"'Cover it up,' he yelled. He was going back to the house for a shovel. I dropped to my knees and scooped snow in my already numb hands. You'd think it would be easy, wouldn't you? Burying a little blood in the snow. Just the opposite. It's like painting a red wall white. Coat after coat and the red still shows. That blood was like a fire burning through every layer of snow I heaped on it. Eventually my dad came back, and by then I was so cold I couldn't open and close my hands, but I knew after he buried that blood, I still had to carry the bucket. If I dropped the second one, I'd spend three nights in the cellar.

"So, as he shoveled snow on the blood, I pulled off my gloves and stuck my hands into my pants, and into my underwear. It was about the only space warm on my body. I carried the bucket to the chamber, and we dumped the blood. When we got home, my hands were like blocks of ice. The tip of my right pinkie had no feeling at all. A few days later, Mrs. Martel told my father I had frostbite on it, and I'd better see the doctor. We didn't have a primary physician. The medical doctor who worked at the asylum came in and treated me. The tip of my pinkie had turned black."

Greta walked to the bed and thrust her hand in Crystal's face. The tip was flat rather than curved.

"They cut it off in a surgical room at the asylum. Afterward, the doctor gave me a lollipop — but when my father saw it, he threw it in the trash and screamed at the doctor for feeding me garbage."

"That's terrible," Crystal told her, and she meant it.

A part of her hated this woman, but another part of her grieved for her suffering.

"Do you understand it?" Crystal asked. "The thing in the woods?"

Greta cocked her head to the side. That sheaf of white blonde hair falling over one cold gray eye. She chuckled and tucked the hair behind her ear.

"He keeps a diary. Did you know that?" Greta asked.

Crystal gazed at her, puzzled. And then realized Greta had shifted to Weston.

Crystal had never seen Weston's diary, though she'd watched him write poems and thoughts on napkins and slips of paper. He pressed them into something, of course, but she'd never seen the book itself.

Greta pulled a leather journal from a large black purse she'd deposited by the door.

"I bought this for him. I had it engraved with his initials, and I gave it to him on our fifth anniversary. And what did he write in it?" Greta asked lightly, holding the journal by its spine.

Crystal watched slips of paper, dried flowers, and even a fortune from a cookie fall out.

She knew what the fortune said: *"Love, because it is the only true adventure."*

He'd read it out loud, lying on his back in Crystal's bed, his head nestled in her lap. They'd made love, and then Weston had gone for Chinese takeout.

The tiny white slip floated down and wedged between two floorboards. It took Crystal's breath away, and a spasm of anguish snaked through her chest.

"He wrote about meeting you. About your hair, the color of the setting sun, and your eyes luminous and hypnotic." Greta rolled her own eyes. "He called mine as expansive and turbulent as the sea crashing against rocks when I first met him."

Greta flipped the pages, glancing back and forth between Crystal and the book.

"You didn't think you were the first woman he felt that way about?"

Crystal said nothing. But no, she hadn't presumed that Weston hadn't loved before. She herself had loved before. Never with the intensity she experienced with Weston, but she knew he had loved before. And she could see why he fell in love with Greta. She was a beautiful mystery, a poisonous flower.

"What happens after I'm gone?" Crystal asked.

A little smile played on Greta's lips.

"Nothing much, except my husband starts making it home for dinner again."

46

1973

Greta Claude

GRETA DIDN'T BOTHER CLEANING up her hairstyle, despite her aunt's insistence that she looked like a molting chicken and Peter's stare of disgust.

When she walked into school, the other students gaped at her. Some of them laughed and snickered. A few looked troubled.

To her surprise, Matt stopped at her locker.

"I like the new look," he told her. "Very Joan Jett."

Greta thought of asking, "Who?" but didn't care to know.

"Can I walk you to class?" Matt asked.

Greta looked at Matt with guarded eyes, but he didn't flinch from her stare. After a moment, she nodded.

As they walked, he told her about the football team, his

brother and sister, and how he hoped to become a veterinarian someday.

Greta had never had a boyfriend. Her father had forbidden it, and life on the asylum grounds didn't offer many eligible bachelors. There were orderlies and doctors. More than a few had taken second glances at Greta, but she'd never considered them as romantic prospects.

Her father knew everything that went on at the Northern Michigan Asylum, and he would have punished her for such a violation.

The first time Matt kissed her, Greta had gone stiff in his arms. His mouth was warm and soft, his touch tender, but her skin crawled as she remembered her Uncle Peter's hands groping her body, pinching and squeezing.

She'd pushed him away and run into the park, to the circle of rocks.

She hadn't cried. Greta rarely cried, but the emotions had risen, huge, like waves crashing against rocks.

When Matt found her, he hugged her and petted her hair and murmured nice things until slowly she told him why she'd run away. She told him how her uncle had raped her for months. Matt had been furious. He'd hugged her tightly and sworn he'd protect her.

And he did. He confronted Peter the next day, carrying his father's shotgun when he arrived at the trailer to pick Greta up for a date. He'd pointed the barrel square at Peter's chest and said if he ever touched Greta again, he'd get a bullet in the heart.

Her uncle had listened. He didn't rape her again, but he did other things to hurt her. He put dirt in her shampoo and threw her new shoes on the porch to get rained on. He stole her books from her backpack and ripped the pages out. He deleted phone messages from Matt and often unplugged the phone from the wall when her aunt was at work, and closed it in the bedroom with him while he drank and watched television.

Greta had thought it would disgust Matt when she revealed her uncle's abuse. Instead, it had the opposite effect. He seemed to fall more in love with her. He surrounded her, coddled her. He picked her up and dropped her off. Bought her flowers and candy and little pieces of jewelry from the gift store in town. He loved her fiercely and hopelessly, and soon she owned him. There was nothing he wouldn't do for her. Well, almost nothing.

Greta had known she would kill Peter since the first morning he'd crept into her bedroom. She might have asked Matt to do it. She could have convinced him, but she also recognized in Matt a weakness. He believed in a certain moral code. If he murdered Peter, he would confess. Even if the police accepted the death as an accident, the deed would haunt Matt until he purged his conscience.

She couldn't risk it. Not only would she be implicated, but the truth of what Peter had been doing would become public knowledge. They would see her as a victim.

~

"PETER," Greta said.

He looked up from his bowl of Franken Berry cereal. It looked like a puddle of sodden pink mush, and Greta's stomach churned with disgust.

"What?" he asked gruffly before scooping another spoonful into his mouth. Pink milk dribbled down his chin.

Disgusting pig, she wanted to hiss.

Instead, she smiled and tugged at her t-shirt. It pulled up, offering him a slight glimpse of her pale belly.

His eyes immediately dropped to the exposed skin, his mouth falling open.

"Matt's not as good as you, not as large."

Greta stared at the table as if her eyes could pass through the cheap wood. His erection had probably already pushed against his dirty sweatpants.

He stood, pushing the chair back, cereal forgotten.

"Not here," she said, gazing at him seductively. "Matt will be here any minute to pick me up. He has football practice tonight. I've always wanted to screw beneath the stars. Meet me at Black Rock. The cliff at the top of the red trail. Matt and I have been there a few times in the afternoon. We have a pile of blankets up there and a bottle."

Peter didn't move. His hands were balled at his sides. His little prick poked against his sweatpants.

Greta's stomach churned again, but she forced herself to lick her lips as she gazed at his hard-on.

"Tell Dolly you're going fishing."

Outside, they heard the rumble of the Pinto as Matt pulled up to the trailer. He didn't honk the horn. He never did.

"This a trick?" Peter demanded, looking towards the window.

The shades were closed, but they heard Matt's car door open and shut.

Greta closed the space between them. She pressed her hand against Peter's erection and squeezed.

"A girl wants what she wants," she whispered. "Meet me there."

She pulled open the door before Matt could knock. She didn't look back at Peter, but she saw Matt's eyes narrow at the man behind her.

~

GRETA GAZED AT HER WATCH. It was a quarter after nine and still no Peter. She stayed in the shadow of the trees, knowing the daylight waned.

Her fury at being stood up grew, but quelled when she heard

loud footsteps on the dirt path. Twigs and leaves stamped under his heavy boots, and his breath came out in ragged wheezes just as she knew it would. Peter was not in shape. Lugging a beer gut up the steep wooded trail would leave him winded and with little fight when he reached the peak. She'd laid the blanket near the cliff's edge, knowing he would go there, straight to the spot of colorful fabric like a bull chasing a red flag.

"Steep climb, huh?" she heard a woman ask.

Greta's eyes shot wider, and she slipped further into the darkness.

"Ugh, yeah," Peter wheezed.

"Great workout, though," another man said.

As Greta watched, two svelte twenty-somethings powered up the hill, their arms and legs pumping as they walked. They both carried walking sticks.

They passed within feet of Greta, oblivious that she stood in the shadow of the trees.

How long did she have? They'd hike to the overlook, surely, another quarter mile up, maybe stay to catch their breath, and begin their descent down. Fifteen minutes, twenty tops.

They disappeared up the slope, and Peter appeared to her right.

He was panting, hunched over. He spotted the blanket but didn't walk to it, choosing instead to lean a hand against a tree. It wasn't night. Wouldn't be for another half hour. She had no time to waste.

She stepped from the forest and pulled her long sleeve shirt over her head, revealing a slinky black tank top. She let one strap drop down her shoulder. She'd taken off her bra, and her breasts hung loose beneath the shirt.

Peter's mouth fell open, still heaving for breath.

"Fuck," he whispered.

"Exactly," she told him.

She grabbed his hand and pulled him toward the blanket. He

started to sit down, but she squeezed his arms and shook her head.

"Not yet," she told him.

He glanced nervously at the drop off behind him, trying to corral her back.

"I want to hear the waves," she told him, holding him steady. "While I suck you off."

He was already hard. He'd probably been hard since she'd spoken to him that morning. She tugged his sweatpants and underwear down to his ankles, feeling his hard flesh press against her hip. He pinched one of her nipples and she gritted her teeth against the sensation.

Taking him in one hand, she used her other hand to prod him back another step. He no longer remembered the cliff edge. He'd closed his eyes. Saliva dripped from the corner of his mouth. She released his penis for only a moment, putting one foot back to increase her strength. She shoved him as hard as she could, ramming both palms against his chest.

Peter's eyes shot open, his arms reached, but he was already over the edge, falling, flailing.

He didn't scream.

There was no time. She heard a grunt as he struggled to catch hold of something, but air surrounded him. He hit the rocks with a far-off thud.

Greta stepped to the cliff edge and studied his broken body. She couldn't see his face, but imagined his eyes open and terrified, staring at her as he died.

She glanced at her watch. Barely five minutes had passed.

Greta savored his broken body for another moment, and then she gathered the blanket and slipped into the trees.

47

Now

NATE WIDENED his eyes and let out a little whistle of breath.

"Oh man, that's bad. I haven't seen Greta in a very long time, but unless she found Jesus or has spent the last twenty years in intensive counseling, I'm guessing she's only gotten more hateful."

"I don't really know her. Her name's Hillary now. Hillary Meeks," Bette admitted. "I met her and she seemed... I don't know, kind of unfriendly. But then I talked to her and she sounded really hurt by the affair. I was convinced that Weston did something to my sister, but now..."

"Weston is Greta's husband?" Nate asked.

Bette nodded.

"Don't count on it," he said. "Greta wasn't the type to date a violent man. She was the violent one. She treated Matt like a horse that needed to be broken. But she played him exactly the right way. She had the perfect sob story. Both parents dead. She was an orphan forced into that trailer. And there was more, lots more. I'd bet my life Matt knew things about Greta that he never told me."

"What do you mean, more?"

Nate scratched his goatee and tugged on his large lower lip.

"I think Greta Claude was getting raped by her Uncle Peter. I went with Matt to pick Greta up a few times, and he stared at her uncle like he wanted to kill him."

"And then Peter died," Bette murmured.

"Yeah, but Matt had nothing to do with Peter's death. He was with me the night Peter Budd fell off that cliff."

At the front of the store, they heard the meow from the plastic cat as someone entered.

"I thought Greta did it. I said as much to Matt. He defended her. I told him she was bad news. She hated me. She hated anyone that came between her and Matt. He kept blowing me off and one night I confronted him. I told him he was pussy-whipped. He told me her whole story, parents dead and all that. I felt bad for her. I did. But I also knew she was twisting it, using it to control Matt."

"You really think she could have done it?"

"Matt was with us that night. We were playing music in my garage after football practice. He didn't go home until like midnight. But we hadn't done that in months because Greta was all over him about spending every waking second with her. It seemed pretty strange that the one night he gets to hang out with us, her uncle ends up dead."

"Did you tell your dad?"

Nate shook his head.

"Not at the time. Only later, after Matt died, did I start to connect the dots. I didn't know Peter personally, but I heard he was a drunk and just fell in the water and died. I was seventeen and still so naïve. After Matt, though… everything changed. I changed. I quit the football team, got involved with drugs for a while.

"I moved to New York and started writing for an alternative newspaper, smoking a lot of dope. I wrote articles about Matt, but only a few of them were ever printed. I stayed away from Marquette for about five years, and then I came back. My older brother had a son, and my mom had been harping on me to come home for a visit. I was running away from this place, running away from Matt's death and the injustice. And honestly, I was mad at my dad. Mad he didn't go after Greta and make her pay."

Nate leaned forward and half-heartedly shuffled the magazines together.

"Now that I'm older, I understand. Our justice system isn't interested in guilt and innocence. It's politics. Who's got the biggest bank account? My dad's as helpless as I was all those years ago. He suspected Greta too, but he couldn't prove it — and she had money to ensure that if you so much as mentioned her name, you'd get your ass sued. He swore if we ever had physical evidence, she'd go down, but we never did."

"What about DNA? I mean, I've heard about cases that were decades old that are getting solved now. Is that an option in Matt's case or—?"

"I've asked my dad that too. But even if they found Greta's DNA on Matt, it wouldn't prove anything. They were boyfriend and girlfriend."

"But if they found her DNA on the murder weapon..." Bette insisted.

"Except they never found the knife. There was no knife at the scene," Nate told her.

"But how could she have gotten rid of it? If she killed him and returned to a party within a half hour, where could she have hidden it?"

Nate smiled kindly.

"I hear you, Bette. And believe me, I asked those same questions after it happened. My friends and I scoured the park, the streets between there and Martin's party. We looked through people's trashcans. We even went out to the dump and spent half a week walking through garbage and looking for a knife or bloody clothes. Nothing. We never found a thing," Nate confessed.

"And that never made you wonder if it wasn't her? If maybe it was a wanderer sleeping in the park that night? A homeless guy or—"

"This is Marquette, Bette. Back then we had exactly one homeless guy, Ralph Simpson. His father owned the bowling alley and Ralph had mental problems. He slept on park benches and the beach. In the winter, he went home to his parents' house. People called him the local idiot. We're not so crude these days, but the man wouldn't harm a fly. That was the extent of our vagrant population around here.

"Not to get on my soapbox, but people love to blame the homeless people and, nine times out of ten, they're the victims, not the perpetrators. Plus, my dad and his deputies interviewed half the town. If there had been a stranger in the area that night, they would have heard about it. People were devastated over Mat's death, devastated. Everyone wanted that murder solved. People would have turned in their grandparents if they thought they were involved." Nate's voice rose as he spoke.

The customer who had walked in peeked around a bookshelf as if to check that everything was okay.

"Hi, Janie," Nate called, waving.

"Hey Nate. Everything good?" The girl, no older than twenty, glanced at Bette.

"Yeah, we're good. Grab me if you need help."

Janie gave him a thumbs up and returned to the shelf.

"The teenagers in this town seem to think I'm the loony uncle they have to keep an eye on," he laughed.

"Were you at the party that night? The one Greta went to?" Bette asked, returning to the subject at hand.

Nate nodded.

"Martin Bayshore, another senior in our graduating class, threw it. He got his older brother to buy us a keg of beer. I was plastered. It's one of those things I've regretted. I don't remember Greta leaving and coming back. I have one memory of her from that night. She was sitting on a sofa in the living room, and this girl from our class that everyone called Babbling Brook, because she never stopped talking, was bending Greta's ear about some nonsense. Greta had this glazed look in her eyes like she'd tuned the girl out hours ago." Nate shrugged. "I don't know if that was before or after Matt died."

"Did Greta have any friends? Anyone she was close with other than Matt?"

Nate shook his head. "Not a single one."

"Matt's sister said he was getting ready to break up with her. Do you know why?"

"The excuse was school, but Matt mentioned something weird to me the week before he died. He said he'd found out that Greta's dad wasn't dead. Apparently, Greta had told him her father committed suicide, but somehow Matt found out her dad was alive and in an institution downstate."

"He wanted to break up with her for lying?"

"Nah." Nate shook his head. "He realized he was in over his head with her. The lie just revealed a side to Greta that he hadn't seen. Everyone else had seen it, but Matt had blinders on. He was starting to see the real Greta, and frankly she scared him."

48

Then

CRYSTAL TRIED to pull the window up, but it had been nailed shut. It didn't budge. She forced her fingers under the frame and tugged.

Greta had left her untied and undrugged. She'd arrive anytime. Crystal never knew when, nor which, Greta would appear. The angry child who recalled life in the old farmhouse, death and blood and a cruel psychotic father. Or the soft Greta who stroked Crystal's hair and spoke to her as if they were sisters. Or the adult Greta, the scorned wife whose eyes flashed with jealous rage.

They were all dangerous, all unhinged, and Crystal knew if she didn't escape soon, she, too, would feed the monster in the forest, the fictitious beast who probably lived only in the mind of the insane woman who'd been groomed to believe it would devour her.

Crystal stared at the floor searching for a ridge or a loose board. But the planks were smooth and firmly locked together.

Heaving, she pulled the bed aside and got on her hands and knees. Near the wall, she felt a slight give in a board. She stuck her fingernails into the crevice and gently pried it up, shocked when the board lifted. A small metal box lay in the dark cavern beneath the board.

The box, once silver, was now streaked by rust.

It screeched quietly as she lifted the lid.

A spiral notebook lay inside, along with other items; trinkets, a bracelet made from pink and white plastic beads, a single pearl earring, a stick of bubble gum hard and flinty beneath her fingers. In the corner of the box, she dug out a misshapen gold ring with two stones, one a half moon diamond and the other a ruby in the shape of the sun.

Crystal opened the book and saw big loopy writing that took up two lines rather than one. It was a diary, and on the inner cover were the initials MRC.

There were only ten or so entries. Many of the pages were filled with doodled hearts, drawings of horses and trees. A few drawings revealed trees with slitted eyes and mouths with sharp teeth.

The entries had dates but no years listed.

December 10

Daddy says I'm bad because I left the blood rag in the sink, and Mrs. Martell found it. Greta lied to Mrs. Martel and said Daddy cut his hand. I wanted to tell her the blood came from the woman in the black dress. I saw Daddy carrying her from his car last night, but Greta said if I talked, the trees would eat me too.

February 21

Greta and I watched the men in the suits today. Daddy calls them the brotherhood. They took a patient to the stone room in the woods. She looked right at us in the trees. She saw us. I know she did. Her eyes scared Greta, but I thought she looked like a fairy princess. She had hair the color of gold.

The last entry was dated August 6.

I kept the ring from the lady in the black dress. Greta says I should throw it away, but I won't. The next time the sheriff comes with a patient, I will show him the ring.

The door opened and Crystal dropped the book.

"Clever," Greta murmured, gazing at the box and the opening on the floor. "This was Daddy's room. The last place I would ever have looked. I thought she buried it in the forest."

"Why did you want it?" Crystal asked.

Greta leaned forward and flicked her fingers through the contents. She pulled out the ring with the two small gems clinging to the gold band.

"It belonged to the woman in the black dress," Greta murmured.

She slipped the ring over her own finger and twirled it around. Maribelle and I saw it in the paper. They had blown up a picture of the woman's hand with the ring on her finger. They thought it was distinctive enough that someone might remember it if they'd received it as a gift or saw someone wearing it. Maribelle called it our white horse."

"Your white horse?" Crystal asked, thinking of Maribelle's last entry, her intentions to give the ring to the sheriff.

Greta laughed.

"I didn't understand either, but she always said we'd get rescued on a white horse. She found this ring in the basement after we cleaned. She hid it in this box. She was going to take it to the police and tell them what Daddy had done. For the first time, she had proof." Greta took the ring off. "I told Daddy that night, and in the morning, Maribelle was gone. They put her in the asylum."

"Did she tell anyone there?"

Greta shrugged.

"Maybe, but without the ring she couldn't prove anything. Lots of kids in the asylum made up crazy stories. Daddy said she was insane, had become a pathological liar. She was seeing things."

"Where is Maribelle now?" Crystal murmured.

Greta snatched the box from the floor, stuffed the journal inside, and left.

49

May 1974

Greta

GRETA WATCHED Matt from the darkness of the trees.

He hadn't heard her approach because she'd removed her shoes and replaced them with flat slippers.

He sat on the rock, his long legs stretched out in front of him, his head tilted back as he gazed at the stars.

She wondered what he thought about. How best to end their relationship? Whether he should tell her at all before he packed his bags and moved seven hours away from her?

She squeezed the hunting knife clutched in her hand. The hard rubber grip pressed into her palm. The knife felt deadly, like a live snake. She knew its power.

Holding her breath, she slipped across the clearing.

He didn't have time to react. Before he'd even lowered his

face from the sky, she'd wrenched the blade across his throat. Blood spurted out, but Greta didn't see it. As Matt slumped forward, she fell upon him, plunging the knife into his back again and again.

She stopped when somewhere far away a car horn blared, ripping her from her rage-filled trance.

Her hands and forearms were sticky, and when she climbed to her feet, a muscle in her right shoulder spasmed and she dropped the knife.

Shaking, Greta picked it up and returned to the dense grove of trees where she'd hidden her supplies. She pulled a black plastic trash bag from beneath high ferns.

Greta had thrown on a black poncho over her clothes before she'd attacked him. She stripped it off and stuffed it into the bag. She'd worn dark jeans and a dark t-shirt on the chance any blood splattered her clothes, but she felt confident she'd remained clean.

She kicked off her black flats and put on an identical pair, throwing the stained ones in the bag. Wiping the knife clean, she fought a momentary urge to taste Matt's blood, before sliding the sheath over the blade and tucking it into the inner pocket of her purse.

The park bathrooms were unlocked, and she ducked inside, gazing at her reflection. Only a single spot of blood had hit her face. It clung high on her right cheek. She pulled a paper towel from the dispenser and wiped it away, adding the soiled towel to the black bag.

As she walked back to the party, careful to stick with the shadows, she paused at one of the many trash bins lining the street. The garbage men would pick up the bins at dawn. She slipped the plastic bag into a bin and walked on.

At the rear of the house, teenagers had trickled out of the house and spread across the lawn. Red plastic cups of beer lay strewn across the grass.

Greta slipped from the trees and rejoined the crowd as if she'd never been gone at all. Most of her peers were drunk. Not one of them focused on her.

She spotted Nate, Matt's best friend, leaning against the wall as he gazed down at one of the bubble-gum popping, gooey-eyed cheerleaders. Her name was Jenny or Jessie, and she giggled as if he'd just made some dashingly clever remark.

Fighting a smile, Greta brushed passed him into the house.

None of them would be laughing tomorrow.

50

Now

BETTE RETURNED to the hotel and asked to use the telephone. She dialed the number Eliza had left on Weston Meeks' phone.

"Sunny Angels Retirement Community. How may I be of service?" The woman's high voice held a false cheeriness that Bette felt sure didn't translate to the person behind it.

"Hi, I'd like to speak with Eliza Sanders, please."

"Phone calls are permitted between the hours of ten a.m. and two p.m."

Bette looked at her watched.

"It's 9:52."

"Phone calls are permitted between the hours of ten a.m. and two p.m."

Bette squeezed the phone and bit back the angry words that exploded in her mind.

"I'll call back," she said tensely and replaced the phone.

She paced away from the phone and back, checking her

watch a dozen times. This time, the number directed her to Eliza's room. An older woman picked up on the first ring.

"Hi, is this Eliza?" Bette asked

"I certainly hope so," the old woman laughed, "but around here, sometimes it's hard to say."

"Eliza, my name is Bette Childs. Could I visit you today? I have questions and I'll be driving downstate from the Upper Peninsula. Sunny Angels is on my way."

"I never say no to a visitor, Bette. I rarely see a friendly face other than my son, and he only makes it once or twice a month. Come on by."

~

BETTE PARKED outside the retirement community. It was located in Harbor Springs, a picturesque lakeside town busy with tourists despite it being a weekday.

The name Sunny Angels felt oddly portentous, as many of the residents would be little more than that when they left the fieldstone house.

The house was high and long, with a gabled roof and clean white shutters on every window. The lawn had the vibrant green color that reminded Bette of limes. She imagined they had to use fertilizer and some other magic powder, aka poison, to produce such an unnatural color.

Inside the front door, Bette found a cheery welcome area. A middle-aged woman with hair dyed red sat in a plush office chair, her manicured hands tapping on the keys of a typewriter. She looked up when Bette walked in.

"Hello there!" She stood and slipped from behind the desk, extending her hand. "You must be Jessica. I'm delighted you've decided to tour Sunny Angels. Your mother will absolutely adore our cozy home."

Bette faltered, gazing at the woman's teeth, which seemed so bright Bette squinted at them. "No, actually, I'm here to see Eliza Sanders."

The woman's smiled vanished, and she placed a hand on a jutting hip.

"Visitors are expected to call ahead, unless you visit on Saturday afternoon, of course. And today, if memory serves me, is Monday."

Bette didn't smile. Crystal would have. More bees with honey and all that nonsense, but Bette had never been one to bow down to rude people, and this woman was rude. She would have been nice to Jessica, because Jessica was a potential check in the mail, but Bette meant no benefit to her.

"I'm sure her son would be disappointed to hear I was turned away," Bette lied. "He's actually in Ann Arbor this week on business. There are some really beautiful retirement communities down there. Have you ever been?"

The woman, named Linda according to the little gold sign propped on her desk, scowled at Bette.

Behind Bette, the front door opened and another young woman entered. She was short and mousy, and wore stiff-looking khakis beneath a white blouse. She looked timidly from Bette to Linda.

Linda's eyes fixed on the woman, and Bette could see her honing in on her prey. She brushed past Bette and held out her hand.

"You must be Jessica," she gushed in the same syrupy voice she'd unleashed on Bette a moment before.

"Yes," Jessica told her, her voice barely a whisper, nearly drowned out by the paddle fan whirring overhead.

"Welcome to Sunny Angels, the loveliest retirement community in Michigan," Linda told her, glancing at Bette as she said it, as if challenging her to disagree.

"Before you get wrapped up, can you direct me to Eliza's

room, please?" Bette kept her voice even, though she wanted to put the woman in her place.

Linda glanced at Jessica and pursed her lips.

"Follow that hallway to the end," she said, finally. "Room 104, the last door on the left."

"Thank you." Bette didn't wait to hear more.

She left the reception area and walked down the hall, gazing at the paintings of sleepy seaside fishing villages and sailboats drifting in still water. Behind the closed doors, she heard the low murmur of voices from televisions. From one room, she heard loud snoring.

She stopped at room 104 and knocked on the door. There was silence within, and she wondered if the woman was sleeping.

Before she could knock a second time, the door swung open and a tall woman with long white hair and bright blue eyes stood glaring at her.

Her eyes softened when she saw Bette.

"Sorry for that look. I reserve it for *Linda*." She spoke Linda's name as if she were describing slimy Brussel sprouts.

"I met Linda," Bette admitted. "I'm guessing she's earned a few dirty looks."

"And a swift kick in the pants; though being a lady, I don't permit myself." Eliza smirked. "Roger across the hall more than makes up for my passivity. He throws his food tray at her at least once a week."

Bette laughed and glanced down the hall, where she saw Linda looking towards them suspiciously.

Eliza leaned out, grimaced and tucked her head back in.

"You better come in, dear. If we loiter, she might give us a ticket."

Bette followed the woman into the little room.

A twin bed stood against a wall, covered in a blanket flecked with blue and yellow flowers. In one corner stood a kitchenette with a mini fridge and sink. A dish-drying rack occupied the tiny counter beside it.

The space was cozy, small for a woman of Eliza's stature. By the window, two wicker chairs sat with a table between them.

Eliza moved easily. It took her only three strides to cross the room and settle into a chair. She gestured to the one opposite her.

"I admit that my mind's not what it once was, but for the life of me, I cannot place you, dear. Have we met?"

Bette shook her head. "This might sound strange, but I'm a friend of Weston Meeks."

Eliza continued to smile at her, puzzled, and then awareness crossed her features.

"Oh yes, yes. The young man who called about the asylum and the Claude family in particular. Well, that's a long story, and I'd offer you a cup of tea, but we're not permitted hot plates. Nor tea kettles. I wonder if Linda fears one of the guests might club her over the head with it. Guests," she repeated with a snort.

Bette took the other chair. "Why do you live here, Eliza? You look healthy. I mean—"

"Not like an invalid?" Eliza asked, eyes twinkling. "I'm not dead, not in the slightest. But I choose to live here, believe it or not. I've been having seizures since an accident at my former workplace, the Northern Michigan Asylum. That happened in the seventies, a long time ago now, two decades."

She shook her head as if disbelieving the passage of time.

"You worked at an asylum?" Bette asked.

"Yes. I was a nurse at the Northern Michigan Asylum for nearly forty years. I went through their nursing school and everything. Such a beautiful place. Have you ever been?"

"No," Bette admitted. "I've seen photographs. It seemed a bit ominous, honestly."

Eliza nodded.

"Oh, yes, it is that. And it's not all in your head either." Eliza winked at her.

"Can you tell me about the Claudes? Did they live at the asylum?

Bette remembered Lisa's claim that Greta Claude had grown up on the grounds of an insane asylum.

Eliza lifted a hand to the back of her head, wincing as if something pained her.

"I'm sorry, are you okay, Mrs. Sanders?"

For a moment, the woman didn't respond. Her eyes had shifted down, and she continued cradling the back of her head with one hand. When she looked back at Bette, an uneasiness had settled over her features.

"I haven't spoken about Joseph Claude in... more than a decade at least."

"But you knew him?"

Eliza nodded. "Oh yes, everyone at the asylum knew him. He was the caretaker. The man we called if the toilet chains broke or a window had frozen shut. That was in the earlier years. Joseph suffered a mental breakdown at the beginning of the seventies. He was admitted to the asylum as a patient. He'd begun to hallucinate. Eventually, one of the doctors diagnosed him as a schizophrenic, but I never believed it."

"Why not?"

The woman folded her hands on the table and looked out at the glossy grass.

"I worked with a lot of schizophrenic patients. Joseph bore little resemblance to them. The only characteristic he shared with those suffering from schizophrenia was visions, but he didn't see all types of things. Not at all. He saw only one thing, one man in particular."

"A man?" Bette asked.

"The man in the blue tuxedo?"

Bette frowned.

"He saw the man everywhere," Eliza continued. "He couldn't use the bathroom without running out, screaming in terror. The man in the blue tuxedo was following him, stalking him, haunting him. He ranted and raved. He had to be kept in a private room and spent most of his final years in solitude because he agitated the other patients. He was also a risk to himself and others. More than once, he attacked other patients claiming they were the man in the blue tuxedo."

Eliza put a hand to her head a second time.

"Joseph Claude is the reason I have seizures. One night, when I was administering his meds before bed, he grabbed hold of my shoulders and started to bash the back of my head into the wall. I have only a vague memory of it. I lost consciousness. I was lucky to have survived."

Bette shivered. "That's terrifying. I'm so sorry, Eliza."

Eliza put on a brave smile that revealed all the lines around her mouth and eyes.

"Water under the bridge, as they say," she said dismissively.

"Did Joseph Claude have a daughter?" Bette asked.

Eliza nodded, rubbing the nearly translucent skin on her knuckles.

"Arthritis," she said. "Odd, I've noticed it flares up when I talk about the asylum. Isn't that funny?" She shook her head. "Joseph Claude had two daughters. Twins, Greta and Maribelle."

"Twins?" Bette asked, surprised. She hadn't heard anything about a sister.

"Maribelle died when she was eight years old," Eliza explained.

51

Then

Crystal lay in the fetal position on the mattress, legs curled close to her body as if she might somehow protect her unborn child from external dangers. But of course it wasn't the external danger that would ultimately destroy her. Crystal's own body would do that when malnourishment kicked in. When her organism realized there was not enough food and water to sustain both beings.

A baby cannot survive without the mother — period — so the baby would be the first to die. Life would cease, and she'd return to that place beyond the stars, that unfathomable realm Crystal sometimes dreamed of, where her mother floated in a gossamer web of light.

She laid her hand on the old, soft and gray wood floor, pressing the nail of her index finger down and embedding her number in the wood. She did it again and again, row after row of six, two, five, one, nine, nine, one. Six, two, five, one, nine, nine, one.

The number's meaning had become known to her that morning as she woke feverish, the sounds of child laughter echoing through the old house. June the twenty-fifth, nineteen-ninety-one. It was a date. The day of her death.

How had she never recognized it?

Or, perhaps she'd known all along and closed her heart to the truth. She'd always known death would come early, but had she realized she held the exact date in her head?

How many days had she been in captivity? Ten, eleven?

As she pushed the grooves into the wood, leaving her mark on the space so filled with horror for the woman who now held her captive, Crystal felt little anger. Most of her pain stemmed from grief. Grief that her unborn child would never take their first shaky breath in a strange, and sometimes unbearable, world. Grief for Bette who would devote the rest of her days to searching for her sister. Grief for her father who would probably slip into his academia and perhaps never re-emerge, as a way to cope with his pain. And grief last of all for Weston, for the love that might have been.

Crystal also felt sorrow for the woman who would take her life. The woman shaped and molded by dark beliefs and even darker deeds.

CRYSTAL WOKE WEAK AND THIRSTY.

Greta stood in the doorway watching her. She said nothing, simply studied her, and the expression in her eyes chilled Crystal.

Greta had come to a conclusion of some sort, and Crystal knew what it was.

"I'm going to die today. Today is June twenty-fifth, isn't it?" Crystal asked.

Greta remained silent. Her eyes drifted from Crystal's face to her raw fingertips and then to the tiny grooves marring the walls and floor. Crystal had carved the date over and over. In the previous days, it had become a mantra, a focus to keep from ruminating on the thought of her baby dying inside her.

She tried not to imagine Bette, her father and, of course, Wes. It was impossible. They filled every space between the numbers, every breath, every moment of pause.

The pot in the corner had begun to stink, and flies buzzed above it and landed on the porcelain rim.

At first it had made her gag, the early pregnancy turning her susceptible to waves of nausea at even moderate smells. Bad smells left her stomach churning, her guts clenching as they tried to release their contents, but she hadn't eaten in days. The only thing she'd managed to spit up was a stream of yellow, bitter-smelling bile. It was in a puddle next to her bed, as she'd grown too exhausted to even creep into the opposite corner to throw up.

"How quickly we become animals," Greta said, eyes traveling the length of Crystal's body. "What we truly are. Do you think he would love you if he saw you like this? If he saw the truth of you? What you are beneath the glossy red hair and the pretty clothes? When your sparkling personality has been replaced by fear and hunger and desperation?"

Crystal didn't respond. She let her eyes drift closed.

Had she intended to fight? To try and overpower Greta and ensure the survival of her child?

She smiled, her lips cracking. It seemed absurd now. The most ridiculous idea she'd ever had — the belief that she could fight this woman off, this woman who'd been murdering people for years and getting away with it.

"Water," Crystal begged, not bothering to open her eyes because she couldn't.

The sand man must have come, her mother used to tell her and Bette on especially sleepy mornings.

"Mr. Sandman, bring me a dream," Crystal murmured.

Greta leaned down and set something on the floor.

Slowly, Crystal opened her eyes and turned to stare at the glass of water. Her stomach cramped at the sight of it.

She clenched her eyes shut and pulled her legs in.

"Dehydration is an ugly death," Greta taunted. "Your eyes are yellow. People beg to die when their body dehydrates."

Greta lifted her foot, clad in a black flat. She pushed her toe against the side of the glass.

"No," Crystal croaked, watching the water, forcing herself to roll sideways.

Greta pushed the glass of water over as Crystal flopped from the bed onto the floor. She crawled toward the wetness already disappearing into the floorboards.

As she lowered her face to press her tongue to the wood, she smelled the liquid and recoiled. It wasn't water at all, but bleach.

She lifted her eyes, an effort that made her head swim and ache.

Greta stepped backwards into the hall, slamming the door behind her.

Crystal listened as the lock slid into place.

52

Now

"SHE DIED WHEN SHE WAS EIGHT?" Bette asked. "That's heartbreaking."

Eliza nodded.

"Indeed, it was. Maribelle was a beautiful little girl. Just full of light. Sometimes I thought she'd been born into the wrong family."

Bette studied the old woman. "Why?"

"The Claudes were… I don't know how to describe them. Hard, maybe. People of the land. Not the salt of the earth, mind you, just hard like the land itself. The kind of people who till fields for two hundred years. Not only do their faces get ruddy and weathered, but their hearts do as well.

"Joseph Claude had a sharp tongue and a stern hand. His wife died shortly after the girls were born. She had been a quiet, stiff woman, and she died a quiet death. I never saw Joseph hug Greta or Maribelle, but still Maribelle sang and danced and laughed. She was precocious. Claude put her in the children's ward when she eight. He claimed she was exhibiting mental problems. Some of us nurses tried to shield her, but..." Eliza shook her head and her eyes filled with sadness.

"What happened to her?" Bette asked.

"It's a mystery. A mystery that was never investigated, of course. The asylum called it a terrible accident. They found Maribelle's body in the steam tunnels. They said she'd been trying to escape and must have fallen and broken her neck."

"But you don't believe that?"

"Her body told another story." Eliza closed her eyes, her features pinched as if it hurt to remember. "Bruises and broken fingernails. She looked like she'd fought for her life. There were rumors a patient had murdered her. A few of us nurses went to the sheriff in town. He listened to our story, but Joseph Claude went in two days later. No autopsy, he said. No investigation. His daughter had gone insane, and he wouldn't have the police making a spectacle of her death."

"And the sheriff listened to him?" Bette asked.

"Two of the sheriff's sons worked at the hospital. The town relied on the asylum. It wasn't just Claude who told the police to back down. There were doctors involved too. A few months later, the police office announced it had received a large anonymous donation."

"And you think someone in the asylum did that?"

Bette thought of the wealthy and mysterious people who'd whisked Greta Claude away from Marquette.

Eliza nodded. "Yes, I do. I could never prove it, and two nurses were fired after they continued pushing the asylum to investigate. Years later Joseph Claude came into the asylum as a patient. A little over a year after that I was injured and had to leave my position. I received a settlement which allowed me to live comfortably, and I still had Jim. That was my husband. He passed three years ago. By the time I left the Northern

Michigan Asylum, I knew better than to speak of Maribelle Claude."

Bette crossed her legs and leaned forward. "I'm trying to understand why the doctors at the asylum would have protected a caretaker. And who could have donated the money? Was Joseph Claude wealthy?"

"I wish I had answers for you, but I was only a nurse," Eliza admitted. "I will say this, the relationship between Joseph Claude and the doctors was an unusual one. He wasn't kind to them. He didn't tiptoe around them like the other asylum staff.

"You have this idea that the caretaker would sort of prostrate himself to the doctors, but in a way, it sometimes felt like Claude called the shots. Never obviously. So many of the goings on happened in secret. I learned of them in whispered conversations with other nurses and orderlies. When Claude was admitted, more than a few doctors seemed downright afraid of him. As far as I know, he didn't have any money, but many of the doctors were very wealthy. I suspect the donation came from them."

Bette frowned. "Would that generosity have extended to Greta Claude?"

"Perhaps," Eliza said.

"What was Greta Claude like?" Bette wondered.

Eliza leaned forward and plucked a stuffed Scottish terrier toy from a shelf near her window.

"Jim and I always had Scotties," she said, smiling and petting the plastic nose on the stuffed animal. "No pets allowed in here, but my son gave me this to keep me company." She snuggled the dog into her lap. "Greta Claude was very quiet, watchful. She spied on the staff at the hospital. She hid in the trees and the woods. Most of us believed she reported everything she saw to her father. Greta and Maribelle were like night and day. When Maribelle smiled, Greta frowned.

"After Maribelle's death, I tried to engage Greta a few times.

I was worried about her. Not only had her sister died, but her twin. The girls were homeschooled. They didn't have friends outside of the asylum. Maribelle played with some of the kids from the children's ward, but Greta never did. After Maribelle died, Greta became even more withdrawn. We rarely saw her. A few patients claimed to see her through the windows at night. As if she were wandering the grounds after dark, but I never saw her myself."

"And what happened to her after they admitted her father?" Bette asked.

"I heard she went to live with family in the Upper Peninsula. The girl's mother had family up there."

"Did a new caretaker start at the asylum?"

"Oh no," Eliza shook her head. "I mean, not in the same way. They boarded up Joseph Claude's house. The hospital hired local men to do the handy work, but no one moved into the caretaker's property."

"Why is that?"

Eliza shrugged. "The world of medicine was changing. By the late seventies, institutions all over the country were closing down. Some of our own doctors left to pursue practices that focused on medication for mental illness. And truth be told, half the patients didn't suffer any illness at all. I mean, in the early days, women were institutionalized for post-partum depression. Men were institutionalized for homosexuality. The evolution of our minds is a big part of what led to the collapse of those asylums. We realized we weren't treating illnesses at all."

"Greta ended up leaving the Upper Peninsula after someone with money came to get her," Bette explained. "Do you have any idea who that might have been?"

Eliza looked mystified. "If I had to guess, I would point towards the doctors at the Northern Michigan Asylum."

Bette stopped near a flower bed outside Sunny Angels. A paper cup of coffee had been thrown toward the trash can, but missed and now hung from a bush of heavy pink roses.

Bette pulled the cup loose and walked it to the trash.

Higher Grounds, the label read, reminding Bette of the coffee shop Crystal worked at, Sacred Grounds.

Bette paused and stared at the cup. Some memory seemed to be forcing its way up from the depths of her mind.

"Gracie," she whispered, echoing the name of the supposed friend Crystal had seen at Sacred Grounds the day she disappeared.

Stunned, Bette dropped the cup and ran back into the retirement home.

Linda had returned to the lobby with Jessica.

"I need to use your phone," Bette panted.

The woman eyed her and shook her head. "Sorry, we don't permit guest use of the phone. If there were to be emergency…"

"Give me your damn phone!" Bette shrieked, and she dove at the desk, dialing the operator.

Linda looked furious, as if she might snatch the phone from Bette's hand, but Jessica had stopped filling out her paperwork, alarmed as the scene unfolded.

Not ready to lose a prospective client, Linda plastered on her faux smile and swept across the room.

"Let's move into the sun room," she told Jessica.

"How may I direct your call?" the operator asked.

"I need the number for Sacred Grounds Coffee in East Lansing, Michigan."

"One moment please, I'm connecting you."

"Sacred Grounds," a woman answered, and Bette's heart dropped into her stomach.

"Is Rick there?" she asked.

"Umm…, you know what? I think he just left."

"No," Bette screamed. "Run to the parking lot. If he's still there, get him, please. It's a matter of life and death."

"Whoa, okay. Hold on."

A minute passed, two.

Bette pulled at her hair and gritted her teeth.

"This is Rick," he said.

When his voice came on the phone, Bette sputtered and tripped over her words.

A jumbled nothing came out.

"Hello? Anyone there?"

"Rick, don't hang up," Bette yelled. "This is Bette Childs. Was her name Greta? Crystal's friend who was in the coffee shop the last day you saw her?"

The man didn't speak. Bette imagined him trying to piece together her frantic question.

When he spoke, Bette's spine went rigid with fear.

"Yes!" Rick exclaimed. "That's it. I've been racking my brain trying to remember it. Greta."

Bette hung up and dialed Officer Hart's number by memory.

"Hart?" Bette demanded before anyone spoke.

"You've got him."

"It's Bette."

The man paused. "Hi Bette. I wish I had some news-"

"I have news," she cut him off. "It wasn't Wes. It was his wife, Hillary. I'm sure of it, Hart. The things I've learned about that woman. You've got to arrest her. Wes is in danger too. I'd bet my life on it."

"Wait, wait. Bette, we already interviewed Hillary Meeks. I told you, she was half a state away from East Lansing. She couldn't have done anything to your sister. She didn't even know she existed, Bette."

"She lied! Understand? She's a liar. She's murdered before," Bette insisted, knowing she sounded manic, but unable to calm her voice.

"Bette..." His tone told her everything she needed to know. He didn't believe her.

Bette hung up once more. She didn't have time to convince him.

She dialed Weston's number in Lansing. He didn't answer.

She hung up and dug through her purse searching for her little flip notebook. When she didn't find it, she dumped the entire purse on Linda's desk. Her fingers flew across the contents, snatching up the little blue notebook.

She searched for the number she'd written down. The home phone number of Hillary and Weston Meek's house in Traverse City.

The phone rang three times. The answering machine would pick up. Any minute she'd hear the crisp voice of Hillary Meeks telling her to leave a message.

Instead, Weston Meeks answered.

"Hello?" he sounded breathless.

"Weston. It's Bette."

"Did you find Crystal?" his voice was desperate, strained.

"No, but listen, Wes, I think... Fuck it. I think your wife is behind this. I think Hillary did something to Crystal."

Silence.

She expected him to disagree, to say she was talking crazy.

"Me too," he whispered.

Bette was stunned and, for a moment, said nothing. Finally, her brain kicked back into action.

"Where is she? Where's Hillary right now?" Bette demanded.

"I don't know. I got sick again last night," Weston confessed. "I think she's drugging me. When I woke up, I was totally out of it. Her car was gone. She hasn't been back."

"She's dangerous, Wes. You need to get out of your house."

"No," he snapped. "No. I need her to come back. I need..." He paused, and when he spoke again, he sounded as if he'd had a brilliant idea. "I need her to drug me again. I'll pretend to eat what she gives me, and then I'll follow her. I'll—"

"What? No, that's crazy. If she knows—"

But before she could finish her statement, he interrupted her. "I've got to go."

Bette listened to the click as he hung up. She stared at the phone in her hand, incredulous. She clicked the button and redialed his number. It was busy. She tried again, and then a third time.

"No," she shouted, banging the phone against the side table. The small plastic mouthpiece broke off and dangled from a series of wires.

"Shit," she muttered, quickly screwing it back on.

Linda poked her head from the other room, fixing Bette with a glare, but when Bette offered her own wild stare, the woman quickly ducked out of sight.

Bette had to drive. She was still an hour north of Traverse City.

53

June 25, 1991

CRYSTAL HEARD the knob turn and knew death had come for her. If she had a mirror to gaze into, she'd see the black shadow had descended.

The knob rattled, but no key turned in the lock.

"Crystal?" Weston's voice whispered through the door.

Crystal lurched to the side of her bed.

"Wes," she croaked.

She would have cried if there'd been water enough in her body to shed a tear.

"Oh God," he murmured.

The knob didn't rattle this time. A loud splintering sound came from the door as he kicked it. The door didn't burst open. He kicked it again, and the wood cracked. The third time, his foot broke a hole through the center of the door.

He peered in.

Crystal fell from the bed and crawled toward him.

"Oh Crystal, oh Jesus. Hold on, just hold on."

He put his hands through the hole and grabbed the splintered edges, ripping the wood back. Only a small piece broke away, and he swore.

"Stay back, Crystal. Okay? Let me try to get this door off."

He kicked close to the frame. The door groaned but held. He kicked it again, howling angrily as the frame bent and pushed slightly into the room. He kicked it a final time, and it crashed inward taking the door with it. It landed with a bang in the middle of the floor.

Crystal braced her bound hands on the mattress and tried to stand. She couldn't pull herself up.

"I'm sorry. I'm so sorry," Weston moaned, kneeling in front of her. He brushed the hair from her face and wrapped his arms around her. "What did she do to you?"

Crystal wanted to hug him back. She wanted to scream with joy and burst into tears. None of it happened. She lay limp in his arms.

"Have to go," she moaned, gazing terrified at the open doorway.

He glanced back, recognized the fear etched in her face and nodded.

"Yeah, okay, we're going." He scooped her up and ran from the room and down the stairs.

She almost laughed when she saw his jeep parked in the high grass.

He pulled open the passenger door, sliding her into the seat.

Crystal lifted her wrists.

"Shit, yeah, sorry," he murmured, reaching beneath the seat and pulling out his hunting knife. He cut the ties and kissed the red welts on her skin.

Weston ran around to the driver's door and climbed in.

"Shit," he muttered as he reached for the ignition.

"I left the keys inside. Be right back."

She reached for him but his shirt slid out of her grasp.

They couldn't leave without the keys, but a wave of horror engulfed her as he disappeared back into the house.

Seconds ticked by and then minutes. Crystal watched the door, hands squeezed together, her breath whistling between her gritted teeth.

He didn't come out.

After an eternity, the door swung open, and she moaned, relieved. But it wasn't Weston who emerged from the house.

Greta, blood spattered, stalked across the porch, her face a mask of fury.

Crystal fumbled to lock the door, hit the wrong button, and unlocked it instead.

Greta yanked the passenger door open and grabbed Crystal by the hair, dragging her from the car.

~

Bette nearly crashed into the old caretaker's house when she spotted Weston's car.

Instead of hitting the brake, she slammed on the gas and her car lurched forward. She shifted to the left pedal and the bumper stopped inches from the peeled white paint on the front corner of the dilapidated farmhouse.

Bette turned off the car and stepped out. Nothing stirred, no breeze, no sounds from within the house.

The day was overbright, the sun blinding her.

"Maribelle, come here!" The voice came from nowhere, loud and commanding. A man's voice.

Bette spun around, expecting to see a man standing on the porch, but it remained empty. Paint peeling, windows boarded or covered in plastic. The house had been abandoned for a long time.

As she turned back to the desolate yard and the forest beyond, she glimpsed the back of a young girl running away, heading towards a barely visible trail in the weeds. As she watched, the girl faded and then vanished. She didn't disappear into the woods. She actually vanished, her entire being dissolving in the air around her.

Bette almost followed the trail of the vanishing child, but goose bumps rose on her arms and neck, and she remembered Crystal.

Terrified, Bette turned and walked to the house.

Adrenaline cast the world into hyperfocus. She saw every board of the rotting porch. A bulky, gray wasps' nest clung to the overhang in the roof's corner. She wrenched the door open and inhaled the musty scent of mold and the acrid scent of bleach.

CRYSTAL WALKED AND THEN FELL, shaking and grabbing at her head to lessen the pain of Greta's hand clutching and dragging her through the forest. Crystal crawled, managed to find her feet, and stumbled behind Greta.

"You ruined everything," Greta spat. "Ruined fucking everything."

"Did—?" Crystal cried out, trying to prise Greta's hands from her hair. "Did you kill him?" Uttering the words felt nearly impossible. But she couldn't take her eyes off the streaks of red on Greta's white blouse.

Greta turned, teeth bared, and attacked her. She slapped and clawed at Crystal's face, screaming.

Crystal fell and curled into a ball. Weak, so weak, her head pounding, she tried to shield the baby who was probably already dead inside of her.

"It should have been you," Greta screamed, pounding on Crystal's back with both her fists.

When she finally stopped, Crystal peered up at the deranged woman.

Greta's eyes were no longer gray. They'd gone black.

"Walk," she hissed, pulling out a bloody knife. "Walk or I'll open you right here."

Crystal struggled onto her hands and knees and back to her feet. She limped through the woods, legs screaming, lungs burning.

When they emerged in the hilltop graveyard, Crystal knew the end had come. Death waited in this field, and it would not go home alone.

"Go," Greta spat, waving the knife at Crystal and forcing her forward.

Crystal saw the hole when they were several feet away. It was a black chasm cut into the green grass.

~

THE STILL, hot day, the vegetation green and bursting. Thorns and brambles pricked Bette's bare legs as she ran down the trail, eyes darting from the dampened grass to the crowded forest before her.

She wanted to call out, to scream Crystal's name, but feared she'd seal her sister's fate if Hillary knew someone was after her.

Bette's hands were sticky from Weston's blood.

The adrenaline, the fear-strength, had subsided, and her legs grew wobbly beneath her. Bits of black, like flies, dotted the edge of her vision. She knew those spots. They were not insects of the forest, but the parasites of her own nervous system, the noxious little invaders trying to steal in and seize control of her body. They wanted to force her face into the lush grass where she would fight for breath until she passed out.

Bette lost the trail of trampled grass and realized they'd turned somewhere. She backtracked, panting, shaking.

"There," she whispered, spotting a fern crushed to the forest floor.

When she broke through the trees into a clearing, the sight before Bette weaved and threatened to disappear into the black hole of panic.

It was a grassy field, devoid of trees. Several small grassy hills poked from the earth.

At the far end, Hillary Meeks stood, sweat glistening on her pale, determined face.

She held a shovel in her hand.

A mound of fresh dirt lay piled beside her. She sank the shovel down, scooped and released a cascade of dirt into a dark hole.

Bette's mouth fell open and a scream of terror and grief erupted from her throat.

Hillary swiveled around. Her face twisted into an angry scowl that made her look like a demon who'd clawed its way up from Hell and was filling in the portal it had used to escape.

"Crystal…" Bette breathed.

Hillary clutched the shovel like a baseball bat as she strode across the clearing toward Bette.

"I've called the police," Bette shouted. "If you kill me…" she stammered, her throat suddenly dry, "they'll…" But she didn't finish the sentence because the mention of the police had not caused so much as a flicker in Hillary's face.

The woman was insane.

Bette turned and ran back into the trees. She ducked behind a thick beech tree and held her breath.

The adrenaline was back. A hot surge burst in her legs and tried to propel her away from the tree and into the forest.

Run, it shrieked, but she held her ground.

Quietly, she lifted the canister of wasp repellant she'd taken from the house.

She placed her index finger on the little plastic spray nozzle, and her hand shook as she held it in front of her.

A twig, only feet away, cracked beneath a shoe.

Then another, closer.

Bette didn't wait; she lunged out and pressed the nozzle, sending an acrid stream in Hillary's direction. The burst hit her in the chest, and Bette lifted the can directing it at her face.

Hillary screamed and swung the shovel, but the repellant blinded her. The blade hit the beech tree and sank into the wood. Hillary tried to pull it free, but her eyes were screwed shut, and she wrenched her hand from the shovel to swipe at her face.

Bette dropped the canister.

She ran past Hillary, who had dropped to her knees and was shoving leaves and dirt into her face to scrub away the toxic spray.

Bette nearly plunged over the side when she reached the hole. It was deep, four feet at least.

She climbed in and started scooping handfuls of dirt. As she threw the dirt behind her, she imagined Crystal curled up, her body ice cold.

When her fingers finally brushed fabric, Bette released the sob that had been trapped in her chest. She grabbed hold of the fabric and pulled.

Crystal's shoulders and head rose from the dirt. Her eyes were closed, but her skin was warm. Dirt filled her nostrils.

"Please, please be alive," Bette cried, as she struggled up out of the grave, pulling Crystal with her.

Trying to remember the CPR training they'd both received at the YMCA as teenagers, Bette turned Crystal over and brushed at her face and nose. She flipped her onto her back and started chest compressions.

"One-two–three-four..." she muttered as she thumped Crystal's breastbone.

When she reached fifteen, she paused, tilted Crystal's head back, and blew two gusts of breath into her sister's mouth.

Nothing happened.

Her sister didn't gasp for breath. Her eyes didn't fly open.

Crystal lay limp on the ground.

Bette's fingers shook as she searched for a pulse —nothing.

She shifted her hands back to Crystal's chest and repeated the compressions.

Bette pushed another two breaths into Crystal's slack mouth and returned her hands to her sister's chest. As she leaned down to start her third set of breaths, the shovel hit her square in the back. The impact made her head snap, and she bit her tongue painfully.

Before Hillary could hit her a second time, Bette fell forward, sprawling across Crystal's lifeless body. The blade cut the air inches above her head.

Bette lurched sideways as Hillary arced the shovel a third time.

The woman's eyes were puffy, the skin on her face shiny and raw. She gritted her teeth as she tightened her grip and stepped toward Bette, raising the shovel over her head. She'd positioned it so the tip pointed straight down at Bette's chest.

Behind Hillary, at the edge of the clearing, Bette saw movement. She strained her eyes toward the figures and realized Weston was coming towards them, limping and bloody. A small girl with cascading black hair tugged on his hand as if encouraging him onward.

Bette kicked her legs out. Her feet connected with Hillary's shins, but like a statue, the woman didn't move. Barely a grimace crossed her mouth as the shovel started its downward spike.

Weston was nearly there now.

Bette screamed and tried to twist away as the shovel plunged toward her. She hunched forward and closed her eyes, expecting to feel the blade sink into her flesh.

It didn't.

Above her, Hillary's mouth dropped open, and she teetered sideways.

Bette scrambled away as the shovel dropped from Hillary's hands. A plume of red blossomed on her white shirt.

Weston Meeks stood behind her, his face and neck slick with red, a blade, blood covered, clutched in his hand.

He gave a loud, grief-filled howl and sank the knife into Hillary's back a second time.

Hillary twirled away from him, losing her balance and falling to one knee.

Weston collapsed onto his hands, heaving, blood dripping from his mouth into the dirt mound beside Crystal's grave.

Hillary cried out and stumbled back to her feet. The dark blade of the knife stuck from her back. She stood, fell, and stood again, half running across the grassy space.

She stopped suddenly next to a mound of grass topped with a pile of rocks.

Bette watched, frozen, as Hillary dropped to all fours and collapsed facedown onto the mound.

"Crystal," Weston's voice bubbled.

Bette blinked, and managed to look at Weston. Unsteadily, she crawled back to her sister.

He rested a blood-smeared cheek on Crystal's chest.

"Get help," he mumbled. "Hurry."

She shook her head.

"CPR. I have to do CPR..."

Weston slid off Crystal.

He thumped his palm against her chest, over and over.

"Go," he gurgled.

Bette stood and started running away. She looked back,

suddenly terrified that Hillary would have found her feet once more to return and finish them off.

Hillary lay still in the grass. Beside her, sat the little girl in the nightgown. She stroked Hillary's blood-matted hair and gazed at her not with fear, but with love.

Bette turned and ran from the clearing.

54

Now

CRYSTAL STEPPED to the edge of the cliff, Weston's hand snug in her own.

He turned to face her, his eyes boring into hers with such intensity, she felt as if she could fly.

He slipped his hand away from hers.

"No," she laughed. "Let's jump holding hands."

He kissed her nose, her mouth, and then shook his head. "Not this time. You're not the only one in that body now. Time to move away from the cliff."

He put a hand on her belly, flat and warm from their day in the sun.

She remembered the baby. How could she have forgotten? She and Weston were having a baby.

"Okay," she agreed. "I'll do the safe thing this time, but our little girl is going to be a cliff jumper."

"Don't I know it," he said, kissing her again and taking a step back.

She reached out for him. He was too close to the edge, but he opened his arms like he might fly and fell backwards off the cliff.

"No," she cried out, running to the edge.

He hadn't jumped out far enough. He might hit the rocks, but as Weston fell, he grew radiant — as if the sun shone from below him instead of above. Bright shimmering light, rather than the dark water of the lake, swallowed him whole.

MOST WOULD HAVE CONSIDERED the red-haired victim a lost cause, but paramedic Steve Fisher had been around a long time. More than once, he'd given CPR to children who'd turned blue or men who'd had heart attacks and were ice cold. More than once, they'd come back to life.

After twenty-three minutes of CPR, Crystal Childs took a tiny shuddering breath. A weak pulse began its rhythmic thrum beneath his fingers.

His partner, Orlando Tustin, didn't have the same luck with the male victim. Although he was alive when they lifted him onto the stretcher, his blood pressure dropped rapidly on the short drive, less than a half mile, to the hospital.

When they wheeled him through the hospital doors, Weston Meeks was DOA.

"I FINALLY GOT up the guts to kiss Brian and right then, as I was leaning forward, you and your friend Collet jumped out of the closet and yelled 'Boo!'"

Crystal heard Bette's words, but they seemed to come from

some far-off place, a back room in a big empty mansion. Walls and hallways and heavy wooden doors between them.

"I was mortified," Bette continued. "And your friend started singing, *Brian and Bette sitting in the tree,* but you grabbed her and ran. I chased you guys for two blocks. I was so mad, but when I got back, Brian kissed me right away. And later, I realized it was better because if you hadn't spooked us, I would have kissed him, and it was way more fun to tell my school friends he kissed me."

A splinter of light slipped beneath Crystal's eyelids. She tried to open her eyes, but they didn't budge.

"Anyway, I wanted you to know that I was happy you scared us," Bette continued, her voice breaking. "It was such a little sister thing to do. And that's why, on top of the other three hundred stories, I've regaled you with in the last forty-eight hours, I need you to be okay. Do you hear me, Crystal?"

Bette's hands pressed into her right forearm. The touch was soft and warm.

Crystal tried again to open her eyes. They stayed closed, but she managed to wiggle her fingers.

"Did you see that?" another voice asked excitedly. It was her dad. "Bette, her hand just moved."

"They did?" Bette demanded.

Crystal felt Bette's fingers entwine with her own. She tried again to move them. When her thumb twitched, Bette gasped.

"Oh my God, they did. She's waking up. Right? Is she waking up?" Bette's voice boomed, no longer far away but so close Crystal flinched.

"Nurse, nurse," her father yelled, followed by the slap of his shoes on the floor. "She's waking up. Hurry, quick."

Another woman's voice joined Bette's and her dad's.

"Okay, calm down. We don't want to get her excited."

A hand brushed across Crystal's face and then pushed one of

her eyelids open. A light shined into her eye and Crystal shrank away.

"Her pupils are constricting. That's good, very good. Crystal, can you hear me?"

Crystal tried to open her mouth. It was so dry. The sound that emerged was barely a rasp.

"Squeeze my finger, if you can hear me," the nurse told her.

Crystal directed all of her strength into her thumb and index finger, managing a weak pinch.

"Good. That's good, Crystal. I'm your nurse at the hospital in Traverse City. You've been asleep for a couple days, but you're with us now."

EPILOGUE

"In total, we've excavated six graves," Officer Hart told Bette. "We haven't identified all the remains, but based on some jewelry, we believe Tara Lyons was one of them."

Bette sighed and pushed her cuticles lower into her fingernail.

The half-filled grave her sister had been lying in careened across her mind. She squeezed her fingers tightly and tried to banish visions of the soft grassy mounds, the bodies within them too late to be saved.

"Crystal's information has been very helpful," Hart continued. "We've identified the man in the blue tuxedo. He disappeared from Traverse City in 1970. He was in town for his brother's wedding that weekend."

"What about the woman in the black dress?" Bette wondered, thinking of Crystal's story as to why Maribelle Claude had ended up in the asylum.

Hart shook his head.

"A lot of the remains are too degraded, but we've tracked down a missing person's report from 1966 that describes a woman who vanished from the Acme area, east of Traverse

City. Apparently, she'd been to a funeral that day, hence the black dress. After the funeral, she disappeared. She wore a ring like Crystal described, but we haven't found the box yet."

"Why do you think she killed all those people? Why did her father?" Bette asked.

"Mental illness often runs in families," Hart said. "Hillary Meeks was raised by a psychopath, and eventually she became one."

"But what about everything Crystal mentioned about feeding the land? And a chamber? She said Hillary Meeks talked about a chamber in the forest?"

Hart shrugged. "Unfortunately, it's out of our jurisdiction. My thoughts? Joseph had psychotic delusions. David Berokowitz claimed his neighbor's dog told him to commit murder. Other murderers have made similar claims. Claude created a story to justify killing people. Maybe he even believed it."

"Hillary, Greta, whoever she was, told Crystal that she helped her father for years and then... and then when he died, she started the killings," Bette said, still trying to come to terms with the torture her sister had experienced at the hands of Hillary Meeks.

Hart's face darkened. "That's the cycle of abuse. I see it all the time in my line of work. Never anything like this. I mean this is just..." He shook his head, disgusted.

"Terrifying," Bette muttered.

"Yeah. It's that. I can look forward to a few sleepless nights after this case. But your sister is alive. That's a victory we rarely see in these cases. How's she doing?"

Bette smiled.

"She's... Crystal. Full of light even on the darkest days."

"Want me to come with you?" Bette asked.

Crystal shook her head.

"I'd like to do this one alone." She leaned over and kissed Bette on the cheek before maneuvering her growing belly from the car.

The hike up to the heart-shaped cliff at Pictured Rocks was a slow one. Her body had not fully recovered from the ordeal at the Northern Michigan Asylum, and the pregnancy often left her weak and longing for sleep.

When she reached the top, she sat on a rock and caught her breath.

Crystal pulled off her backpack and took out a velvet pouch. Tucked within the pouch was a plastic bag containing some of Weston's ashes. The rest she'd placed in an urn with the words from his fortune cookie inscribed in the dark wood: *Love is the only true adventure.*

She opened the bag and stepped to the cliff edge, remembering her last glimpse of him in the world between worlds as she returned to life and he left it.

The breeze lifted the silty gray ash and carried it away.

Crystal rested one hand on her belly as she watched the dust of her beloved disappear into the sky.

ALSO BY J.R. ERICKSON

Read the Other Books in the Northern Michigan Asylum Series

Some Can See

Calling Back the Dead

Ashes Beneath Her

Dead Stream Curse

Rag Doll Bones

Dark Omen

Let Her Rest

Available in Ebook, Paperback and on Audible!

ACKNOWLEDGMENTS

Many thanks to the people who made this book possible. Thank you to Scott Roberts for contributing his true paranormal experience, which inspired the story of the man in the blue tuxedo. Thank you to Rena Hoberman of Cover Quill for the beautiful cover. Thank you to C.B. Moore, for copy editing Dark Omen. Many thanks to Will and Donamarie for beta reading the original manuscript. Thank you to my amazing Advanced Reader Team. Lastly, and most of all, thank you to my family and friends for always supporting and encouraging me on this journey.

ABOUT THE AUTHOR

J.R. Erickson, also known as Jacki Riegle, is an indie author who writes stories that weave together the threads of fantasy and reality. She is the author of the Northern Michigan Asylum Series as well the urban fantasy series: Born of Shadows. The Northern Michigan Asylum Series is inspired by the real Northern Michigan Asylum, a sprawling mental institution in Traverse City, Michigan that closed in 1989. Though the setting for her novel is real, the characters and story are very much fiction.

Jacki was born and raised near Mason, Michigan, but she wandered to the north in her mid-twenties, and she has never looked back. These days, Jacki passes the time in the Traverse City area with her excavator husband, her wild little boy, and her three kitties: Floki, Beast and Mamoo.

To find out more about J.R. Erickson, visit her website at www.jrericksonauthor.com.

Printed in Great Britain
by Amazon

29887157R00196